Hampton, Westbrook Publishing

Princeton Junction, New Jersey

ISBN 978-1-4951-7632-6

EBOOK ISBNL 978-1-68222-361-1

For those who put their lives on
the line every day.

God bless.

Widow-Taker

R.H. Johnson

Hampton, Westbrook Publishing

MANHATTAN WOMAN FOUND SLAIN IN UPTOWN MANSION

by Andrea Wilson

Vivian Schuyler Latourette, a prominent Manhattan socialite who sat on the boards of several major New York City charitable organizations, was found murdered in her posh Upper East Side home late yesterday morning. A source close to the investigation has confirmed that the billionaire widow's death is "extremely likely" to have been the work of the East Coast serial murderer known as the Rosebud Killer.

The crime was discovered by the victim's housekeeper of thirteen years, Elva Stokes of the Bronx. Mrs. Stokes said that when she arrived for work early yesterday, Mrs. Latourette failed to unlock the front door to the brownstone mansion on East 73rd Street. After trying unsuccessfully to contact her employer by phone, she dialed 911.

New York Police Department officers who responded to the call were also unable to gain entry and notified the Emergency Service Unit. When ESU personnel finally entered the home, they found the woman's body on a couch in the main-floor library. According to an NYPD spokesman, she had been dead for at least two days.

Prologue

The middle-aged man with graying hair climbed the front stairway of the handsome East Side brownstone.

Twilight. The gentle passing of another languid summer day in Manhattan.

He rang the bell and waited patiently. When the old woman looked through the peephole of the massive front door, she saw a stocky, smiling gentleman in tan blazer, pale yellow shirt, and patterned green tie. In his hands he cradled a blue Tiffany bag, its gift tag hanging prominently from a white silk ribbon.

Ten minutes after opening the front door the woman lay dead. Thirteen minutes after that her murderer came down the stairs from an upper floor, gazed at the body, then showed himself out.

He calmly disappeared into the shadows.

1.

I liberate the souls of three women in the space of six weeks, yet the best the *New York Times* headline writers can come up with is **THE ROSEBUD KILLER.**

They are sinfully wide of the mark.

I am to a killer as Michelangelo is to a circus freak who paints with a brush held between his toes.

Ah, well, I accept that there are things I cannot change. The *Times* beat the other newspapers in correctly linking my first two successful missions of mercy. So the *Times* claimed the privilege of creating this highly misleading *nom de guerre* for me. Given the choice, I would have asked for something loftier — something reassuring, perhaps even a touch biblical. But the "Rosebud Killer" has stuck. I cannot change this, so I have moved on.

I have far weightier concerns than this.

A man must wake up each day with his life's purpose firmly in mind, and I am fortunate to have dual purposes — one infinitely nobler than the other — that keep me fully engaged and intensely active even as I approach my 63rd birthday.

I spend much of my time earning a modest but adequate living. I teach English literature to endless hordes of unremarkable college students who would rather text lewd photographs to each other than muddle through a line of Chaucer. Each day they swarm from subway stations like worker ants, then joylessly follow each other's pheromones to the University's classrooms

— dusty, ill-lighted spaces crammed into anonymous gray buildings on the streets of Downtown Manhattan.

I do not dislike teaching. Not at all. It is a perfectly respectable way to pay the bills. And since I carry the enviable title of full professor, I am able to choose the classes I teach each semester, and in this way can usually put myself in front of the least awful students that the University has to offer. The students who register for my classes are typically upperclassmen, usually English majors, and generally as literate as one can be after having been raised by an iPhone and iPad instead of a mother and father. All things considered, I suppose that I am overcompensated for guiding these 21st- century post-adolescents through musty phrases crafted by men whose bones long ago disintegrated in Britain's soil.

But my life's true purpose, God has assured me, is the deliverance of widows.

The *New York Times* would have its readers believe that I murder people. But it is nothing so crass as this. What I do in God's name is set free the women whom I serve. I release them for all time from fear, want, and vulnerability. I spare them the brittle loneliness of unkind years in empty homes. I allow their souls to sing by reuniting them with departed loved ones.

The widows in my growing flock would thank me if they could.

Of this I am absolutely certain.

Detective Javier Silvano, a twenty-three-year NYPD veteran who early in life escaped the mean streets of the South Bronx and earned a college degree in criminology, headed the team tasked with ending the Rosebud Killer's string of murders. One of the department's most experienced and most decorated homicide investigators, Silvano had been partnered three years ago with a younger detective, Pete Nazareth, a man widely recognized as one of the department's rising stars. Together Silvano and Nazareth had successfully worked some of the City's highest-profile cases, and it came as no surprise when Deputy Chief Ed Crawford put his A Team on this latest one.

Silvano cut an imposing figure in the drab, windowless conference room at One Police Plaza where he and Nazareth met on a Monday morning with Chief Crawford to update their boss on the Rosebud Killer case. At 6'4" and a chiseled 225 pounds, the 44-year-old Silvano looked like a pro tight end and was exquisitely capable of using brawn when brains alone couldn't get the job done. A sharp dresser, he had a fondness for tailored suits that showcased his impressive frame in classy, understated fashion. He enjoyed looking the part of a man who was going straight to the top.

Nazareth was by far the quieter of the two, a listener and thinker whose mind was capable of assimilating and organizing seemingly unrelated facts more quickly than anyone Silvano had ever worked with. He and Silvano made a somewhat odd couple: the strapping and outspoken Silvano with his thick black hair, brown eyes, and caramel skin; and the fair-skinned, blue-eyed Nazareth who at 5'10" and 165 pounds looked even younger than his 33 years.

Nazareth's boyish appearance had more than once invited his adversaries to mistake the former Marine for an easy mark. But those who had underestimated him had consistently learned the hard way that he could hold his own in any company. Four months earlier, while making an arrest in the Brownsville section of Brooklyn, Nazareth had been jumped by three men armed with box cutters and broken beer bottles. He crushed the first attacker's sternum with a thunderous spinning back kick, then fractured the second man's skull with an elbow strike to the face. The third man dropped his weapon and disappeared into an alley.

Despite their impressive record, Silvano and Nazareth had been under serious pressure for weeks. The mayor, the NYPD chain of command, the press, and the public had been clamoring for an arrest and conviction. Silvano and Nazareth understood the urgency, but they couldn't change the facts: what they knew about the Rosebud Killer remained infinitely less than what they didn't know.

At the morning briefing in Lower Manhattan, Chief Crawford sat, as usual, at the far end of the conference table, where he could take in everyone and everything at a glance. A blunt, glowering sort who wore his impatience badly, he alternately chewed a fat Cuban cigar and sipped bitter black coffee that he brewed at his desk.

"So where are we, Javi?"

"Still trying to identify a meaningful pattern, Chief. But nothing's coming into focus yet," said Silvano. It was not his style not to sugar coat the truth, which in this instance meant the absence of meaningful progress.

Chief Crawford knew from experience that Silvano never talked just to hear the sound of his own voice. He saved his energy for the hunt.

Crawford turned to Nazareth. "Pete?"

Nazareth nodded and offered his quick take on the investigation.

"At the moment we have only a few common threads linking the three murders. One, the victims are all widows. Two, they're all killed by lethal injection. And, three, after death the body is carefully posed: eyes shut, victim on her back, hands folded at the waist holding a red silk rosebud. Beyond that," he said, "lots of facts but no possible conclusions."

The facts that Nazareth referred to were plentiful but seemingly unrelated. The first woman was murdered in late April in Hallstead, PA, a small town that the detectives had never heard of, much less visited, before the investigation began. Eleanor Martinson, 78 and recently widowed, was found by a realtor after two days of not answering her home telephone. Her body, fully clothed and artfully posed, was on the family room couch. The woman's dead hands clutched the stem of a silk rosebud.

Two more widows were murdered in May — one on Staten Island, one in Manhattan. If there was a connection between the two, Silvano and his team had not yet found it. The victims were 86 and 77 — Rita Marconi and Lenora Fairchild. So far the investigation suggested that the two women had never met, probably had never even heard of each other, and had no friends, clubs, or doctors in common.

The *New York Times* had picked up on the story following the first May murder on Staten Island, when reporter Andrea Wilson remembered reading about a similar crime that had been committed in some rural Pennsylvania community back in April. After several days of badgering the right people, Wilson had confirmed that the two victims were both widows and that both had been posed after death with a red silk rosebud. In her front-page article the reporter referred to the murderer as the "Rosebud Killer," and a criminal legend had been born.

The NYPD brass wasn't convinced they had a serial killer on their hands until a third dead widow was found in Manhattan. At that point they became believers. Also at that point the story got picked up by every media outlet on the East Coast, and Deputy Chief Ed Crawford called on Silvano and Nazareth to fix the problem.

Crawford sipped his burnt coffee and stared at Silvano, whose face, as usual, revealed nothing of what was going on inside his head.

"Well," Crawford said as he set his cup down, "let's all hope the new week brings us some answers, because the Mayor and the Commissioner are out for blood. And if we can't bring them this damn Rosebud Killer's blood, they may decide to settle for ours."

"Understood, Chief," Silvano replied, glancing over at Nazareth, who calmly studied his third cup of coffee. Nazareth looked up at his partner and offered a sympathetic smile. Both men understood that if widowhood was the only common denominator in these murders, they could be light-years away from solving the case.

At the moment they were absolutely nowhere.

Eleanor Martinson, God bless her, was my first. In some ways she was the easiest, but in other ways she was the most difficult. Either way, of course, she played a key role in guiding me to the true purpose of my earthly life.

She was my younger sister's mother-in-law, and during the months leading up to her husband's grim death from pancreatic cancer, Eleanor tumbled ever deeper into a black abyss of fear and hopelessness. I know this because my sister, Chelsea, often spoke of Eleanor during our weekly phone conversations. It became increasingly clear to me that Chelsea and husband Art were obsessing over what would happen to Eleanor, and more specifically to her mind, when 80-year-old husband Jake finally passed.

Jake and Eleanor had spent the past forty-three years tending a modest place — what real estate agents would most likely term a *gentleman's farm* — on a winding, two-lane country road on the outskirts of Hallstead, PA. Hallstead is a bucolic, eye-blink of a town, population 1,000, on the state's northern border, and for Jake and Eleanor it had long been their own bit of heaven.

The Martinson farmstead featured a gently used two-bedroom ranch-home, a weathered 170-year-old gray barn, and several small outbuildings, all of it set on five acres of hay, wildflowers, and lovely private woods. This area of Pennsylvania was first settled in 1787 — at least according to the non-native Americans — and retains much of what I presume was its Colonial flavor: quietude, conservatism, and lily-whiteness.

But as Eleanor faced the certainty of life without husband Jake, Hallstead's endearing qualities made it seem more like a living hell than paradise. She knew that she would be intensely alone 24/7, three miles from the nearest neighbor and five from the town center. And she feared not having either the energy or the income to keep the property in good repair. Life as she knew it was about to end, replaced by a measure of hardship and loneliness for which she was ill-prepared.

I had not spent a great deal of time in Eleanor's company, but what I remembered of her prior to Jake's funeral was a charming, well-read woman who kept joyfully busy with her baking, her vegetable garden, and her fair share of the simple farm chores that beckoned to her and Jake each day throughout the year. She would have enjoyed caring for grandkids as well, but Art, their only son, and Chelsea had not cooperated on that score. In all, she was a companionable and earnest woman.

That was long before Jake's funeral.

The woman I encountered on the chill, rainy morning that they lowered Jake into his hole in the ground had changed utterly. Joyless, yes, naturally. But also skeletal, as though in recent months both she and Jake had been devoured by cancer. And her eyes, once lively and inquisitive, now reflected the growing terror of a hollow life. As the minister offered comforting words about a man who had been a loyal member of the congregation, I could hear Eleanor's thoughts. Would she find a buyer for the property she had hoped never to leave? And if she did, would she then agree to live with Art and Chelsea, who had invited her to do so . . . but who probably hoped it would never happen? Or would she settle anonymously into some sterile continuing-care community where she could shuffle around in her small apartment, pretending to feel fortunate to be alive, until ultimately she had to move into the facility's nursing unit? Her lips didn't move, but I heard her words nevertheless.

So it was at this solemn ceremony on a bleak day in March that I was washed by the divine light of understanding, much as Saul must have been while traveling the road to Damascus more than 2,000 years ago. At that moment I knew to the very core of my being that mine was not only the power but also the responsibility to rescue Eleanor from a living death — from an existence alien to everything she held dear.

No, I could not turn back the clock or raise Jake from the dead. But surely I could, indeed must, end Eleanor's suffering and reunite her with the man she loved.

Yes, I do believe in life after death. Without question the energy of our existence, that which some of us call the soul, is everlasting. It remains vital after clinical death . . . retains its full, glorious essence. And I held the means of lifting Eleanor's soul to the higher plane it deserved.

Back in Manhattan after the funeral, I spent nearly a month assessing the most efficient means of fulfilling the mission that now inspired me. I needed to devise a process that would assure success on several levels. To begin with, of course, the method of freeing Eleanor, as well as other women suffering from the same death-in-life existence, needed to be swift, as pain-less as possible, and certain. In addition, I needed to keep my actions hidden from a world that would badly misread my motive. After all, I would not be able to pursue God's work from a prison cell. Finally, I wanted somehow to mark the act of liberating each widow's soul as a truly transcendent experi-ence — as a matter of the spirit, something quite apart from the biological machinery that most people mistakenly accept as life.

Yes, Eleanor would be my first rescue. I suspected that working with her would help me through the nervousness that any novice, no matter how well trained, experiences prior to his or her first real-world enterprise. Surely every expert in every field is the product of many years of anxiety, error, and practice. This is as true for violin virtuosos as it is for neurosurgeons.

By working with Eleanor, I would actually be able to feel the enormous pain that I had seen in her face at Jake's funeral. That pain would serve as a constant reminder to me that my mission, even if poorly understood by others, constituted an act of supreme mercy. And since Eleanor would surely welcome me into her home when I arrived unannounced, I would not have to deal with any front-door hysterics that could — though I hoped not — accompany later encounters with widows who, like Eleanor, were in desperate need of my ministrations. In every way possible it made great sense to operate in this controlled environment the first time around.

On April 22nd I drove the pleasant country road that rises gently from the center of Hallstead to the long, sleepy curve at the front of Eleanor's property. The drab tan Ford Taurus that I had rented in Manhattan was practically invisible amid the brilliant landscape of sap-green trees, lavender meadows, and golden roadside daffodils. In the unlikely event anyone noticed my arrival, no one would be able to remember a car — was it a Chevy, a Toyota, a Nissan? — that was merely one of thousands just like it motoring through Pennsylvania that day.

Mountainous clouds rolled toward Hallstead from the southwest, troubling the late afternoon sun, as I pulled onto the gravel at the back of Eleanor's home and parked close to the kitchen door. That kitchen door, she once told me, was reserved for family and friends. The formal front entrance, on the other hand, had always been a standing joke between Eleanor and Jake. If anyone rang the front doorbell, she had said, they immediately knew it was someone not worth bothering over — an annoying salesman, a whiny student intern representing some local politician, or perhaps a Jehovah's Witness who had not yet figured out that Hallstead is, was, and always will be Presbyterian.

Family and friends always knew to use the kitchen door. And that's precisely what I would do.

Although the day had turned murky and rain had just begun spattering the brick patio, Eleanor recognized me through the window over the kitchen sink. She offered a weak smile and waved me in. The door, as always, was unlocked. This surprised me a little. In these early post-Jake days I had expected her sadness to be accompanied by wariness. She was, after all, an old woman alone at the edge of a forest, miles from the security afforded by neighbors. The simplest explanation, it seemed to me then as it does now, was that she no longer really cared what happened to her.

"Tom, what a surprise," she said as she met me at the door. "What are you doing all the way out here on a stormy evening?"

"I've spent the last two days at a conference in State College," I replied, closing the screen door behind me, "and I found myself practically passing by your front door on my way back to Manhattan. It occurred to me that a cup of your coffee would fortify me for the final three hours of my trip."

"Excellent," she said, though nothing in her countenance suggested excellence. Her face was gray, drawn, hollow. She was in every way a cruel caricature of the old Eleanor, and on her I could practically smell the mustiness of death, as if damp clay from Jake's grave still clung to her shoes. "Let's go sit in the family room while it brews."

The family room adjoined the kitchen at the back of the house, invisible to anyone who might approach the front door. A large floral-print couch stood alongside the picture window that looked out on the rear gardens.

Closest to the house were her flowers, early blooms that would grow riotous in the weeks just ahead. Beyond them were two larger gardens, now idle, where she and Jake had grown all of their vegetables each year.

She would grow nothing there again.

I sat on a comfortable maple rocker next to the couch, soothed by the low, homey sound of an antique grandfather clock that marked time in the darkest corner of the room. Eleanor carefully set a place mat on the coffee table and began lowering herself to the couch right next to me. As she did, I leaned over and touched her rib cage with my 15-million volt stun gun.

I knew precisely what to expect, because I had tested the device late one night a week earlier near the corner of 22nd Street and 8th Avenue in Manhattan. The surly drunk sat on a bed of grimy cardboard and leaned against the brick wall of a Korean deli that had been shuttered for the night. He held the obligatory bottle of cheap wine to his mouth as he eyed me. I saw no one else in any direction, so I bent forward as if handing him a dollar and held the terminals of the stun gun to his chest. He immediately mutated into a quivering mass, more jellyfish than human, and it was clear to me that at this point I could do whatever else might need doing.

As Eleanor arched painfully on the couch, I took the syringe from my jacket, found the most prominent vein on the inside of her right elbow, and injected the diazepam. This had an immediate calming effect on both of us. As soon as she relaxed, I felt free to continue my work at a more leisurely pace.

After gently positioning Eleanor on her back, I administered the second injection. Sodium pentobarbital, the drug that would rescue her from this life, is readily available to the patient shopper, and I had purchased my modest supply in Mexico. The drug worked its blessed magic. No movement, no breathing, no heartbeat. Eleanor was at peace in death, and I was refreshingly at peace with the humane service I had performed on her behalf.

I knew then that I could easily do the Lord's work again and again.

Eleanor actually looked lovely in her perfect rest, all the more so when I placed the stem of the silk rosebud under her crossed palms. I was greatly moved by the scene.

I can now state as absolute fact that when you first set out to take someone's life, no matter how righteous your motive, you find butterflies fluttering in your stomach. I'm no fan of clichés, but I had, indeed, felt butterflies in my stomach when I imagined the things I would need to do in order to rescue Eleanor from this world.

But that was all behind me. I now knew that I could go forth and do God's good work without fear. The widows I served would experience a few moments of fear, then soar on angels' wings to their heavenly homes. In this world they might not understand what I was doing. In the next, however, they would praise my name.

My motives are pure.

4

The Staten Island murder — the first Rosebud Killer slaying within the five boroughs of New York City — had been discovered on a Monday afternoon and given three paragraphs buried deep in the Tuesday edition of the *New York Times*. But after successfully linking the Staten Island and Pennsylvania murders, the *Times* broke its front-page story about the Rosebud Killer on Wednesday, and the police commissioner immediately demanded that the City's top homicide team handle the case.

On Thursday morning detectives Silvano and Nazareth sat in Eleanor Martinson's kitchen with State Trooper Matt Duncan, the officer who had first responded to the call about the widow's murder. The detectives hoped that something about the Pennsylvania murder would shed light on their Staten Island case.

"A local realtor, Beth Simmons, had an appointment with Mrs. Martinson," Duncan explained, "so that they could talk about putting the house on the market. When Beth got here the back door was wide open. So she called for Mrs. Martinson, got no response, came in and found the body on the couch. By this time Mrs. Martinson had been dead for about 24 hours, according to the medical examiner. Beth didn't touch the body. She just called 911."

"When you got here," Silvano asked, "where was Beth Simmons?"

"Sitting on the back steps, crying into her cell phone. She was on with her mother, who lives a few miles up the road and was real good friends with Mrs. Martinson."

"Did you ask Ms. Simmons whether she had disturbed anything at all? Furniture, objects on the coffee table, kitchen items?"

"Oh, yeah," he nodded, "that's the first thing I did after making sure that Mrs. Martinson was definitely dead. At that point I didn't know whether we had a homicide or a suicide, so I wanted to preserve any evidence that might be there. As soon as the ME told us it was a murder, we had our crime-scene guys come in. They hit every room in the house but found absolutely nothing that could point us to a suspect."

"And you had no reports of strangers in the area that day," asked Nazareth, "or vehicles that didn't look familiar?"

"We went door to door for miles, Detective, hoping that maybe one of the neighbors had driven by on the day of the murder. But we came up with nothing," he said, shaking his head. "We don't get a whole lot of traffic out here, so the odds of someone seeing anything important were pretty slim."

"Especially if the killer used the back door," said Nazareth, "which apparently is what the victim's friends always did. If that's the case, then we're probably dealing with someone she knew."

"Agreed. But we interviewed damn near anyone local we could think of who might have had a motive to come out here and do this," he said. "I'm talking about utility workers, the UPS driver, mailman, lawn guy — you name it. We haven't found anyone who shouldn't have been out this way, and we still haven't come up with a motive.

"The house was pristine," Duncan continued, "so we ruled out burglary right away. And I have to tell you the body was treated very gently. This actually looked to me more like an assisted suicide than a murder, and that's exactly what I thought until the ME found the taser marks. After that, I had to agree that it was a murder."

"And you're confident the real estate agent wasn't involved?" Silvano asked.

"We know she was here," he shrugged, "but there's absolutely no motive that we can think of. Beth Simmons is the one who called us, and when I arrived on the scene she was a complete mess, let me tell you. If what I saw was just an act, she deserves an Academy Award. Trust me."

Silvano and Nazareth spent two hours walking room to room through the house and around the property, not really expecting to come away with more than the state police had already told them. They were no closer to finding a link between the Hallstead murder and the Staten Island case that they had picked up the day before.

Silvano pulled the unmarked Chevy out of the driveway and turned toward Manhattan. Nazareth looked out the passenger window, lost in thought. After a minute or so, he turned to Silvano.

"Two victims. No connection that we know of. One murderer, although that's still a maybe." He shook his head slowly. "Javi, if we have some nutcase who's choosing random victims simply because they happen to be within driving distance, you and I aren't going to sleep a whole lot."

"Can't disagree," Silvano said. "If this guy, or woman, is smart AND decides to pick victims at random, we're going to need as much dumb luck as police work."

That ugly thought hung between them like a dull headache all the way back to Manhattan.

5.

What did I feel after injecting Eleanor with sodium pentobarbital? I posed the question to myself in a variety of ways for nearly a week following my Pennsylvania mission, and each time the answer surprised me.

I felt nothing.

No thrill. Certainly no elation. But no guilt either. I was utterly detached from the event, like a ghost hovering near the ceiling of an operating room and looking down dispassionately at its former body on the table. I was simply pleased to have done God's work. Nothing more.

During this period of enlightening self-inquiry I began searching through online obituaries, waiting for signs that would point me toward other widows in need of salvation. My searches required only minimal skill, since there are a number of fine websites whose sole purpose is to display death notices by city and by date. All one needs to do is pick a city, then read each of the online write-ups. Some death notices say almost nothing, of course, but others contain highly detailed and extremely useful information — things like the names of surviving relatives, viewing days and times at the local funeral parlor, and interesting tidbits about the deceased's memberships, hobbies, and employment. With this sort of information in hand, it is a remarkably easy leap to current phone numbers, addresses, and driving directions.

Each time I searched online I quickly identified at least two or three worthy candidates. But I am just one man. I cannot help everyone.

I didn't plan for Rita Marconi's home to be my first stop on Staten Island, but on the appointed day hers was the home that best served the purpose. Over a period of ten days, as time permitted, I had driven past the homes of three recent Staten Island widows, Mrs. Marconi among them. Two of the homes were virtually lost amid the boxy rabbit warrens that pass as residential neighborhoods on the City's fifth and often forgotten borough. I thought it highly unlikely that I would be noticed visiting either of these two places, since both had entryways shrouded by tall shrubs that provided excellent cover. They seemed ideal. But on the day I arrived to offer one of the widows God's everlasting peace, I found cars parked in both driveways.

So I drove to Mrs. Marconi's home instead. A bent and irreparably broken 86-year-old whose husband had died roughly three months earlier, she lived in a small, shabby bungalow near the edge of Great Kills Harbor. I had seen the old woman four days ago as I drove past during my final scouting trip. On that day she had struggled to drag a small metal garbage can to the curb, and it was obvious that Rita Marconi was a woman very much in need of rescue. I had smiled to think that her suffering might nearly be over.

God would decide.

And then . . . there I was. Darkness had already fallen, and the lights were on inside Rita's house. Her shadow moved slowly across the shades at the front of her home. On one side of the building was a weeded lot littered with worn tires, broken bottles, and a soggy couch whose upholstery had been shredded by vermin. On the other side was a bungalow that might have been abandoned but which in any event showed no evidence of human habitation. The dilapidated homes directly across the street had lights on inside, but their wildly overgrown hedges made it impossible for anyone to see Rita Marconi's front steps.

I parked alongside the vacant lot and walked back to the house. On this warm, humid evening all that stood between Rita Marconi and me was a battered screen door with flaking paint. I could see the old woman fussing at her kitchen stove at the far end of the house. Hoping not to startle her, I knocked just loud enough to be heard.

"Who's there?" she called down the narrow hallway.

"It's Charlie, Rita." Charlie, I knew from my online research, was the name of one of her adult grandchildren. But there was certainly no way she could see me in the low light by her front door. As expected, the familiar name and a bit of early evening confusion — a common problem for folks her age — outweighed any suspicions she might otherwise have harbored.

"Oh, come in, Charlie," she called to me. "I'm here in the kitchen."

I closed the inside door behind me and turned the dead bolt. I passed the small living room to my right and walked purposefully along the hallway. When she turned to greet me, Mrs. Marconi slowly discerned the shape, then the face, of a man who was obviously not the Charlie she knew.

"You're not my Charlie," she said, concern registering in her voice.

"I'm Charlie from up the street, Rita," I said soothingly. "Mary's husband." She gave me a confused smile, and then I placed the stun gun against her ribs and lowered her slight, quivering frame to the floor. Her eyes tried but failed to focus, and in short order I had the diazepam coursing through her veins. Her brief moment of fear was over. She was now only moments away from perfect joy.

After placing her on the tattered living room couch, I administered the second injection, then carefully slipped the rosebud stem under her hands. I turned the kitchen light off and walked calmly back to my car. Not a single neighbor in sight. No one peering through window blinds. Just the tentative chirping of small birds settling in for the night.

As I drove across the Verrazano Bridge and headed home, I thought back on the details of the evening's work. With God's help my actions had been swift and sure, but I knew that I could always improve. Above all I needed to avoid detection and thereby preserve my ability to sustain this holy mission. And avoiding detection meant being extremely careful in my selection of widows. Rita Marconi had been an ideal widow in an ideal setting.

I would remember her fondly as I went forth to do His work.

6.

Two days after their trip to Pennsylvania, Silvano and Nazareth paid their second visit to the Staten Island murder scene, desperate to pick up something, anything, they had missed the first time.

"How in the hell did the murderer even find this place?" Silvano asked, stepping over a pile of fallen branches that Rita Marconi had been meaning to clear from her narrow side yard. The tall, untended hedges that shielded her home from the next-door neighbor were heavy with new growth. A towering oak leaned ominously toward her rear screened porch. The air was thick with the stench of debris that had washed onto the beach at the end of the street — decayed driftwood, mounds of blackened seaweed, and the rank skeletons of countless horseshoe crabs.

Nazareth turned slowly from the harbor to the vacant lot next to the Marconi place, then to the homes across the street. Like Silvano, he wondered what odd circumstance had led the killer from a bucolic farmstead in Pennsylvania to this rundown backwater on Staten Island.

"I can't tell you what brought him here," said Nazareth, as he stood in the deep shade of the back yard and examined the porch door, "but this place was made for murder. Isolated. Overgrown. No neighbors hanging around."

"Right, it's a damn ghost town," Silvano replied. "When's the last time you saw crime-scene tape and no crowd? Maybe never?"

"Well," said Nazareth, "you have a low-rent area and some really old people who've seen just about everything they're going to see in this life. Maybe they no longer really care what happens around them . . . or even *to* them."

"If I ever get there," said Silvano, shaking his head, "please remember to shoot me."

The crime-scene unit had gone over every square inch of the property, both inside and out, but had found nothing that could point to the killer. One moment Rita Marconi had been making spaghetti sauce, and the next moment she had been murdered and placed on the living room couch. Just like that. End of story. No evidence of a struggle. Just some skin irritation on the woman's body from a stun gun and two needle marks on her right arm. Whoever killed her had left no prints, had treated the woman's body respect-fully, had evidently turned off the kitchen stove, and had locked the front door on the way out. Had Rita's daughter not stopped by, no one would have had any reason to suspect something was wrong in the house.

Officers from the local precinct had gone door to door and interviewed everyone in the neighborhood, but the findings were underwhelming. The average age of Rita's neighbors was something north of 80, and no one had seen or heard anything unusual. Of course, most of them never looked out-side, for fear something might frighten them, and all these people ever heard, both day and night, was the endless jabber of their loud TVs. These folks would soon be in a nursing home or dead. They knew it and were past caring.

"Both here and in Pennsylvania," said Silvano, "this guy just walks into a home, kills a woman, and leaves without a trace. I get that. What I don't get is that the two places are so far apart geographically and that we can't connect the victims."

"Even though we're working with very few facts," Nazareth responded, "I'd like to run this by one of the FBI profiling guys. Could it just be a coincidence that both victims were old and widowed? Yeah, sure. But there's something about the two crime scenes that suggests to me a high degree of precision and planning. I think we're dealing with someone who knows exactly who he's going after . . . and why . . . and how . . . and when."

"If that's true, then this is even worse than I'd thought. It means we're up against someone who's highly capable and who doesn't plan to give us any clues about his motive."

Nazareth stared off into the distance, waiting for at least one piece to fall into place, then nodded at Silvano's comment.

"It's definitely a lot easier when we're dealing with some nut who can't resist telling us what axe he's trying to grind. In a case like that we always get some strong clues. But when the perp keeps his motive a secret," Nazareth said, shaking his head, "the odds are pretty good that we're going to get more victims before we track him down."

"Well, maybe your FBI profiler can get us in the game."

"May it be so, Javi. May it be so."

7.

Spring is gloriously present in the Downtown breeze as it passes through the open windows of my classroom and washes enticingly over the nineteen students in my Modern British Lit honors class. These, I had been told early in the semester, were the crème de la crème of our English majors, and their outstanding grades were offered as evidence. But reality came crashing down in a hurry. The young women, it was clear after just five minutes in their presence, were destined to spend more time wriggling into torn $200 jeans than preparing for my class. And the young men would undoubtedly remain more interested in the young women's asses than in any literature I might set before them.

This is a pity, for today we are examining my favorite poem, Philip Larkin's "If, my darling." The opening lines frame a tantalizing premise:

> If my darling were once to decide
> Not to stop at my eyes,
> But to jump, like Alice, with floating skirt into my head . . . .

From here the speaker reveals, in a torrent of masterful images, a simple truth: he is most definitely not the man that people believe him to be. The world that prissy Alice would discover in the looking glass of his mind would most definitely leave her numb, confused, and shattered.

I marvel at the words the poet has knitted together. No one has described the human condition more succinctly or more imaginatively. But his message is hardly news. For more than a century psychiatrists have told us that we are all madmen when we fall asleep and become, if only for a few minutes at a time, the inner beasts that actually control us.

The wisest of us, of course, recognize that we don't need to fall asleep to become madmen — that even awake we are forever creatures of bestial cravings. This is fact, not fiction.

Whatever stalking beast resides within me is at this precise moment aroused by blonde, lithe Elissa Fairchild, who sits before me braless in a filmy white tank top whose thin straps curve softly over her magnificently sculpted shoulders. But I am a wary veteran of this old game between aged professors and nubile coeds. I have seen faculty colleagues destroyed by innocently hopeful glances that metamorphosed into animal gropings in shadowy campus places. The end is always ugly, even when no spouse is involved, as in my present case. So I never do more than steal a quick look, savor the momentary thrill, and force myself to turn back to the text.

The arousal I experience while noting the lines of Miss Fairchild's tender body is only partially driven by hormones. Something more compelling is at work. Several weeks ago Miss Fairchild missed two successive classes, the second of which called for turning in a short paper on Yeats. Although I do not take attendance, I noted her absence because she is generally one of the more active participants in class discussions. What her comments lack in depth they compensate for with frequency, and this provides welcome relief in a room filled with dullards.

On the day she returned to class I asked whether she had been ill.

"No, my grandfather died suddenly," she said with tears in her eyes, "and the whole family is still in shock. The funeral was yesterday."

"Oh, I'm awfully sorry to hear that," I said, quite sincerely. "Please accept my condolences, Miss Fairchild. And please don't worry about the Yeats paper. You can turn that in whenever you're feeling up to it."

"Thank you so much, Professor Mercer. I tried to work on it this week, but I got absolutely nowhere. We had relatives in from all over the country, and I just couldn't focus on anything but the family and the funeral arrangements."

"As I say, please take your time," I told her. "How old was your grandfather?"

"He was 79, but he acted a lot younger," she said, offering a sad half smile. "He liked to jog, play tennis, racquetball. He was in really great shape as far as we all knew. One afternoon he came home, told my grandmother he was totally beat from running, and died an hour later. The doctor said it was a massive stroke and that there was no way anyone could have known this was coming."

I shook my head sympathetically. "Was this your mother's father?"

"No, my father's. And my father is absolutely numb over this. He had expected Grandpa to live to 100. Seriously. So did I, actually. And my grandmother," she continued, "is beyond inconsolable. She and Grandpa got married when they were in their late teens, and she has never been without him. I don't know how she's going to get through this."

"Well, it's going to take a long time and a lot of family support," I assured her. "Comfort her as much as you can. That's about all you can do."

"Yes, I think so. Well, thanks Professor Mercer. I really appreciate your kindness."

That night I went online and devoured the obituary for Laird Fairchild of East 38th Street in Manhattan. Managing partner of a white-shoe law firm, member of all the correct clubs and societies, and director of two Fortune 100 firms. Survived by his wife, Lenora, two sons, a sister, and five grandchildren, among them Elissa Fairchild.

Whereas Rita Marconi had been a bit of an unknown — a widow whose pain I could only imagine after reading her husband's obituary — in Lenora Fairchild I had a woman whose suffering had been fully revealed to me in her distraught granddaughter's face. In just a few words and glances, Elissa had told me more about Lenora Fairchild than weeks of study could have, and I had no doubt whatsoever that this was a woman who required what only I could provide.

I also had no doubt that my visit would need to be carefully orchestrated. Manhattan brownstones obviously lack the sort of seclusion and anonymity that I had found during my visits to rural Pennsylvania and suburban Staten Island.

I would need all of my brain cells fully engaged for this one.

8

The latest NYPD briefing on the Rosebud Killer case came three days after the murder of Lenora Fairchild of Manhattan. Joining Silvano and Nazareth on this late-May morning at police head-quarters were Chief Crawford, a small group of detectives and uniformed patrolmen who had done some useful legwork on the case, and Mavis Underhill of the FBI's National Center for Analysis of Violent Crime. Underhill was a highly regarded behavioral analysis veteran who had played a major role in solving a number of high-profile cases — a series of Washington, DC, shootings among them — but on this day she was oper-ating somewhat outside her comfort zone. With only minimal facts upon which to base her preliminary conclusions, she wanted everyone to know that the margin for error was uncharacteristically large.

"I'm sensitive to the pressure that you're all getting on this case," she began, adjusting the notes in front of her, "and I assure you that I will con-tinue incorporating new details as you feed them to me. But at the moment I assign a low probability of accuracy to my assessment. In plain English, we're still flying blind."

Since she had found no similar cases in the FBI's huge crime database, she based her profile of the Rosebud Killer exclusively on visits to the crime scenes and photographs provided by the various forensics teams.

"Here's what I'm thinking today," she continued, "but keep in mind that this could change dramatically if, or I should say when, the killer strikes again."

Chief Crawford's eyes grew larger, and he pounced on Underhill's words. "Wait, you say it's a when, not an if?" "Correct," she nodded. "We're dealing with what the FBI calls an *organized* murderer — meaning, an intelligent individual who plans ahead rather than an impulse-driven, spur-of-the-moment killer. And remember also that so far your Rosebud Killer has not tried to engage either law enforcement or the press in any way. That's another sign we're dealing with someone intelligent and very much under control. So, yes, I would say that this person plans to keep on killing."

The Rosebud Killer profile that Agent Underhill laid out did almost nothing to shrink the suspect pool. White male, almost certainly. Most likely 45 to 55 years old. Intelligent, possibly extremely intelligent. Single but socially connected — in other words, not a brooding loner who would stand out in polite company. Meticulous, well-groomed, and gainfully employed.

But her next point attracted most of the attention.

"I also believe it's possible we're looking for someone whose first victim was either his mother or a close proxy — grandmother, aunt, someone like that." This detail created enough of a stir among the assembled officers that Chief Crawford had to shout everyone down.

"Hey, time out! If you have something to add, you'll get your chance. Let's get on with it," he said as he turned the floor back over to Underhill.

"The three victims have been widows," she continued, "and this is no coincidence. He's targeting them. And this introduces the strong possibility of some trauma that triggered his behavior. It's conceivable that his mother was the first widow. But, as I said at the beginning, I'm building hypotheses on the foundation of just three recent incidents, and that's a statistically inconsequential sample."

"Well, from what I've heard you say so far," said Crawford, whose temper was set to low boil, "the killer could be damn near any man walking anywhere in the tri-state area."

"Not quite anyone," she responded patiently. "I would definitely focus your attention on someone who lives in Manhattan. We're dealing with a person who probably functions best in the City. From a purely practical standpoint it's easy to get lost in the crowd here. And that certainly helps if you're planning to murder people. But there's also some suggestion of — how should I put this? — a measure of civility or refinement in his behavior that would play better in Manhattan than, let's say, in either Hallstead, PA, or Staten Island."

Silvano smiled for the first time since the meeting began. He found the enormity of their challenge so unquantifiable as to be almost amusing. "So we look for a civil and refined serial killer?"

"It's actually quite common," Underhill said coolly, maintaining the joyless demeanor that must have been issued with her FBI credentials. "We often find it in terrorist leaders, who need to move in the right circles in order to secure donations for their causes. You can't mingle with the uber-rich in places like London, Paris, or Riyadh if your interpersonal skills are lacking. These people may be sociopaths, but they tend to be highly polished and exceptionally smooth.

"Of course, you can probably find the same skill set among U.S. Senators and Congressmen. They are the epitome of civility, even though they are willing to vote for war on a moment's notice." She let her uninvited political jab sit for a moment. "In any event, I believe the killer is a highly polished individual who could become practically invisible in Manhattan."

After the meeting Silvano and Nazareth shared coffee and danish at a deli around the corner. They sensed a long, frustrating road ahead. But even more they recognized that so far they had been reacting rather than acting. They needed to take charge in some way, no matter how small.

Nazareth broke the ice.

"Obviously she didn't give us much to work with," he said, seeming to meditate on the steam rising from his coffee cup, "but it's something. So for the time being I say we should assume that she's on target. Obviously the guy we're looking for has some issue with widows. But right now it doesn't matter *what* issue. Hell, it may never matter, and in fact we may never know. But at least we have a highly specific victim pool."

"Okay, we have a victim pool," Silvano replied, "but have you ever wondered how many new widows there are every day in Manhattan alone? I don't pretend to know the answer, Pete, but I do remember from some damn briefing that about 200 people die every day in the City. If 25% of them are husbands, that means we get 50 new widows every day. That's, what, 1,500 a month? So all we need to do is find the one he's going to kill next? Talk about going after a needle in a haystack."

"All right, fine. Glass half empty. The half-full version is that instead of having millions of potential victims, we now have thousands. What we need to do next is shrink the pool even more."

"And you have a plan for doing that?"

"Ah!" he grinned as he raised his right index finger in a gesture of mock enlightenment. "I'm still working on that."

9.

The trip from my one-bedroom Cornelia Street apartment on the Lower West Side to East 38th Street took less than twenty minutes by way of the Lexington Avenue subway. From there it was a short, comfortable stroll to Lenora Fairchild's $7-million brownstone in one of Manhattan's tonier neighborhoods. My research indicated that the Fairchilds had never been in the same league as some of their fantastically wealthy neighbors, but they had always fit in nicely, in large part because of their generosity toward popular local causes, among them the Morgan Library, which was located practically around the corner.

Ever since speaking with Elissa Fairchild about her grandmother I knew that I would need to plan my moves with impeccable care, because there is nothing at all remote about Manhattan's Murray Hill section. Unlike Hallstead, PA, or a down-at-heel neighborhood on Staten Island, East 38th Street provides no seclusion whatsoever. The stately residences, all of them worth $5 million or more — in some cases vastly more — stand shoulder to shoulder like the Queen's Guard at St. James's Place. Snooping eyes could be anywhere. And then there's the traffic: cabs and commuter vehicles throughout the day and much of the night. And pedestrians, of course. Almost always pedestrians.

Finally, I considered the possibility of advanced security systems up and down the block. Surely the residences would be well protected, but did the security extend to the street itself? How many cameras might be hidden along the route, capturing every movement for posterity?

So my first visit to the neighborhood was as casually furtive as I could make it. I arrived at dusk and maintained a leisurely pace toward Rossini's, one of my favorite Italian restaurants. I didn't plan to dine there that night unless I inconveniently bumped into someone I knew and was compelled to explain why I was wandering so far from home. My goal that night was simply to observe, assess, and remember as many details as possible.

I employed the same process on three more occasions, twice during mid-afternoon and once more at dusk. Each time I gleaned an additional scrap of knowledge but found no striking differences from one visit to the next. I never saw a police car cruising the street, even though I found it unimaginable that the NYPD would not be providing limitless TLC to the gentry. I noticed a few delivery trucks calling on several of the homes — furniture, appliances, and such. But above all I found that those who truly belonged on this street invariably looked like the knights and ladies of this genteel kingdom. I actually saw very few residents either leaving or returning to their homes, but the ones who did appear always seemed ready for a photo shoot, or perhaps cocktails at a nearby embassy. Priceless watches glittered from wrists. Both men and women were draped in designer clothes. And all of them wore shoes that probably cost more than my monthly rent. I smiled at no one as I passed, and no one smiled at me.

An inoffensive old man always goes unnoticed in Manhattan.

The most meaningful bit of intelligence that I gathered during my visits to Lenora Fairchild's street is that four of her neighbors used the same firm, Cogent Security Systems, to protect their property. So I decided to call Cogent, using a disposable cell phone bought solely for this purpose, and I told the polite young man that I would be moving into a $5-million home on East 38th and needed to know just how much home security would be enough. He seemed quite knowledgeable and patiently answered each of my detailed questions. After fifteen minutes I knew the following: street cameras are unnecessary, since the in-home security systems are quite robust; rarely do Cogent's clients request in-home cameras, because most people view them as offensively intrusive; and Cogent's own armed personnel respond to alarms, usually within ten minutes.

I also learned that I cannot afford Cogent. But, then, who wants to rob an old English professor anyway?

On June 7th I paid my fifth and final visit to East 38th Street. On this occasion I wore an innocuous, slightly baggy tan suit purchased online for less than $250 along with a pale blue shirt and a dark blue paisley tie that I bought on sale at Macy's for $31. I had also slipped on a pair of clear-lens glasses with nerdy, thick brown frames in order to alter my appearance just a touch. I needed to look presentable but in no way conspicuous, and in this pleasant outfit I knew that I would virtually disappear.

Truth be known, I have always been a man who seems to disappear without even trying. There is nothing the least bit remarkable about me. At 5'9" and 183 pounds I am neither slim nor fat; my round face and pasty complexion attract no attention since I am neither handsome nor homely; and my hair, once brown but now mostly gray, is neither too long nor too short to merit a second glance.

I am disarmingly average in every way. Put me in a crowd of a hundred people, and I will invariably be the man everyone forgets.

I had decided to gain entry to Lenora Fairchild's home by delivering a lovely bouquet of spring flowers that I purchased at 6:10 p.m. from a florist on 35th Street near Second Avenue. After leaving the shop, I attached a small card that read, "To Lenora, with much love, Preston and Julia Carrington."

She would not recognize the names, of course, but they sounded proper enough to give her pause if she actually read the card. That moment of hesitation could be the key to a successful visit.

What I did not know, of course, was whether Lenora Fairchild would be home or, if so, would be alone. I chose not to call ahead under some pretext for fear that this might alarm her. So if she didn't come to the door, I would leave and take the flowers with me. If she came to the door but had company, I would leave the flowers and wish her a good evening.

But if she came to the door and was alone, I would fulfill God's will to the best of my ability.

At 6:42 I climbed the stairs to Lenora's regal front door — a grand wooden creation the color of Vermont maple syrup — amid the customary rush-hour frenzy. Cars and trucks inched along East 38th Street while subway-bound commuters walked past me without noticing, since their faces were glued to their iPhone screens. I had chosen this time of day with the utmost care. What could possibly be suspicious, after all, about an aging man with a bouquet in his hands? In this place and at this time of day I might actually belong. To those who passed by on the street I could have been a husband bringing his wife a small token of his affection. To the neighbors I could have been an aged friend calling on an East Side matron. And to Mrs. Fairchild I would simply be a delivery man bearing gifts. Whatever people might see in me, they would soon forget.

As I reached the top of Lenora's stairway my heart nearly stopped when a cheery voice from behind shouted, "Hi, there!"

Good God! It sounded like Elissa. Had she already recognized me, or would she do so when I turned around? What would she think about the flowers and the fake eyeglasses? Would she approach or avoid? If she and I both entered her grandmother's house, what would I do with her? Could I devise any plausible explanation for my presence?

These thoughts and a hundred more like them jolted from synapse to synapse in the space of a single heartbeat, and I suddenly realized that I had not prepared at all properly for this visit.

I steeled myself for the fateful confrontation with Elissa, then looked over my shoulder at a young woman who waved to an older man some twenty yards away. She was smartly outfitted in a trim black cocktail dress and sensible heels, wore minimal jewelry, and carried a small beaded purse. She looked nothing like Elissa and, as she passed, paid no attention to the man at the brownstone's front door.

I began to breathe again, and I momentarily considered bolting. But the thought quickly passed. I rang the doorbell and heard a faint chime behind the large door.

A voice from the intercom said, "Yes, who's there?"

"Good evening," I replied as pleasantly as possible. "It's Eric from Hill Floral Design with a delivery for Mrs. Fairchild."

She looked through the peephole and saw a presentable, neatly dressed man with a colorful bouquet in his hands. Would she tell me just to leave the flowers? I think not. She was, I knew, the sort of well-bred woman who would receive her flowers graciously, offer me a $5 bill for my effort, and then shuffle off to the butler's pantry to fetch a $25,000 Daum crystal vase.

She opened the door and smiled. It seemed to me the smile of a woman for whom a gift bouquet was commonplace. She was pleased though not especially enthusiastic. Yet her smile was, I could tell, sincere. She wore a loose silk periwinkle blouse over black slacks, no doubt a wealthy woman's version of lounging attire. On her feet were sparkling ballet flats that cost more than many people in rural America earn in a year.

"What a lovely surprise," she said as she accepted the bouquet. "I can't imagine who sent them." She peeked inside the green cellophane wrapping, seemed pleased, and turned toward an antique sideboard in the foyer.

"Please wait a moment," she told me. "Oh, they're quite lovely."

She set the flowers on the sideboard as I quietly stepped in and closed the front door behind me. A startled yelp sprang from her lips when I pushed the stun gun against her upper back, and she began to collapse. With my free arm I caught her before any damage was done either to her or to the furnishings, and I gently lowered her to the Italian marble floor that glowed under the light of an extraordinary Tiffany table lamp.

The diazepam injection immediately removed all fear from her face, and the sodium pentobarbital shot delivered her to the Creator and, I hope, her late husband.

She weighed no more than one hundred pounds, so I easily moved her to the living room couch. The front blinds were fortuitously tilted down at a 45-degree angle, making it impossible for anyone from across the street to see me posing Lenora. Every hair in place. Blouse smoothed free of wrinkles. Elegant shoes placed side by side on the floor next to the couch.

I removed the single silk rosebud from the inside pocket of my sports jacket and slipped it gently under her hands.

Throughout this process I wore inexpensive latex gloves that I had snapped on immediately after helping Lenora to the floor. The police would find no fingerprints or, as far as I could tell, any other evidence that might place me at the scene. I removed the green cellophane from the flowers, folded it neatly, and placed it inside my jacket. Then I carried the flowers to the kitchen, along the way discovering an ornate crystal vase that stood empty in a magnificent 18th-century china closet on a side wall of the formal dining room. I removed the vase, filled it halfway with water, and quickly arranged the flowers.

As I prepared to place the vase of flowers at the center of the kitchen island, the phone rang, nearly causing me to drop my handiwork on the granite counter top. Once again my heart did a back flip. Clearly this latest venture had me more on edge than I had anticipated.

After four rings the phone call jumped to an answering machine on the kitchen counter, and I heard Lenora's voice offer a polite greeting: "You have reached the Fairchild residence. Please leave a message, and we will return your call shortly." The "we" stood out. She had never changed the message after her husband died, and this suggested to me that I had successfully rescued the woman from a life she never would have chosen to live.

"Lenora, this is Beth. You're probably getting ready. I'm leaving home shortly and should be in front of your place in about fifteen minutes. See you soon."

The phone call was alarming, but my time at Lenora Fairchild's home was almost over. I did one more meticulous walk-through to make sure I hadn't left anything out of place — except Lenora, naturally — or dropped something that could identify me. No, everything seemed very much in order. I opened the front door slightly, still wearing a latex glove on my right hand, and checked to see whether anyone was looking closely in my direction. No one. I pulled the door closed and removed the glove before turning toward the street. I took each step carefully — a tumble wouldn't have been helpful at this point — and walked along East 38th Street toward the subway station. I reminded myself to stand tall, look calmly about without making eye contact with anyone, and in every way possible become a ghost on this charming spring evening.

I did not look back to see whether anyone had pulled up in front of Lenora's home. That would happen soon, of course, and I suddenly considered how fortunate it had been that the call had come after my arrival. What would have happened, I wondered, if Lenora's friend had already been on her way before I showed up on the doorstep?

The mere prospect left me mildly nauseous.

10.

On a stuffy, overcast mid-June morning, Detective Silvano stood at the front of the large briefing room in One Police Plaza and addressed a group of twenty-five officers representing all five boroughs. These men and women, each with at least five years on the force, were going to spend the next week on a focused effort to gather intelligence in support of a plan that Detective Nazareth had proposed. After bringing everyone up to date on the Rosebud Killer case, Silvano would introduce Nazareth to outline the work that needed doing.

"Pete's idea is to shrink the victim pool so that we can try to predict who this guy will target next," Silvano began. "Is it a Hail Mary pass? Yeah, it is. But right now it's the only play we've got. This killer is making all of us look bad. We've had two New York City murders in two weeks — one on Staten Island, one in Manhattan — and we have no leads. And this has a whole of people, including the mayor and the commissioner, jittery as hell. So, please, help us get this nut off the streets."

Nazareth walked over to a large whiteboard and drew a rough outline of three states: Pennsylvania, New York, and New Jersey.

"Here are the facts we're working with. Three murders: one in PA, two in the City," he said as he marked the spots on his crude map. "Three old and fairly recent widows. Identical M.O. each time. That's it. Everything else is speculation.

"So we have a choice. We do nothing until the guy screws up and gives us some evidence — in the process of killing more women, that is — or," he reasoned, "we identify as many potential victims as possible and try to get to the right one before he does. That's a tall order, but Javi and I can't justify scribbling notes and waiting.

"I wish I could tell you that this plan has a high probability of succeeding," Nazareth said as he looked from officer to officer around the room, "but that's not the case. On the other hand, if you've ever played roulette, you know that there is absolutely no way to predict what number will come up next. Odd, even, red, black, whatever.

"But with our Rosebud Killer we know he'll be going after a widow, right? This is like knowing for a fact," he emphasized, "that the next number on the roulette wheel will be even. The odds of guessing one right number are still against you, but they're better than they had been. If this guy's next target is a woman inside the five boroughs, there's a chance we can get to her before he does."

Nazareth saw the unmistakable skepticism in the faces before him. "We certainly need some luck," he nodded, "but very often hard work creates its own luck. And the work ahead of us is certainly going to be hard."

The plan that Nazareth laid out for the team incorporated reasonable but admittedly arbitrary criteria that he and Silvano had agreed upon before the meeting. First, they would focus on women who had been widowed within the last six months. Since the number of New York City widows who met that first test would still be large, they would narrow the pool of potential victims further by looking only at women 60 and over.

Second, they would work only on potential crime scenes that seemed ideally suited to the Rosebud Killer based upon two of his first three murders. To begin with, the location should be relatively secluded, maybe even remote. Although the killer had already struck in a busy Manhattan neighborhood, Silvano and Nazareth believed that this would prove to be the exception rather than the rule. The Pennsylvania and Staten Island crime scenes were a far better match for someone with murder on his mind.

Beyond this, they would not be looking at high-crime areas within the five boroughs. If the FBI profiling was on target, the killer was someone who looked and felt at home in polite society. Silvano and Nazareth could not picture this guy stalking his victims in the South Bronx or in some homicidal housing project on Staten Island.

Silvano had arranged for each of the twenty-five officers to receive a list of the relevant widows for his or her borough. The assignment was straightforward. First, drive by each address and rate its attractiveness as a potential crime scene. On a scale of one to three, with three being extremely attractive, was it a place where the Rosebud Killer could work comfortably? Second, have a local officer visit each of the highest-profile widows to explain the situation — hopefully without frightening them to death — and then arrange for as many patrols as possible until further notice. If nothing else, increased vigilance by the widows and a greater police presence could make the killer think twice about operating within the five boroughs.

Silvano and Nazareth suffered from no illusions. The plan had gaping holes in it, and they might be many months — and many murders — away from their first break.

11.

I always do my best to avoid the University's utterly nonsensical monthly Faculty Round Table meetings whenever I can decently do so. Sitting still in the faculty club's sun-dappled conference room and pretending not to be bored while a colleague of little substance holds forth on a topic of little merit is surely one of the supreme challenges of my life. Chardonnay helps, but not nearly enough. When I do attend, I do so merely as a matter of form. I do not want to be regarded as a self-satisfied loner. That could invite undue scrutiny, and scrutiny is precisely what I do not need.

For thirty-seven years I have survived the brutal warfare that masquerades as collegiality in academia. Campus infighting is a given, not just at this university but everywhere, and you must battle heroically without seeming to do so. If you are overly fierce, you will never attain the rank of full professor, a position akin to divinity at a major institution in New York City. You make too many enemies that way, and your enemies will eventually destroy you. Why would they not? You and they compete for the same few places of high honor.

On the other hand, if you are overly meek and are perceived to be kissing too many asses, you will be taken for a lightweight, a midge, a mere thing not to be taken seriously. In this event you will remain an assistant professor until they finally get around to firing you in order to make room for someone younger, cheaper, and more ambitious.

I made full professor not on the strength of my publishing, which had been no more than adequate, but by virtue of my highly vocal role in opposing the University's plan to sell off part of the campus some years ago. The sale would have raised millions – to help pay the president's obscene salary, I thought at the time – by helping a rapacious developer create a glass and steel monument to his fanatical excess. I was instrumental in launching a campaign of moral outrage – letters to Congressmen, press coverage, and the like – and briefly served as a campus hero to all but the Administration. This brief moment of glory had coincided with my having met the minimum requirements for promotion to full professor, and the rest, as they say, is history.

If I am no longer a hero, I am also by no means a pariah, and I think it useful to remain a colleague, if in name only. So here I sit, sipping a glass of low-budget wine and listening to Prof. David Ellis of the art department explain why subway graffiti rival the early sketches of Leonardo da Vinci. I consider David a friend, but if I had a gun right now, I would have no choice but to kill him.

Following a mind-numbing Q&A session marked by much intellectual bellowing, David and I enjoy a celebratory drink at O'Mara's, a homey Irish-tinged bar that is too sedate for students and therefore a safe place for faculty to congregate.

"So, Thomas," he begins, far more seriously than the situation requires. I roll my eyes and interrupt David before he can go where I already know he's going.

"David, I'll finish the thought for you, because every time you raise this subject I am suddenly no longer Tom, but Thomas. You and your lovely wife want to know why I am reluctant to get something going with Myra Gentry. Am I right? Yes, of course I am. Myra, you are thinking, is a lovely middle-aged woman, a tenured member of the biology faculty, and, most of all, quite available. This is all true, especially the part about being available. Myra could not be more available if she wore a *Husband Wanted* sign on her back."

"I don't think that's true at all," he whines defensively. "Has she made it clear that she enjoys your company? Yes. Did Anne and I like the way you two hit it off at our house a few months ago? Yes. Do we think you should find someone before you're a surly old man? Yes. But I don't believe Myra has been overly aggressive toward you."

"I haven't needed to get a restraining order, if that's what you mean. But she has an uncanny knack for bumping into me wherever I go."

"Well, gee, maybe that's because you work at the same place and live three blocks from each other." David smiles at me across the small table. "Really, the two of you seem wonderful together."

"You obviously forget that I was married for what seemed to be three thousand years but was actually only three. This is how I learned that tigers have the right idea. Mate quickly, then sneak back into the jungle."

"It's not all about mating, of course."

"Of course. There's all that quality time spent arguing about who should take out the trash, or where to go on vacation, or how many times a month it's best to visit your wife's parents in Paramus, New Jersey. Yes, I do miss those tender moments."

"Well, I never knew your first wife."

"True, but you've certainly suffered a paper cut. Imagine a million paper cuts every day of your life, and you will understand what my marriage was like."

"So why did you get married in the first place?"

I take a sip of my Guinness and grin. "We mated, of course. And I was naive enough at the time to believe that humans should mate for life. Having been thoroughly disabused of that notion, I am now and forever quite content to travel, read, write, or do anything else that pleases me."

"When you're a bit older and lonelier, you're going to miss having a companion."

"If so, I'll buy a cat."

I am, in fact, as content as a man can be. I have my health, my books, and a divine mission. And, yes, I also have nagging concerns about the way things went at Lenora Fairchild's home. I did not adequately expect the unexpected, and as a result I found my emotions somewhat out of control. That must change.

In addition, I worry about this Rosebud Killer task force that the *Times* has mentioned more than once recently. Has the NYPD actually made significant progress on the case, or is this, as I suspect, mere window-dressing for the press? I am not absolutely certain. And I am never comfortable when I am not absolutely certain.

I replay the details of my visits to the three widows, and I remain satisfied that I have left no amateurish clues for the police to pursue. At the same time, I do believe it may be time to broaden my horizons a bit.

I have not been to Maryland for years.

12.

Silvano and Nazareth caught their first apparent break in the Rosebud Killer case when a witness showed up unannounced at One Police Plaza two weeks after Lenora Fairchild's murder had made page one of the *Times*. Bud Grant, a veteran UPS driver, had delivered to an East 38th Street address on the day that Lenora Fairchild was murdered, and he told the officer at the front desk that he had seen someone at the victim's door. Ten minutes later Grant sat in the upstairs conference room with the two detectives, dumping a third packet of sugar into his vile NYPD coffee.

"Thanks very much for coming in, Mr. Grant," Silvano said as he shook the guy's hand. "We can certainly use your help."

"Hey, I would have been here sooner," Grant said between sips, "but my wife and I just got back from Disney World with the kids. I didn't read about Mrs. Fairchild until last night when I went through all the old newspapers."

"And you're sure it was Mrs. Fairchild's door where you saw this guy?" Silvano asked him.

"No question," Grant nodded. "I've been delivering to the Fairchilds for years, and they give me a hundred bucks every Christmas. They're really nice people. I, uh, mean they were."

"Exactly where were you when you saw this person?"

"Across the street, two houses down. I had just taken a package out of the back of my truck and was locking the door. I looked across the street, and I noticed this guy at the Fairchilds' front door."

"What was he doing?"

"Standing there, you know, waiting for someone to answer the door-bell, I guess. I went around the truck with my package and up the front steps, and I was standing there because I needed a delivery signature. I happened to look across the street again, and now the guy was gone."

"Were you suspicious at the time?"

"Nope. I just happened to notice him there. And the next time I looked he was gone."

Nazareth had been taking notes but looked up toward Grant.

"You weren't suspicious," he said somewhat warily, "but you noticed this guy for some reason. Do you know why?"

Grant took his time, trying to remember the scene.

"No particular reason. He was wearing pretty old clothes and just didn't look like someone who belonged there."

"When you say he was wearing old clothes," Nazareth said, "do mean like a homeless person?"

"No, he definitely didn't look homeless. He could have been a work-man maybe."

"Did he have a tool box?" Silvano asked.

"No, I didn't see him carrying anything."

"And what time of day was this?"

"Late afternoon. I remember that because I was nearly finished for the day and had a doctor's appointment that night. So I needed to get home."

"All right," said Nazareth. "This is really important. We need you to describe this guy in as much detail as you possibly can. If he's the killer, you're the strongest witness we've got. So please think back and try to see the guy standing there on the front steps. Is he facing the street? Is he facing the door?

Is his hair long or short? Is there anything about his clothing that might stand out? Anything at all you can remember, Mr. Grant."

Grant closed his eyes, tilted his head back, and began describing what he could remember.

"He wasn't a kid, wasn't old, either, so maybe 45 or 50. I'm not very good at picking ages."

"That's fine," Nazareth said. "What else?"

"Average height, a little too heavy. Short hair. Gray maybe. Not sure about that."

"Tell us about his clothes," Silvano said.

"Okay. Baggy dark pants, maybe black." He paused, then began nodding. "There was something about his shirt. Let me think. Yeah, his shirt was green, dark green maybe. And when he turned sideways, just kind of looking around, I could see something red on the front of the shirt. Like a red design or red lettering maybe."

"Some kind of uniform top maybe?"

"Could be, yeah. I mean not like a police uniform or anything, but some kind of company shirt. A work shirt — long sleeves, looked kind of old to me."

"Did you happen to see a truck parked anywhere? Maybe this guy was with a local company?"

"No. Didn't notice that. As I say, I didn't see anything really suspicious, just some guy who looked a little out of place. And a minute later he was gone. I wasn't especially looking for him. I just noticed some things and thought this might be helpful."

"It's tremendously helpful," Silvano said enthusiastically, "and we really appreciate your coming in today. We could use more guys like you."

Silvano and Nazareth compared notes after Grant had left them.

"Okay, so we've now got someone at Mrs. Fairchild's door on the day she was murdered," Silvano began, "and it's someone who's definitely not trying to blend in with the locals."

"A guy in old clothes pushing his way into a home on East 38th Street on a weekday afternoon," Nazareth said skeptically. "I understand that damn near anything can happen in this world, but I really can't see that happening."

"I'm with you, but this is what we've got. Let's track down a green shirt with a red design."

"Shouldn't be more than ten million of those in Manhattan," Nazareth grinned. "But, hey, we're detectives."

13.

I had never heard of White Marsh, Maryland, until two days ago, and now I am driving there in accordance with His grand design.

My online search of recent obituaries has touched on at least fifty towns and cities within a comfortable driving distance of Manhattan, and I have identified more than one hundred widows in need of rescue. This leaves me free to choose the very best candidates on the basis of several criteria, chief among them my ability to avoid arrest.

Fewer than 10,000 people call White Marsh home, and two of its eldest male residents recently departed this world, each leaving behind a suffering widow. I will gladly help either of these unfortunate women, but my decision awaits the results of today's preliminary visit.

White Marsh is a relatively easy drive — a bit more than three hours when the Lincoln Tunnel cooperates — along I-95 and I-295. And since I think it supremely unlikely that the NYPD has much reach beyond the borders of New York City, I view Maryland as a place where I can safely do God's work. This could change over time, of course, but I derive much comfort from the fact that in America there are far more places than detectives.

As long as I keep moving, they will never catch up.

After a leisurely ride along one of America's busiest Interstates, I arrive in Fallston, Maryland, which is roughly ten miles from White Marsh. I leave my car in a McDonald's parking lot, then walk several blocks to a Budget office, where I rent a bland white Ford Fusion with Maryland plates. Even though I will not actually call on anyone today, I refuse to risk having someone remember an out-of-state vehicle that slowed down as it passed a widow's home. As I see it, the rental car is inexpensive insurance.

I drive almost due south through leafy, underpopulated neighborhoods until I cross Maryland 40, the Pulaski Highway, and turn off onto Marsh Line Road. Here I find abundant solitude. I slowly motor along a sleepy two-lane road that passes through a stretch of deep woods before reaching a tiny residential neighborhood of exceedingly modest old homes, most of them standing at the water's edge. An unusually high number of the residences, I notice, have *FOR SALE* signs at the street.

The home I'm looking for, Doris Healy's, is on my left. It, too, is for sale. A decrepit two-story bungalow covered by bleached cedar shakes, the structure stands next to a large, grassy lot that stretches at least a hundred feet from the nearest home on the right. The home to the left is disagreeably close for my purposes, but it is essentially walled off by a row of tall, overgrown boxwoods and a wide old spruce that entirely blocks the view to the Healys' front porch.

I continue past the home, never exceeding twenty miles per hour, until the roadway dead-ends on a narrow peninsula that reaches into the Bird River, part of the Chesapeake Bay's 100,000 miles of tributaries. After making a U-turn, I again pass slowly by the Healy home on my way back to the highway. I could easily take a quick photo or two with my iPhone, as though I were a prospective buyer looking for a summer home. But I will have no difficulty remembering the key details, and I have no wish to call attention to myself.

Would anyone actually notice? Not likely. The few people I see, all of them quite old, pay no attention whatsoever to the man in the white car who has detoured from the main road in order to view the Chesapeake's backwaters. Two men scrape old paint off a green dinghy that rests on two-by-fours and cinder blocks. One woman in a summery house dress plants flats of impatiens along the front flower garden, while another walks a black Lab that has almost as much gray hair as she does.

I don't need to visit the second widow on my list. Doris Healy's neighborhood is everything I could wish for.

14.

Over the space of three days Silvano and Nazareth worked the phones, calling officers in all five boroughs in an effort to track down a green shirt with some sort of red design on the front. Throughout the process the two detectives had found themselves waist-deep in the major-league sarcasm that abounds in New York City.

"A green shirt. Whoa, baby!" said Silvano's former partner Ed Lembo, who now headed a Brooklyn unit. "Man, you've really got this case nailed down, don't you? What time is the press conference?"

"Right, just pile it on, Ed. I haven't heard any of this before. No, seriously, you're the first wiseass who's busted my chops over this."

"Hell, I can't understand why. It's not like you're looking for just any middle-aged fat guy with gray hair. You're looking for a middle-aged fat guy with gray hair who's wearing a green shirt. That gets us down to, what, maybe four million guys in the Metro area?"

"Yes to all that," Silvano said. "But this is the hand I'm playing. Unless, of course, you have a better idea."

"Actually, I do. Come over to Brooklyn and work with me. Because if you stay where you are, my friend, you're going to get your ass nailed to the mayor's wall on this one. Nobody likes seeing little old ladies murdered," Lembo told him, "and we both know the odds against finding the killer are about a billion to one. This guy's not just really sick. He's really smart. I've seen the file, Javi, and I'm telling you this thing doesn't end anytime soon."

"But just the same you'll ask around about the green shirt, right? If we ask enough people, maybe the shirt rings a bell for someone."

"You got it, pal. I wish I could do more for you. But I'll get my guys following up every which way they can."

"I know you will, and I appreciate it. Stay well, Ed."

"You too, Javi."

Less than two hours later Silvano took a call from a young patrolman, Jeff McCloskey, who had devoted his first year on the force to hoofing around the streets of Times Square. He spent most of every day asking tourists not to step in front of moving buses while taking pictures with their iPhones.

"Hey, Detective, I'm calling about that green shirt we were briefed on a couple days ago."

"What have you got for me?"

"A few minutes ago I noticed this green-and-white van parked on West 43rd. Kelly's Plumbing. New York plates. Midtown address. As I walked past, the driver got out, and he was wearing a green work shirt with red lettering on the front. Two lines: *Ralph*, and underneath that, *Kelly's Plumbing*."

"Did you say anything to him?" Silvano asked, the excitement rising in his voice.

"No, I didn't want to spook him, so I just called you."

"Outstanding! Listen, what I'd like you to do," Silvano explained, "is go back past the truck and see if there's a phone number on it."

"Yep, there is. I already have that: 1-800-PLUMMER. That's *plummer* with two *M*'s."

"P-L-U-M-M-E-R?"

"Right, either Kelly can't spell, or the other phone number was already taken."

"Gotcha. This is great stuff, Officer McCloskey. I really appreciate your help, and I'll be sure to have Deputy Chief Crawford get word to your captain about this."

"That would be really great, Detective. I've been walking Times Square for about a thousand years, if you know what I mean."

Silvano hung up and wound his way through a maze of desks. He found Nazareth at a computer screen reading an article entitled "Multivariate Statistical Analysis."

"I'm afraid to ask what that's all about," said Silvano.

Nazareth shook his head slowly and kept looking at the screen.

"Please don't," he said. "One hour of this stuff, and my brain is orbiting some planet in another galaxy. Multivariate statistical analysis is basically a way of searching for answers when you're dealing with lots of moving parts. And it says here all we need to do is use a non-metric multidimensional scaling procedure to find the Rosebud Killer."

"Right," Silvano nodded. "And what the hell is that?"

"No clue, Javi. I've read this three times, and I still have no idea. I guess it means we should do detective work."

"Speaking of which, I just got a call from a uniform up at Times Square, and it looks as though the guys who work at Kelly's Plumbing wear green work shirts with red stitching on the front."

"Well, hot damn! So I guess we're going to visit Kelly's Plumbing?"

"As soon as you're finished studying for your Ph.D."

Nazareth closed the browser on his laptop. "I'm good to go."

15.

I spend another hour touring the back roads within five miles of Mrs. Healy's home. I have no particular reason for doing so, but also no reason not to. The day is still early, and the more I know about the area, the better prepared I will be for any unexpected developments during my next visit.

Most of the neighborhoods that border the Chesapeake's tributaries have a gritty, working-class feel to them. Take away the cars — the only clear evidence of modern civilization — and you could be in mid-19th century Maryland, where hard-working folks earn modest livings by taking crabs and fish from water that has not yet been befouled by toxic runoff from both industry and the heavily fertilized lawns of the wealthy. The Chesapeake today is dying, and the only people who will tell you otherwise are commercial fishermen who are content to deplete whatever fish remain. They have a right to fish as much as they choose, they will tell you, until one of them catches the last fish ever to swim in the Chesapeake.

I pass a large gated community whose carefully planned views of the water must be breathtaking at certain times of day, and I see extravagant homes whose square footage is probably ten times that of my Manhattan apartment. Each home is a monument to something that I can't quite put my finger on. Avarice? Smugness? Entitlement? I'm not sure. But I know that I would not want to do the housework in any of these grand homes, much less pay for the annual upkeep. I also would not want to face the daily chore of smiling at Ken and Barbie next door, or continually trying to own a better BMW than everyone else, or waving benignly to some neighbor who watches approvingly as his Irish Setter defecates in my pachysandra.

My pleasures are simpler than these, and my work is more enduring.

I drive another twenty-five minutes to Nottingham, Maryland, where I enjoy an inexpensive Italian meal at the local Olive Garden. Many of my Manhattan acquaintances turn up their noses at places like Olive Garden, but I always find the food and the surroundings quite comforting. Whenever I'm on the road, I look for places that consistently deliver the expected. McDonalds for breakfast, Olive Garden for lunch or dinner, that sort of thing. I'm definitely not someone who likes to discover new places, especially when I am alone — which is virtually always — or in a strange city. I have relatively simple tastes and feel no pressure to spend more than the next person.

By the time dusk arrives I reach the Budget office in Fallston and return my rental car. I then walk to McDonalds, where my car has been parked all afternoon, and buy a cup of coffee that I enjoy in the comfort of my own vehicle. I sit in the car listening to a local classical station until darkness falls, then begin the drive home.

On the way I must make one very important prolonged stop. I leave I-95 and after a few minutes pull into the Holiday Inn Express in Aberdeen, Maryland. I choose a parking space in back of the hotel, as close to the corner of the building as possible. From this angle it will be especially difficult for guests to look out their windows and see me at work later this evening.

This vantage point will also keep me away from most of the hotel's evening traffic, since people generally like to park near the lobby entrance. Only a daring few, I know from experience, will venture toward the back of the hotel. I lock my car doors, take a few sips of bottled water, and fall asleep listening to a Telemann CD.

The alarm on my iPhone wakes me at 11:15 p.m. The parking lot is perfectly still and poorly lighted at this back corner. The sky has grown overcast since I first arrived, and a gentle rain begins to fall. I sit quietly for another few minutes and through my side mirror keep watch on the windows nearest to where I am parked. Almost all of the rooms are dark. And in those that aren't, the heavy drapes are pulled shut. In less than two minutes I can be on my way again.

I step out of my car and close the door just enough to turn off the interior lights. I walk to the front of the car, then bend down and move quickly to the Toyota SUV two spaces away. Using a small rechargeable Craftsman screwdriver, I remove the SUV's front Maryland license plate. If anyone should pull into the parking lot right now, I will be quite invisible. The rear license plate is the more dangerous of the two, because while I work on that one I will be utterly exposed should anyone drive back here before I finish. I am not concerned about someone who might be looking out a hotel window, because I will be long gone before he or she can call the front desk or the police. But if a car pulls quickly around the corner, I will have some explaining to do.

I crouch and listen. In the distance I can hear highway traffic, but here at the hotel I detect no voices or car engines. All I need is thirty seconds. Two screws, and I'm finished. My heart rate rises as I crab-walk toward the other end of the SUV. I pause and listen once last time before I come around the corner and set the screwdriver into the first screw. If I were attempting to do this with a conventional screwdriver I would fail, without question, because the screw holds fast to the license plate. But my Sears screwdriver easily jolts the screw and twists it out. The second screw releases more readily, and I return to my car and toss the license plates into the back seat.

Is it rain or sweat dripping from my forehead? I can't tell. My heart is pounding inside my chest, and my hands are trembling. Yet what I feel isn't fear. On the contrary, I have never been more energized in my life. The Lord's work is exciting as well as fulfilling.

An hour later, still tingling from the experience, I stop for coffee in a rest area on the highway. Before leaving my car, I slip the two Maryland license plates into a large brown envelope, which I seal and place under the trunk carpeting. When I pay my official visit to Mrs. Healy, the vehicle I use will be virtually untraceable.

How quickly should I return to Maryland? That's the operative question. Is Mrs. Healy my next widow? Or do I dare to work closer to home once again before returning to White Marsh?

I await His sign.

16.

Silvano double-parked the unmarked cruiser outside Kelly's Plumbing, located in a typical 11th Avenue war zone of steel-shuttered store fronts and trashed high-rises. He and Nazareth walked through the open garage door into a cavernous space that served as warehouse, parking garage, and front office for the busy plumbing company. A heavyset guy with white hair and a boozer's florid complexion sat at a grimy desk pecking away at a computer keyboard. His name was Tim Kelly, or so said the red stitching on his green work shirt. He looked up at his early-morning visitors and without missing a beat said, "Good morning, detectives."

Silvano and Nazareth smiled good-naturedly as they flashed their shields. "That obvious, huh?" said Silvano.

"Hey," Kelly snorted, "two well-dressed guys, not carrying meat cleavers, arrive in a late-model black sedan for a morning stroll on 11th Avenue. Right. Either I'm hallucinating, or you're cops. So how can I help you guys this fine morning?"

Silvano explained why they were looking for a heavyset guy wearing a green work shirt, and Kelly asked for the victim's address. A few taps on the keyboard and he said, "The guy you're looking for is Pat O'Reilly. He was at the Fairchild home for forty-seven minutes, minimum charge for one hour, to repair a leaky connection on a new Bosch dishwasher. Service call and labor $235, paid by Citibank check #1372," he continued reading.

"Customer told Pat that she'd be calling again in a week or two because she was having new granite countertops installed and needed us to disconnect and reconnect the plumbing. And, let's see, uh, fifteen minutes after leaving Mrs. Fairchild, Pat was at his next call two blocks away. I'll print you out a copy of the service report."

"That would be great," Silvano said. "Is he around here right now?"

"Should be. Hey, Frankie," he yelled across the garage. "Patty still here?"

"Just loading his truck, boss," Frankie shot back. "You need him?" Frankie looked warily from Kelly to the two detectives.

"Yeah, ask him to come on over." He turned to Silvano. "Pat's one of the best. Been with us for about ten years. Knows his stuff. Never gets complaints or call-backs from customers. A serious workhorse."

"Is there someplace quiet we can talk with him?" Nazareth asked as he looked around the immense space. "This probably won't take long."

"Yeah, there's a break room right across the way. Oh, hey, Patty," he said as O'Reilly walked up to the desk. "These two detectives need to speak with you about one of our customers. Go talk in the break room."

Pat O'Reilly stood not quite six feet tall and seemed to match the UPS driver's description of the man he saw at Mrs. Fairchild's on the day of the murder. Graying hair, beer drinker's gut, and a well-worn green work shirt with *Pat* and *Kelly's Plumbing* in red script over the left pocket. What the UPS driver wouldn't have noticed from a distance, but Silvano and Nazareth did right away, is that Pat had a great smile. He smiled a lot, like a man without a care in the world.

Nazareth kicked off the interview. "We're investigating an incident that took place recently at this address." He showed O'Reilly the top of the service call report. "Do you remember being there?"

"Sure, Mrs. Fairchild. Super person," he said as he gave Nazareth a thumbs-up. "Very first thing she did was hand me a bottle of cold water, because it was a hot day. Most customers never bother with something like that — especially the rich folks, you know. Anyhow, she'd just bought a $2,000 Bosch dishwasher, top of the line, and let two dumb-ass delivery guys install it for her. Big mistake. Always a big mistake," he emphasized. "Don't ever do that.

"Those guys are always happy to take a fifty-buck tip," he continued, "but they don't know jack about plumbing. So, naturally, she had a flood in her kitchen three days later. She thought maybe the machine was a lemon, but it wasn't. Just two guys who should stick to delivering stuff. Hey, did those guys do something besides screwing up the installation?"

Nazareth didn't answer right away. He wanted to see whether the pause would prompt the guy to fidget the way the guilty almost always do. But O'Reilly just looked back and forth between Nazareth and Silvano, smiling the whole time

"How long were you there, Mr. O'Reilly?" Silvano asked.

"Less than an hour," he said as he thought back to the visit. "It should be on that service report."

"And was anyone else there while you were hooking up the dishwasher?"

"Not that I could tell. Mrs. Fairchild brought me into the kitchen, gave me the bottle of water, and told me what was going on with the dishwasher. It took me half a minute to see what was wrong. After that she went off to another room, and I fixed the problem. When I was finished, I called for her, and she came in and wrote out a check. She also gave me a twenty dollar tip, which I didn't want, but she insisted. Very nice lady, like I said."

"Did you notice anything special about the kitchen while you were there? I mean," Nazareth said, "was there anything that really stands out in your mind?"

O'Reilly thought about that, then said, "Aside from the fact that her kitchen is worth more than my whole house?"

"What makes you say that?"

"Let me tell you, this kitchen should be on a magazine cover. Best refrigerator, dishwasher, double oven, floor, even the countertops. She already has granite countertops," he said, somewhat shocked, "but she told me she's getting new ones because she wants a different color. Big money, you know. Great taste."

"Any decorations that stand out in your mind?"

"You mean like paintings?"

"Anything at all," said Silvano.

"No." He shook his head. "Can't think of anything. I was working, not snooping around, you know?"

"How about a large crystal vase filled with flowers. It was right in the middle of the kitchen island. Did you see that?" Nazareth asked.

O'Reilly shook his head vigorously. "No, no flowers there. *That* I would remember."

"Why so?"

"Because that's where Mrs. Fairchild put the water bottle. And that's also where she laid out the paperwork that came with the new dishwasher. She thought I might need it, I guess. I definitely would have noticed a big vase of flowers. It wasn't there."

"Did you go back for any reason once you had left her house?" Silvano asked.

"Nope. Before I left she told me I'd need to come back in a couple weeks because she's doing the new counters, and I wrote that on my report. So what's going on, detectives?" O'Reilly stiffened noticeably when Silvano told him about Mrs. Fairchild's murder. His smile finally disappeared. "Hey, wait, you think I killed her?"

Silvano shook his head slowly. "All we think is that we need to interview everyone who was with Mrs. Fairchild that day. That's why we're here."

"Listen, guys, I have never — and I mean never — been in any kind of trouble, not once in my life. And I sure as hell wouldn't hurt a woman as nice as Mrs. Fairchild. She was perfectly fine while I was there, and I didn't see anyone else come or go."

"Let me ask you something," Nazareth said. "If we go over the parts you listed on the service report, will we find those parts on the dishwasher?"

"Hell, yes," he replied, obviously offended. "We never play games with our customers. We don't need to. We're so damn busy here we can hardly handle all the calls that come in. You think we charge people for work we don't do?"

"And if we ask your boss how long Mrs. Fairchild's job should have taken, he's not going to tell us ten minutes, is he?" Silvano asked. "Because if this type of job should take only ten minutes, you would have had a lot of extra time on your hands."

At this point O'Reilly seemed truly concerned. "Listen, detectives, please believe me. Except for saying hello and goodbye and drinking my water, I worked on Mrs. Fairchild's dishwasher. I took no more time than I needed, and I did the job right. I never waste time, because I always have more calls than I need. I like to see my family at night, you know?"

Silvano thanked O'Reilly for his cooperation, asked him to call if he thought of any details that hadn't been covered, and told him they'd be in touch if they had any other questions. O'Reilly left the room a bit shaken, but Silvano and Nazareth already knew that this wasn't their Rosebud Killer.

"Someone brought her flowers after the plumber left," Nazareth said. "O'Reilly couldn't have missed a large bouquet of spring flowers in a big crystal vase. It wasn't there yet."

Silvano nodded. "Absolutely. I'm thinking the killer needed a way in, so he brought flowers. But we didn't find any wrapping paper or card or delivery receipt. And there's no way in hell the killer brought that big fancy vase with him. No, he brought a bouquet and put the flowers in the vase before he left. But he left no prints on it."

"Even if he bought those flowers within walking distance of Mrs. Fairchild's home, which I doubt," Nazareth reasoned, "we're still talking about standard, everyday spring flowers that you can probably find in thirty Midtown shops. We can go shop to shop forever, but we're not going to find someone who remembers one bouquet of spring flowers . . . sold on June 7th . . . to some guy who walked in, paid cash, and left two minutes later."

Silvano shrugged. "Unfortunately, I think we need to ask around,"

"If we have the manpower, sure. But I think we'd just be spinning our wheels, Javi. This guy is smart, he's careful, and he blends in."

"Blends in? Or is invisible?"

17.

Death closes all: but something ere the end,
Some work of noble note, may yet be done,
Not unbecoming men that strove with Gods.

"**M**r. Edwards."

The dolt looks up from his cell phone, which has occupied his full attention for the past thirty-five minutes. I teach only two summer courses, including this one, *Survey of English Literature,* because I don't have the stomach for three. The pay, though welcome, scarcely compensates for the pain and suffering I endure.

Summer survey courses attract two, and only two, types of students. First are the over-achievers who are planning to graduate in three years. I have a few of them in this class, and they almost restore my hope for our species. Second are the mollusks, Mr. Edwards chief among them, who are taking the course for the second time — perhaps seeking to pull an F up to a D — and hoping that a summer course is a diluted, vacation-friendly version of the real thing. If I average the talent and potential of the two groups, I am able to convince myself that I should wait another week before hanging myself in disgust.

"I don't mean to interrupt your texting, Mr. Edwards."

"Uh, that's, uh, okay," he says. A few students snicker, as indeed they should, but Edwards is clueless.

"I was being ironic, Mr. Edwards."

"Uh, okay."

Trading witticisms with the brain-dead is hardly sporting, so I get back to the lesson at hand.

"Mr. Edwards, the lines that I just read to the class represent perhaps the most powerful statement in *Ulysses*." His eyes are glazed. Is he high, I wonder, or merely stupid? "Okay, let's go back to the beginning. Who wrote *Ulysses*, Mr. Edwards?"

A dim bulb lights his face. "Uh, James Joyce?"

"Is that a question or an answer?"

"An answer."

"Right answer, wrong class, Mr. Edwards. James Joyce did indeed write a novel entitled *Ulysses*, but Alfred, Lord Tennyson wrote the poem *Ulysses*, and we have been discussing that poem for most of today's class."

I leave Edwards wearing his characteristic deer-in-the-headlights look as I turn to another student.

"Miss Klein, please tell me about the lines I just read to the class."

"The speaker is an old man who remembers all the great things he once was and once did. And he decides not to just fade away. He wants to go out in style, doing some work of 'noble note,' instead of just rocking in a chair."

"And do you believe that this is simply Ulysses who is speaking," Miss Klein, "or do you suppose Tennyson is speaking as well?"

"Yes, I think Tennyson was thinking about his own life and what it would mean to him as the years went on. He wrote the poem right after a good friend of his died, and he wanted to say that he would fight on despite this loss."

"And the friend's name was?"

"Arthur Henry Hallam?"

"Question or answer?"

"Answer," she smiles sweetly.

"Quite right," Miss Klein. "Well done. It's amazing how much you know when you read an assignment and stay awake in class, isn't it?"

Everyone glances at Mr. Edwards, who is no longer texting. He is now dozing in a comforting shaft of sunlight that streams through the window and shines upon him like a spotlight.

I take a deep breath and look at the clock high on the rear wall. Soon, I tell myself, you will be away from this absurdity and doing your own work of noble note.

18.

On the Monday following the visit to Kelly's Plumbing in Manhattan, Pete Nazareth sat in a classroom in Falls Church, Virginia, at the start of a five-day counterintelligence program that had been on his calendar for almost a year. The program was offered only to a small group of hand-picked officers, so cancelling at the last minute wasn't an option for someone looking to make his mark at the NYPD.

Silvano and Nazareth agreed that the timing wasn't all that bad, since for the moment much of the day-to-day Rosebud Killer work was being handled by the twenty-five precinct officers who were trying to identify the most seriously at-risk widows within the five boroughs. So Nazareth settled in to learn as much as he could from this program for rising stars.

Nazareth had, in fact, been a rising star all his life. As a kid growing up on Staten Island he was a standout in every sport he tried, including football, even though he was always one of the smallest players on the team. He proved to be a ferocious competitor who was willing to push himself to the limit. Once he reached high school he fell in love with track, and by the outdoor season of his senior year he regularly ran under 4:10 for the mile. That and straight A's earned him full ride at Fordham University.

He continued his winning ways at Fordham, graduating summa cum laude, earning a black belt in Taekwondo in his spare time, and running a personal-best 3:58 mile during his team's final week of practice. The mile mark would never appear in the school's record books, since he had achieved it in practice. But he knew, and that's really all that mattered to him.

After Fordham it was the Marine Corps, where as a young captain in a Special Operations Battalion he earned a Silver Star while leading troops on a high-risk operation among the cave complexes of Eastern Afghanistan. In an area known by the Marines as the Valley of the Shadow, Nazareth went hand-to-hand with three Al Qaeda hostiles who were dragging off one of his injured team members. His action resulted in a small scar on his chin, three very dead bad guys, and a rescued Marine sergeant whose account of the incident made Nazareth a living legend within the Special Ops fraternity.

Toward the middle of his week in Falls Church, Nazareth managed to catch up with Mavis Underhill, the FBI profiling expert who had continued to sift through the details of the Rosebud Killer case. The two shared an early dinner at an outdoor café in DC, where Underhill worked and lived.

"A couple of things have been gnawing at me lately," she said. "First you have the silk rosebud that this guy leaves with each victim. Initially I thought this was just a publicity gimmick of some sort, and maybe it is. But I now think it's more likely to convey the rosebud's traditional meaning."

"Love?"

"Not quite," she explained after a sip of Merlot. "A fully opened red rose symbolizes love. But a red rosebud, I have recently learned, actually represents purity or perhaps a combination of purity and love."

"Interesting," he said, deep in thought. "Is it possible he knows each of the victims and that this is where the love and purity idea comes in?"

"I don't think so. From what we've seen so far I think he's too smart to kill women that we can trace back to him through some common thread. What he's doing, I believe, is showing tenderness, or respect, or love — something in that general direction — for each of the women. It's as though he thinks that what he's doing represents an act of goodness or purity in some perverse way."

"As though he's helping them?" Nazareth said. He looked off into the distance while he considered Underhill's theory. "I guess anything is possible, but I have trouble buying into this."

"No need to buy into anything right now," she replied. "Just keep your mind open to all the possibilities. What we're doing is triangulating. We keep identifying potential variables until the right ones cross each other on the grid."

"Okay, that's fine. What else has been gnawing at you?"

"Something I believe could prove to be important in your investigation," she told him. "We're obviously dealing with someone who is both smart and careful. But," she paused and locked Nazareth's eyes with hers, "somewhere along the line he has taken an enormous risk. Follow me on this. Let's assume he lives in New York City — and I do believe that's the case — and let's also assume he drove to Pennsylvania for the sole purpose of killing his first victim. That sets up three possibilities.

"First possibility: he knew the victim, and he called ahead to arrange a visit. That way he'd know for sure she would be home when he arrived. No wasted trip, right? But," she shook her head, "that would be an exceptionally high-risk approach, because he would have no way of knowing whether she might tell someone about his visit. So I rule out this possibility.

"Second possibility: he had a victim in mind, went to Pennsylvania simply hoping she would be there, and got lucky. In this case he probably drove out and back the same day, because he didn't want to stay overnight and thereby increase the likelihood that someone would remember him. But if you think about it, this is also a very high-risk strategy. What if she hadn't been home? What if someone had been with her? Lots of what-ifs. And lots of ways things could have gone wrong.

"The third possibility is a variation on the second: he had to drive back and forth several times before he got the perfect opportunity — meaning the woman was home, she was alone, there was no traffic in front of the house, and so forth. But this, too, is a risky strategy. The more he went back and forth to Pennsylvania, the more likely it was that someone out there would remember him or his car and notify the police after the murder. So no matter how you slice it, he was gambling."

"Unless he was just incredibly lucky," Nazareth said after thinking through the three scenarios, "I think your third possibility is the likeliest. He had to make several trips before everything lined up properly."

"Yes," she nodded. "That seems the most plausible."

"But if he did that, he also created multiple opportunities for someone to notice him."

"I agree."

"Well, it sounds as reasonable as anything else we're working with," Nazareth said as he jotted down some notes. "I'll talk with Silvano and see if we can't knock on some doors in Pennsylvania. If this guy made multiple scouting trips, let's hope somebody remembers the car."

Nazareth decided not to call his partner until morning. That way maybe Silvano could enjoy a relaxing night with his wife and two young kids at their modest co-op in Riverdale.

19.

Silvano's phone rang on the table next to the bed shortly after midnight, and he snagged it in the dark before Charlene woke up. His wife was actually a pretty good sleeper — something about running after two kids, 5 and 3, all day every day — and, like most NYPD wives, she had long since learned how to tune out Silvano's late-night crisis calls.

"Yeah, Silvano here."

"Javi, Tucker from the 20th. We have something going down right now, and it might be your Rosebud guy."

Bobby Tucker and Silvano had gone through the police academy together and remained buddies who still saw each other now and then at the family barbecues that made the rounds of cops' homes each summer. Tucker worked in the 20th Precinct, whose turf was a mixed bag of residential, commercial, and cultural neighborhoods on Manhattan's Upper West Side.

Silvano was already up and pulling on his pants.

"Talk to me, Bobby."

"We got a 911 call about twenty minutes ago. A woman on that high-priority widows list of yours. She heard someone in the kitchen, and she locked herself in a safe room off the bedroom. Brownstone near Lincoln Center. Big, big money."

"Okay, so who's where?"

"I'm at the front door, and I've got two guys at the back. No sirens, no lights. We know the woman is safe, but we don't know whether the guy is inside. If he is, no way he gets past us."

Silvano memorized the address as he closed the apartment door.

"Outstanding, Bobby. I'll be there in fifteen."

Silvano hit the flashers on the Impala as he roared down the Henry Hudson Parkway. The highway was virtually empty at this time of night, but he used the lights anyway so that no one would try to pull him over. He shut the lights off as he turned onto West 73rd. The brownstone was on the corner, where two uniformed officers were using their blue-and-white for cover. Next to them, in civilian clothes, was Bobby Tucker.

"Javi," said Tucker, waving Silvano over. "Officer Ramos here thinks he saw movement at the first-floor drapes a few minutes ago. Not sure. But if someone's in there, he knows he's got lots of company. Maybe he's thinking he can shoot his way out. Two of my guys hopped the fence and are in the back garden."

"If this is our guy," Silvano said, "I don't think he'll try to go out in a blaze of glory. The perp we're after is very careful, very smart, and most likely scared shitless right about now. We can probably talk him out."

"We didn't try the front door," Tucker said as he peered over the car's hood, "but one of my guys checked the back door. Lock was either picked or never set."

"No alarm?"

"Standard wireless system, not worth a damn. Place like this," he nodded to the multi-million dollar home, "should have top shelf stuff, not pure crap. We've got eighth-graders disabling these wireless systems."

"And the woman is okay?"

"Yep. Officer Davis has been on the phone with her since I called you. She's relatively calm now. They had a safe room installed about five years ago, and you'd need a nuclear warhead to get in."

"Okay, how do you want to play this?"

"Not sure, Javi. We really don't know whether anyone's in there, so do we want to call in ESU yet?"

Silvano weighed the options. If this turned into a shoot-out, having the Emergency Service Unit on hand would prove to be the right decision. Those guys played for keeps and had all the right training and equipment. But if the whole thing was merely the figment of a frightened old woman's imagination — definitely a possibility — neither Silvano nor Tucker would enjoy explaining why they had hit the panic button.

"Okay," said Silvano, eyeing the five-story brownstone, "how about we hold off on calling in the big guns until we know what we've really got?"

"Suits me."

"Let me go around back," he said. "I'll open the door just a crack and use the megaphone to let this guy know exactly where things stand. If he cooperates, we'll handle it. If we get nowhere, we call ESU."

"Sounds good. I'll go with you." Tucker grinned. "I hope you have your climbing shoes on, Javi, because the fence might be a little tricky for an old guy like you."

Silvano smiled and gave him the finger.

The two detectives slowly made their way to the rear patio, a moonlit oasis of lush trees and manicured shrubs surrounding an opulent expanse of Italian marble.

"This garden is worth more than my house," Tucker said as he motioned for the two uniformed officers to hold their positions.

"God bless America," Silvano smiled. "Keep buying that lottery ticket, Bobby."

The two detectives inched toward the darkened back door, and Silvano assessed the layout.

"Okay, the back stairs are too narrow for both of us," Silvano said, "so you hang here for a minute. Here's what I do: I hug the fence until I get to the stairs. I go up, push the door open, and tell him to get his ass out. If we get nothing, I come back, and we call ESU. Plan?"

Tucker gave an encouraging thumbs-up. "Just make sure you stick real goddamn close to the fence," Tucker said as he drew his weapon, "and stay far to the left side of that door when you open it. We have no idea what this asshole is thinking."

Silvano nodded. "If he's my guy, I think he just caves. Either way, I don't see anyone thinking he can shoot his way out. You've got this place locked down."

"Agreed."

Silvano put his right shoulder to the fence, crouched down, and slowly made his way to the rear stairway — poured concrete with wrought iron handrails on both sides. *Why doesn't this woman install motion-sensor lights out here?* he wondered. *Save a couple hundred bucks? It's dark as hell.* He cautiously went up the left side of the stairs. At the top he reached across to the knob on the right side, turned it quietly, and gently nudged the door open forty-five degrees. If Silvano had been able to see inside the dark entry way, he would have noticed the business end of the Glock 20, a hunting gun whose massive firepower can stop a charging rhino.

Before Silvano could raise the megaphone to his mouth, he took a 10mm round to the face and flew back dead onto the patio.

The shooter sprang from the door like a wild animal released from its cage. Before he had taken five steps, Tucker and the two patrolmen had put eight bullets in him, including three to the head.

White guy, mid-fifties. Blood and brain tissue everywhere.

20

The next morning Nazareth nearly lost his breakfast when he called in and learned that his partner had been killed on the job. He had always understood the risks that come with police work, but death in the abstract had not prepared him sufficiently for the death of a partner — especially someone of Silvano's quality.

His first stop when he got back to New York City was Silvano's place in the Bronx. He didn't know whether Javi's wife Charlene would be home, but that didn't matter. He needed to be there. Whenever he and Silvano had talked about something other than the Rosebud Killer, it was usually Charlene, Javi, Jr., and Nita. The guy's life away from work was 100% family, so if his life essence was still floating around somewhere, Nazareth figured this is where it would be.

A sweet-faced woman with long, dark hair and red eyes answered his knock. She balanced Nita on her hip. Javi, Jr. was on the couch behind her, sitting next to an older man and woman, both gray-haired, probably her parents. Something like this should never happen to a good family man, Nazareth thought, and he caught himself tearing up before Charlene could say anything.

"Oh, Pete," she said, forcing a sad smile, "we lost him. We lost our Javi."

He just nodded. He knew that if he tried to speak right now, he'd lose it. And he didn't want that, for her sake as well as his own. Anyway, she had no trouble reading the pain in his eyes.

"Come in, Pete."

He put his hand up and searched for the right words. They had been right there on the tip of his tongue before he reached the apartment door, but now his mouth wouldn't cooperate.

"Please, it's okay," she said gently, urging him to enter. "I think Javi loved you as much as he loved me. He called you the original All American boy. And you were the partner of his dreams."

Nazareth took a few tentative steps into the apartment.

"I felt the same way, Charlene, and I'm obviously having trouble accepting this. I'm so sorry for you and your family, and I'm so sorry I wasn't there with him."

Tears rolled down Charlene's cheeks, and daughter Nita began to wipe them away.

"Come. Meet my Mom and Pop."

Nazareth stayed long enough to know that Charlene and the kids would eventually triumph over Silvano's awful death. She came from a strong, loving family that would hang in with her. And a long time ago she had come to terms with what every officer's wife knows can happen. Throughout his brilliant career her husband had always believed deeply that what he did on the streets of New York City would make the place better, safer, more welcoming for his family and everyone else who went there. This was a guy who desperately wanted to live, and who had everything to live for. Yet he had never failed to put his life on the line.

After leaving Silvano's home Nazareth drove to Lower Manhattan and hit the office for the first time in over a week. His first stop was Silvano's desk. Nothing had been touched since last night's shooting. It felt almost like another Monday morning to him, and he half expected Javi to walk in with his cup of Dunkin' Donuts coffee.

One minute you have the world perfectly under control, he thought, and then you blink. In that fraction of a second everything can change. Laughing, then crying. Succeeding, then failing. Living, then dying. You just blink, and the world changes forever.

Nazareth was a guy who often sat alone at night and thought deeply about these kinds of things. He was the consummate warrior when the situation demanded it of him, but he was also exceptionally comfortable inside his own head and continually asked himself questions that "real men" are presumed to ignore.

Does a good man's death ever change anything?

Did we create evil, or was it always there, festering in the primordial soup that ultimately became *homo sapiens*?

Why am I on this planet?

"He was a very good man, Pete," said Deputy Chief Crawford, who walked up alongside Nazareth. "One of the best I've ever worked with."

"You've seen more than I have, Chief, but I can tell you he was *the* best I've ever worked with. I wish it had been me instead of him."

"I know," Crawford said softly, no longer the chief who terrorized his subordinates. "Let's go talk in my office."

Nazareth declined a cup of coffee from the throwback electric pot on Crawford's credenza. Crawford poured himself a cup, then looked gravely at the young detective.

"I brought Javi here when I became Deputy Chief," he began. "I worked with him before he made detective, and I saw him grow stronger, better, smarter, every day . . . especially after he got promoted. So I knew he was someone I could build this place around. Like recruiting a star center for the Knicks, you know? That's what it was like. He was the key recruit. I built everything around his skills and his leadership."

Crawford was not someone to share his feelings easily, and this unchar-acteristic openness left Nazareth unprepared for what came next.

"You're the same kind of guy, Pete. I spent enough time around the two of you — the two of you as a team — to see that you were two sides of the same coin. You both wanted the really tough cases. And I knew that you two would bring this Rosebud son of a bitch in.

"Well, now we have a dead cop-killer in the morgue," Crawford said bitterly, "and we don't know whether he's the guy you and Javi were after. My gut tells me he's not. But we need to know for sure. If he's not, then we still have a nasty case on our hands. And I need you to take it from here.

"It's your team now. Keep the people you've got, add if necessary, but get the job done."

Nazareth nodded gently as he looked the chief in the eyes.

"You can bet your life on that, Chief."

21.

I walk the four blocks from my apartment to the garage. For $400 a month I have the privilege of trekking through rain, snow, or blistering heat whenever I need to use my car. $4,800 a year, not including an indecent tip to Ramon at Christmas if I want my car kept in one piece. Since when do you deserve a tip for doing your job? Never. But that's New York City for you. Pay five dollars for a cup of coffee, and some cretin in a black apron glares at you unless you put another dollar in his jar. Walk into a florist and pick up some flowers, and they give you the finger behind your back if you leave without dropping a couple bucks in the "tips appreciated" box. Are tourists supposed to tip cops who provide directions to Radio City Music Hall? Not yet . . . but soon.

I'm feeling peevish, no doubt because I have another long day of driving ahead of me. It would be easier if I could just use my own car throughout, but that's not an option. No. I'm doing this the right way. So at 3:45 p.m. I pick up my car, head down to the Battery Tunnel, and eventually crawl over the Verrazano Bridge to Staten Island. From there it's the Goethals Bridge to New Jersey, where I pick up I-95 and head to Maryland. As I had on my first trip, I leave my beige Nissan Altima at the McDonald's in Fallston and rent a car — a gray Toyota Camry this time — a few blocks away.

Today before fulfilling my mission I enjoy a leisurely and highly satisfying early dinner at Jody's Crab House, about ten miles from Doris Healy's home in White Marsh. No alcohol, just clam chowder, crab cakes, and a small salad. I make a bit of small talk with a waitress whose two young children, she informs me, don't appreciate all that she has done to raise them by herself. But I cut the conversation short, tell her I'm on my way to see my father in Baltimore, and leave a 20% tip. Anything larger or smaller might jog her memory later, and I wish not to be remembered.

Twenty minutes later night has fallen, and I am parked very much alone on the long, narrow road that leads to Doris Healy's home. The street is heavily bordered on both sides by tall marsh grasses and a few gnarled trees that don't seem to mind the salt water. Certain that no cars are heading in my direction, I take out my electric screwdriver and switch license plates. My rental car is now perfectly secure from any prying eyes I may encounter during my visit to the aged widow.

Nine minutes later I pull up in front of her house and notice that only a couple of relatively dim lights seem to be on. Is she home? Is she alone? I can't be certain from the street. I get out of the rental car and follow the weathered slate walk to her unlocked screened porch. I step inside and see that the old wooden front door is wide open, but the glass storm door is closed. I cannot tell whether it is locked, and I don't dare try it in case she has company.

Directly ahead of me is a staircase that leads to the second floor. Toward the right is a large open space that I assume is a combination dining room and living room. I ring the doorbell and wait to see which plan will unfold tonight. Will I talk myself into her home and fulfill my mission of mercy? Will I find a visitor with her and need to excuse myself as a lost tourist? Or will I find no one home and have to try again another day? Improvisation and patience are two of my great strengths.

Ah, she walks toward the front door. I note that she moves more unsteadily than she should at 76. I often see older men and women who are far nimbler than Doris Healy. I take this as a sign that I have been guided to someone who truly needs me.

She squints at the door but doesn't see much. No porch light. A silly oversight for any old widow.

"Robbie?" she says as she reaches the storm door.

"No, ma'am. I'm Special Agent John Wilson, FBI." I unfold my wallet and hold it to the glass door. Even a close inspection will show my ID card to be a perfect representation of the real thing, courtesy of the Internet and my scanner. But, frankly, who but an FBI agent would recognize a forgery anyway?

"I'm looking for Mrs. Doris Healy," I say crisply. I choose my words carefully. The phrase *looking for* is authoritative, perhaps even a bit ominous. It is therefore preferable to something along the lines of *would like to speak with,* a timid phrase that makes compliance sound optional. The words have their desired effect. I can see that she is startled to be the focus of an FBI investigation.

"I'm Doris Healy," she says meekly, her anxiety evident.

"Mrs. Healy, I'm with the FBI's Baltimore Field Office, and we have reason to believe that you may be in some danger."

My voice is flat and businesslike. I don't want her to panic. I just need her to open the door.

"Danger? Oh, my. What kind of danger?"

"Well, ma'am, that's why I'm here." I hold up the first of several meaningless 5x7 images that I have printed off the Internet. It shows a biker type with a jagged scar on his left cheek and a spider tattoo that reaches out from under his T-shirt and wraps around his bull neck. "I would like to show you a few photographs unless you're busy or expecting company. I'll need about fifteen minutes, and I can always come back."

"Oh, Lord, no. Please, please come in. I'll get my glasses. I can't imagine why I would be in danger."

She turns toward the living room, and as she does so I quietly close the inner door and turn the lock. When she reaches the coffee table next to the couch, I am at her side, stun gun in hand. All of the shades are down, and we are very much alone. She utters a brief squeal as the current jolts her. I regret any pain this causes, but it will be short-lived and quickly forgotten. I lower her to the couch and, still holding the stun gun to her chest, administer the diazepam. Time stops for her, the great blessing of this particular drug. Next is the sodium pentobarbital and eternal rest.

I leave the lights on after I have posed her on the couch with a silk rosebud in her hands. She looks relieved. Her face is peaceful, and the barest hint of a smile graces her lips. She is beyond all pain now. I pray that she is already with the man she loved for more than fifty years.

As I step into the darkness of the screened porch I listen carefully, then look up and down the street. I hear muted voices down where Marsh Line Road dead ends at the water's edge, but all is wonderfully quiet near the Healy home. I walk casually to the street and drive off. Within thirty minutes I have changed the license plates, returned the rental car, and settled onto I-95 for the trip home. At this time of night I should be able to make good time. Back in the apartment by 1:30 a.m., I believe.

A long but praiseful day.

22.

Two days after taking charge of the Rosebud Killer case, Nazareth sat with Detective Tara Gimble, his new partner, at a deli half a block from One Police Plaza. Brooklyn born and raised, Gimble had been on the force for nine years and had gotten her ticket punched on a string of high-profile assignments. Her resume incorporated everything from armed robbery to sex crimes to undercover narcotics work. She was blonde, unpretentiously attractive, and athletically built at 5'7" and 120 pounds. During her senior year at Stanford she was a first-team soccer All American, and the word was she could still run forever in cleats, sneakers, or high heels.

She had also proven herself to be remarkably handy with her Smith & Wesson 5946, partly because she practiced a lot and partly because she had spent many weeks of her younger years hunting in the Adirondacks with her dad, a retired NYPD sergeant. The gun's twelve-pound trigger was no impediment for Gimble, who could squeeze off rounds all day with vise-grip hands that had been crafted by years of judo training. All things considered, thought Nazareth, what's not to like?

After a few sips of black coffee and small talk about running, Manhattan life , and professional backgrounds, they settled into the details of Nazareth's plan for taking down the Rosebud Killer.

"I want to pick up exactly where Silvano left off," he told her. "He planned to go back to the very beginning — the Pennsylvania killing

— because something out there set this whole process in motion. Among other things, with the help of the local and state police you and I will interview every person who might have any scrap of information about either the victim or the day of the murder. If it's there, we need to find it. You and I drive to Hallstead, PA, tomorrow."

Nazareth had spoken the day before with Captain Wayne Miller of the Pennsylvania State Police and been assured of PSP's full cooperation. The investigation of the Hallstead murder hadn't ended, Miller told him, but it hadn't gotten very far either. It was clear to Nazareth and Miller that shared resources would benefit everyone.

"What about Silvano's killer?" Gimble asked. "No chance he's our man?"

Nazareth shook his head as he studied her face.

"No way. Tucker from the 20th will eventually ID the body, but I already know he's not our guy. No syringes on him, no silk rosebud, nothing at all that would connect him to the serials. This guy was after money and jewelry in the right neighborhood. The woman just happened to fit our profile."

"Okay," she said, "what's the drill for you and me in Pennsylvania?"

"Tomorrow, late morning, we meet with Capt. Miller to get whatever documentation he can turn over to us," he explained, "and then you and I split up. We visit everyone who has already been interviewed and, more importantly, try to identify potential witnesses who were overlooked. I figure we'll go our separate ways each morning, compare notes at lunch, then go back to interviewing for the afternoon. We'll finish each day comparing notes again."

"Sounds reasonable to me. How many days are you thinking?"

"Two, maybe three. Longer if we're on a roll."

"You still want to have someone visit Midtown florists?"

"That was Silvano's plan, so we'll go with it," he said. "I'm not expecting much, but let's give it a shot."

"Sounds good." She smiled encouragingly.

Nazareth put the lid on his coffee. "Then let's go find us a killer."

23.

I am greatly saddened by the report of Detective Silvano's death in today's newspaper. In trying to hunt me down he was merely doing his job, no less than I have been doing mine. Although he might not have understood why, he and I were brothers — two honest men trying to make life better and safer for the weak. To be torn from a young wife and two small children like that is unspeakably wrong. It disgusts me that he was slain by the sort of trash that one routinely finds nowadays all over America, most especially in cities like New York, where viciousness is the new normal.

My father died when I was 9 and he but 37. He was in his old Toyota, stopped at a red light, when a tractor-trailer loaded with frozen meat plowed into him from behind. The trucker had been driving for twenty-nine hours — making up time lost in a Kansas snowstorm, he said tearfully in court — and was numb from a combination of fatigue, NoDoz, and pot. He was sentenced to twenty years, was released after three, and killed five more people — himself and a family of four — when he drove a stolen car through a red light less than a month after leaving prison.

Life is never normal again after you lose your father when you are nine. Adolescence is a grim enough ordeal for a boy without losing the father who could have helped make sense of it. But things were worse, I came to realize, for my mother, who was forced to hold down two jobs while raising her children in a house that was sinking under the weight of a huge mortgage. Had my father died with more than $10,000 of life insurance in place, perhaps our lives would have been gentler. But he hadn't, so they weren't.

My mother lost the best of her jobs when I was eleven; she lost the home when I was twelve; and she was a crack addict before I reached high school. She eventually beat the addiction and kept the family afloat by alternating between small jobs and welfare. She died of AIDS during my sophomore year at state college. After that I worked full time, went to school full time, and took care of my sister.

Here I am.

Detective Silvano and I would never have been drinking buddies, I am certain, but I mourn his untimely passing. I also deeply regret that the NYPD suspects, if only for the moment, that I may be his killer. I was in Maryland when he was shot, but more to the point I am not a murderer and never will be.

Tonight I will pray for Silvano. I will also pray for widows — those who still suffer as well as those who enjoy everlasting peace.

Amen.

24.

Nazareth and Gimble drove to Hallstead, PA, in one car, then rented another so that they could each have wheels while calling on witnesses. They checked into the Colonial Brick Inn and Suites, which offered a splendid view of a big, lazy bend in the Susquehanna River about a quarter of a mile away and stood just a short walk from Dunkin' Donuts. They were soon joined by Capt. Miller of the PSP, who gave each of them a thick file folder that contained copies of all the interviews that had been conducted right after the Martinson murder along with crime scene photos and forensics reports. As an added courtesy, Miller included in each folder a letter signed by Jed Sanders, the Susquehanna County D.A., asking local citizens to assist Nazareth and Gimble in any way possible. The letter didn't seem necessary to Nazareth, but he appreciated the strong indication of support just the same.

The three officers batted ideas around for a while, then were joined by Art and Chelsea Martinson, who had agreed to meet with Nazareth and Gimble. Eleanor Martinson's son and daughter-in-law plainly had not gotten over the shock of the murder. When they were first interviewed on the day that Mrs. Martinson's body had been found, they were barely able to speak, much less consider who might have wanted to harm her. This time around they were better able to handle questions, but the whole episode remained surreal, a bad dream from which they were unable to awaken.

"I'd like to ask you what we'll be asking everyone else we meet with," said Nazareth. "First and foremost, can you think of anyone who had issues with your mother? Anyone she had argued with? Anyone who owed her money? Anyone who might benefit in some way from her death?"

"Mom's death hurt everyone who knew her," Art said, his voice cracking slightly. "You couldn't have had a better friend. If you needed help, she was there. If you needed someone to talk to, she was a phone call away. If you were in the hospital, she was the first person who brought you flowers. Whoever killed her didn't know her."

"That's what's so horrible about this," Chelsea quickly added. "If there had been a believable motive, something that would allow us to connect the dots and understand why this happened, I think we could move on. We'd still be heartbroken, but we could at least understand how this whole thing came about. But it was just random. Someone picked her out of a phone book or saw her as she drove by, and he decided to kill her. What kind of sick, awful person could do that? What kind of world do we live in?" She began to sob. When Art leaned over to put his arm around her, she stiffened as though she wanted to be left alone in her grief.

"Right now we have plenty of questions and very few answers," said Gimble. "But Agent Nazareth and I are determined to go away with a lot more than we have. We're going to meet with everyone who has already been interviewed, and we're going to identify additional people who need to be visited while we're here."

"And I should say at this point," Nazareth added, "that I don't believe we're dealing with a random act. We have a growing list of victims who are somehow connected. The picture is still hazy, but it's getting clearer. That's all I can tell you right now."

Chelsea handed Nazareth a thin set of papers that he had asked for in advance of their meeting: photocopies of the pages from the funeral parlor's guest book. She had annotated as many names as possible with relationships to Eleanor Martinson — neighbor, cousin, banker, and such — along with phone numbers. Nazareth and Gimble would spend the rest of the day scouring the list to see whether anyone popped up as a high-potential witness. Had the killer actually signed in and stood alongside Eleanor's coffin? Not likely. But then, thought Nazareth, it's not impossible either.

By 9:30 that night, working with their laptops at a cluttered desk in Gimble's room, they had generated a matrix that cross-referenced each visitor to the funeral parlor by sex, address, and relationship to Mrs. Martinson. More importantly, they had rated each person by his or her presumed importance to the investigation, from low-probability to high-probability. At the bottom of the matrix were Eleanor's relatives who had flown in for the funeral from Ohio, Colorado, and Oregon, along with couples who had driven distances that seemed to require overnight stays. Nazareth went with the assumption — and it was nothing more than that at this point — that the killer was someone who had been able to arrive, murder Mrs. Martinson, and leave on the same day. If that assumption proved faulty, he and Gimble would need to backtrack at some future date and expand their "possible" list.

Of reasonable interest were nine men who lived in the immediate area and who were single and listed as "acquaintances" rather than "friends." Gimble had called Art Martinson and asked him to clarify the difference. "Friends," he said, "are the people I know for a fact she was closest to for many years. Acquaintances are people she simply knew, or who apparently knew her, or who worked for her now and then — like Ted Waters, the plumber who installed a new gas boiler last year. When Chelsea and I didn't know for sure, we listed people as acquaintances, because we figured they'd need to be looked at more closely than Mom's friends."

Gimble reserved comment. She knew that in many cases the murderer is someone close to the victim and not just a passing acquaintance. All nine of these local men would require a visit. For his part, Nazareth couldn't stop thinking about Art Martinson. Something about this guy's attitude was just a bit off. At times his show of grief seemed overacted. Yet at other times he seemed unusually detached from his mother's death, as though he had more important things on his mind. Nazareth knew that this wouldn't be the first time that a son had killed a parent for money, and it wouldn't be the first time that a poor acting job had helped unmask a killer.

At the top of the matrix, however, were four non-locals — three men and one woman — who lived no more than four hours away by car. One of the men, from New Jersey, was married and had come to the funeral parlor with his wife, or so the guest book indicated. Nazareth and Gimble needed to check with Art and Chelsea Martinson to see if they remembered whether both husband and wife had attended. If so, the guy would be of less interest to them. One of the women, the one from West Virginia, was also married, but she had driven in for the funeral without her husband — again assuming the sign-in register was correct. The detectives didn't think the killer was a woman, but they needed to keep open minds.

This left two men who stood out on the short list. Both, it appeared, were single. One lived on Staten Island, and one lived in Manhattan. If the FBI's profiling was on target, someone from New York City should be the prime suspect. But Nazareth knew that profiling is a crude tool at best, so he was not about to consider the case solved. These two men would be looked at carefully, but in the meantime he and Gimble had more than enough work here in Pennsylvania to keep them busy for several full days.

The next morning they went their separate ways, each accompanied by a local officer, hoping that the day's meetings would turn up shreds of evidence that had been overlooked earlier. After a total of eleven interviews — four for Nazareth, seven for Gimble — they were back at the desk in Gimble's room with iced tea and a small sausage pizza from Tedeschi's. They agreed that the choice of pizza had gone better than the morning's business. Everyone who knew Eleanor Martinson seemed genuine in his or her praise and remorse. And no one could imagine anybody wanting to harm her, much less kill her. If the afternoon interviews were no more productive, Nazareth said, he might vote for trimming the remaining list and heading back to Manhattan.

"I don't disagree," said Gimble as she scanned her notes from the morning's meetings. "I wasn't necessarily expecting a lot of new information, but I did think I would pick up some vibes. You know, something that wasn't being said — a disconnect, maybe, between the words and the look."

"Intuition."

"Yeah, I guess. That works better than forensics sometimes."

"I hear what you're saying," he nodded. "In fact, my intuition tells me that we need to look more closely at Art Martinson. He's spooked about something."

Gimble's eyes lit up. "Yes, absolutely. I got the same feeling. The guy is definitely edgy. And something wasn't right between him and his wife."

"Okay," Nazareth said, genuinely excited, "let me make a phone call and get some background on him. While I'm doing that, how about you let him know we'd like to stop by his mother's place while he and his wife are still there. Maybe 5:00 or 5:30 today, right after we finish the day's interviews."

"That sounds good. I'd like to walk around the property anyway to see if anything stands out."

Nazareth gave that some thought as he stirred his iced tea.

"I like that idea a lot. Why don't you take a long, slow walk with the wife while I try to get a better fix on the husband? Getting them away from each other would be good. But I definitely don't want to raise any alarms for them."

"Sounds like a plan."

"You want that last piece?" he smiled.

"I was only in the fitness center for an hour this morning," she replied. "So I'd better pass."

"Well, I did five miles before breakfast, so I need my carbs."

Back in his room before heading out again, Nazareth called an FBI friend in DC and asked for as much info as possible on Art Martinson. Twenty minutes later, as he drove to his first afternoon appointment, Nazareth glanced at the information that had already found its way through cyberspace to the iPad on the front passenger seat. Something toward the end of the report grabbed his attention, and he pulled over to give the summary a closer look. Then he speed-dialed Gimble's number. He caught her just before she went in to see Margaret McCutcheon, the 81-year-old president of the Hallstead Garden Club.

"I just got the background check on Art Martinson," he told her, "and this guy definitely does not have a money motive."

"Really?"

"You bet. He's chief financial officer of a small software company that was bought last year by Google. Art Martinson is currently worth somewhere in the neighborhood of $40 million, so unless he's one greedy son of a bitch, the mother's property is more trouble than it's worth."

"We're thinking the house and the land are worth maybe $700,000."

"Exactly. Meanwhile, his net worth grows by maybe $5 million a year. So we just lost a motive."

"But we still agree that there's something off about the guy, right?"

"Most definitely. So we still meet."

"All set. He and his wife will be there at 5:00."

"Later."

25.

I cannot predict how, or even whether, Detective Silvano's untimely death will affect the investigation. Will things move faster, a show of resolve in the face of adversity? Or will the process grind to a halt as the NYPD hunts for a suitable replacement? Impossible to say. The safest thing to do, I believe, is stay away from New York City for a time, even though doing so may cause some inconvenience for me. White Marsh, MD, was, in fact, quite a haul. Three hours each way, not to mention all the effort in between. I don't relish the prospect of another long drive just yet. And there's the bothersome issue of trying to find news stories that are published in some insignificant burg in another state. I cannot, after all, just walk to my corner newsstand and buy a copy of whatever rag of a newspaper one might find in a place like White Marsh. To read about Doris Healy's death along Maryland's Bird River I need to go online, and that's something I refuse to do at home. In the highly unlikely event the NYPD ever looks my way, the consequences of having searched for news about each of the rescued widows could prove unpleasant. So I am forced to use the computers in the university library. How much easier it would be to read the *New York Times* after each of my visits. But I cannot allow convenience to trump caution.

This morning I examine the map on the computer screen with a mind toward trimming back the mileage for my next mission. New Jersey and Connecticut beckon. Each is hospitable enough, and each offers an abundant population of senior citizens. But so does the state to which I pay my taxes each year. New York State is lovely and quite diverse in its offerings — mountains, lakes, streams, forests, small town, big cities. I can easily travel the roads of New York State while doing God's work, and it has been years since I drove north out of Manhattan into the fresh air and winding open roads of the Empire State.

So many choices within easy reach of Downtown Manhattan! Newburgh, Monticello, Ellenville. Don't ask me why, but Ellenville catches my eye. It has quite a pleasant ring to it. I have never been there; of this I am certain. Yet it strikes a chord. The woman's name, perhaps? Yes, possibly. Whatever it is, I am not one to ignore a sign.

I search for Ellenville obituaries and quickly find more than a dozen from the past six months. Among them is one for Harvey Karcher, 88 at the time of his passing. Harvey's sole survivor is Ellen — yes, Ellen — age 83.

Ellen Karcher from Ellenville! If this is not God's voice whispering in my ear, what is it?

Before leaving the University library I jot down several cryptic words on a sticky note — a few scribbles to jog my memory when I get home — then erase the computer's history. Could some high-tech investigator tear the machine apart and tease out evidence of my search? Surely anything is possible in an age when men have supposedly walked on the moon. But will someone actually do that with all fifty computers in the campus library? Of course not.

Ellenville is slightly less than a two-hour drive from Manhattan, and I am suddenly eager to make the trip and study the area. Although a preliminary reconnaissance visit is not absolutely essential, I see no harm in taking extra precautions, especially since I have detectives on my mind.

I will allow nothing to stop me from doing His good work.

26.

After saying goodbye to the state police officers who had accompanied them on the day's interviews, Nazareth and Gimble arrived at Mrs. Martinson's forlorn Pennsylvania home within minutes of each other shortly after 5:00 p.m. Art and Chelsea Martinson sat waiting for them in the back yard at a redwood picnic table in the dense shade of a sprawling old maple. Alongside them was a red cooler that contained bottled water, Gatorade, and Yuengling beer. They didn't know whether the two officers could drink alcohol while on duty, but Art decided that there was no harm in offering. On the table was a bowl of Wheat Thins and a small plastic container of cheese dip.

"Please help yourselves," Chelsea said pleasantly. "Just a little something that I picked up before I left town this afternoon."

"That wasn't necessary," Nazareth smiled, "but we appreciate it." He took one of the Gatorades, and Gimble grabbed a bottle of water. After they had all sampled some cheese and crackers, Gimble announced that she wanted to walk the property out back and asked if Chelsea could join her. Art glanced quickly at his wife, then back to Nazareth.

"Should we walk with them?" Art asked as he began to get up from the bench.

"Actually, no," Nazareth replied firmly, "I'd rather go over some additional details with you while Detective Gimble and your wife look around."

"Uh, okay, that's fine." His words said fine, but the look on his face said not at all fine. But there was nothing he could do about that now.

"I don't really know what you told the police when they interviewed you right after your mother's death," Nazareth began, "so if you don't mind, I'd like to go back to the very beginning and start out fresh."

"Sure, I'll do whatever I can to help."

"I appreciate that. One thing that's not clear in the files is where you were on the day your mother was murdered."

Art was offended. "Wait, you think I might have had something to do with it?" His question was a bit more aggressive than necessary, and Nazareth took this as a sign of defensiveness.

"Not at all. I'm just going back to the beginning, and this is a routine first question."

Art was slow to answer.

"Chelsea and I were just basically home." His tinny response sounded more like a question than an answer. "I don't recall every detail now."

"Understood. But you live over an hour from here, so you'd certainly remember driving to and from Hallstead that day, wouldn't you?" Nazareth stared, allowing Art to process the message that had just been delivered.

Art looked around, then took a deep breath.

"All right, look, can I assume that this discussion is strictly confidential?" he asked.

"On the contrary," said Nazareth, shaking his head. "You should assume that everything you say will become a matter of public record. If there's something that doesn't need to be public, I can use my discretion. Otherwise, this goes where it goes."

One of the people Nazareth had interviewed that afternoon remembered seeing Art Martinson filling his tank at a gas station at the edge of town on the morning of Eleanor Martinson's murder. The witness had thought nothing of this, however, since Art often visited his mother. It was nothing unusual.

"I actually was in Hallstead that day, but Chelsea doesn't know," he said. "In fact, Chelsea doesn't know I have been coming here every now and then for the past few months."

"To visit your mother?"

"Sometimes my mother, yes. But not always."

"And when you came here but didn't see your mother, who were you visiting?"

Art saw that Chelsea and Gimble had stopped walking and were deep in conversation over by the woods that bordered the Martinson property.

"I've been seeing a woman I dated in high school. It's not serious, but, you know, we've just been seeing each other on and off for a while. Listen, Detective, Chelsea doesn't know, and there would be hell to pay if she found out. This woman and I have already agreed to stop, so do you and I really have to pursue the whole thing?"

Nazareth shrugged. "Detective Gimble and I have to pursue any evidence that we believe is relevant. And the fact that you were in Hallstead on the day of your mother's murder is highly relevant, especially since you didn't tell anyone this before."

"Wait," Art pleaded, "no one ever asked me."

"Wrong. I asked you less than two minutes ago, and you told me you were home with your wife."

"Well, I was. Most of the day and all of the night. But I was also here for a while. I didn't always see my mother when I came here. And on those days I was very careful about not being seen."

"And yet you were seen. I know when, I know where, and I know by whom. All you've done is confirm what I already knew. Would you like to have a local police officer sit in for the rest of our conversation?"

"Oh, God, no! Detective, I swear to you I had nothing to do with Mom's murder. I loved her, and I'll miss her every day for the rest of my life. I was just screwing around with someone. And now I want to keep my marriage together."

"Because you assume Chelsea doesn't know what was going on?"

"She doesn't."

"Has she said that?"

"She doesn't need to because she's never suspected anything was going on."

Nazareth slowly shook his head.

"I think you're wrong," he said, "but that's neither here nor there. I don't care about your personal life. I care only about tracking down a murderer. So if you give me this woman's name and address, I'll determine whether the two of you are murder suspects."

"It's nothing like that!"

"What's not like that?" Chelsea said coolly as she walked up behind her husband. Gimble shot her partner a knowing look and nodded just once. They thanked the Martinsons for their hospitality and cooperation, then headed back to the hotel.

"She knew something was going on?" Nazareth asked after they had parked their cars.

"Well, let's see," Gimble grinned. "She may have mentioned something about a gold-digging bimbo that her husband has been screwing."

"So why didn't she do anything about it?"

"At the beginning all she had was hearsay, and she wanted more than that. Then his mother was murdered, so she put the issue on the back burner temporarily. She was getting ready to wage serious war when we showed up and said we were going to start questioning people. At that point," Gimble said, "she believed the truth would probably come out. He seemed to be getting edgier every day."

"Well, we had that part right, but I'm certain he had nothing to do with the murder."

"So based on everything we've learned here, where do we go next?"

"I think we take a hard look at the two City guys who came out here for the funeral."

"The ones from Staten Island and Manhattan."

"Yep. They're probably both long shots, but we should play this thing out. Let's run a background check on both of them." He thought for a moment, then added, "I'm also going to have them followed for a week or so and see where that takes us. I can have teams on them tomorrow."

Thirty minutes later Nazareth phoned Gimble in her hotel room.

"We need to pack up and leave," he told her.

"Why's that?"

"I just finished talking with Crawford. The local police from some Podunk in Maryland just got around to letting us know that our Rosebud Killer claimed another victim there on the same day Javi was killed."

"You're shitting me!"

"I wish I were. Crawford got lots of apologies. Apparently their two top cops each thought the other had called us. Whatever. We need to drive down and check things out ourselves."

"So we're heading to Maryland now?"

"Afraid so. It'll take us about four hours, but then we can visit the crime scene first thing in the morning."

"How the hell many women can one guy kill, Pete?"

"Unfortunately, Tara, I think he's just getting warmed up."

27.

I could not ask for a more beautiful day for my scouting trip to Ellenville. Not a cloud in the sky, low humidity, high today near 80, and a lovely breeze in my face as I walk to the garage for my car. Good man, Ramon. The car is freshly washed and awaiting my arrival. "Have a fine day, Professor," he says as I hand him a five, and I can tell he's sincere. It's that kind of day. Manhattan always has some sort of buzz, but not usually this kind. We've gotten a reprieve from a string of disgustingly hot, humid days, thanks to a cold front that passed through the area late yesterday. First came powerful thunderstorms that pounded and crackled all the way from the canyons of Wall Street to Columbus Circle, and then came a cool, steady breeze that bathed the City in a whole new frame of mind. Miraculous, really.

Mid-morning traffic is relatively light as I head up the West Side Drive toward the George Washington Bridge. I plan to take the bridge over to Fort Lee, then pick up the Palisades Parkway for the first third of my trip to Ellenville. I am pleasantly distracted by thoughts of Catskill villages and winding roads when quite by accident I notice that the same black sedan has been behind me ever since I left the garage. It's not the sort of thing that would normally capture my attention, especially in a city that houses more limo services than most small nations. But a couple of thoughts sneak into my consciousness. First, there are two front-seat passengers. In this particular city, limo passengers would rather be chained to the rear bumper and dragged than sit up front with the driver. It just isn't done. Second, because I am a genuinely cautious driver, virtually every car on the road passes me. But not the black sedan. The driver has had numerous opportunities to do so, but he keeps falling back, sometimes two cars, sometimes six or seven.

My sister has dutifully kept me informed of progress, or lack of progress, on the investigation into her mother-in-law's death. She recently told me, in fact, that two New York detectives had requested my phone number and address in case they needed to reach me. Routine questions, they said. Routine, indeed. Then what does it mean that they have not yet spoken with me but are now following me up the West Side?

What I feel is not quite panic. But the prospect of being scrutinized by two men in an unmarked car has certainly put a dent in my earlier mood. And I am unhappy about that. I remain thoroughly confident that Detective Nazareth and his new partner have no evidence linking me to Eleanor's death. Yet here I am being followed. Or am I not being followed? How can I know?

Given the uncertainty, I believe it unwise to continue today's trip to Ellenville. This is only a minor problem. I need to be flexible and change paths as conditions warrant, so I adjust. I drive over the bridge as planned, but rather than head toward the Palisades Parkway I turn off in Fort Lee and pull into the first gas station I see. The black sedan drives past me.

While the attendant fills my tank, I scroll through a list of New Jersey places worth visiting — at least according to the state's tourism website. The Old Barracks Museum. No, I believe I'll pass on that. The Jackson Premium Outlets. Pass. Claremont Distillery. Pass. Ah, Atlantic City casinos. How many years has it been since I donated $50 to the slot machines in Atlantic City? Fifteen or more, I think. From here to Atlantic City will take just about two hours, according to Mapquest. I can spend some time in a casino, eat well, and still be home before 10:00 p.m. I don't like having to interrupt the Lord's work like this, but I must be patient.

My gas tank is not quite full when I note that the black sedan's driver has made a U-turn somewhere out of my sight and is now idling on a side street diagonally across from me. So, this is not my imagination at all. I am enormously pleased, I must say, to have detected my police "escort" all the way back in Manhattan. And I am even more pleased that my two new NYPD friends — well, I assume they're NYPD, though I suppose the FBI could be getting involved in this effort — will be taking a long ride to the Jersey Shore with me on this fine day.

I set the GPS for Atlantic City and make my way toward the NJ Turnpike. The first part of my drive along the Turnpike offers some of the most wretched views of any highway in America. Factories belching smoke, abandoned warehouses with their windows shot out, and putrid flows of oil and refuse that masquerade as rivers. Finally the Turnpike's southern end produces a stretch of inoffensive suburban scenery before I turn onto the Garden State Parkway. Most of the Parkway is rather scenic as it makes long looping turns through the pine barrens and alongside marshes whose emerald grasses reach far out toward the Atlantic. It's a pleasant drive, all in all, and I hope that my friends in the black sedan are enjoying it with me.

They stay well back, attempting to hide in the light midweek traffic. Are they really foolish enough to believe that I haven't seen them? Perhaps. Or are they simply trying to send me a message? "We know who you are and what you've been doing."

I doubt it.

They are no match for me.

28.

Detectives Joe Russo and Lyle Stormer dutifully followed Mercer's late-model Altima over the GWB, then into Fort Lee, and then down the NJ Turnpike and Garden State Parkway. Nazareth had told them that this surveillance would most likely be a royal time-waster, since at first glance Prof. Thomas Mercer seemed an unlikely murderer. On the other hand, so did Staten Island sculptor Raphael Black. Both Mercer and Black had attended Eleanor Martinson's funeral in Pennsylvania, and both lived in New York City — in Black's case only on a technicality, since most Staten Islanders believe their home is a separate country rather than one of the City's five boroughs.

Stormer drove while Russo worked the phone. He twice called Nazareth, who was on his way back from a time-wasting visit to Maryland with Gimble, and explained what was going on in New Jersey. He put the speaker on for the third call so that he and Stormer could both trade ideas with Nazareth and Gimble.

"So Mercer is still cruising the Parkway?" Nazareth asked as he blew past a line of sixteen-wheelers on I-95.

"Slow and steady," Russo replied. "He has only one speed: 67. Everyone else is doing 85, and we're moping along at 67. Lyle hasn't touched the cruise control for about 50 miles."

"Well, at this point I think we all agree he's headed to Atlantic City," Gimble said.

"There's not much else between where we are and the ocean," said Stormer cheerfully, "so I guess we'll all be playing roulette pretty soon."

"Just remember," Nazareth joked, "that you can't expense your losses, Lyle. That's your nickel."

"Last time I was here it cost me a whole lot more than a nickel, I can tell you that. No," he shook his head, "I think I'll just follow the professor."

Nazareth turned back to the business at hand.

"Tara and I have spoken with ACPD Chief Del Blount," he said, "and he's going to have two plain-clothes guys meet up with you as soon as you're ready for them. When you're in position someplace, call Detective Larry Ellison."

Gimble gave Russo and Stormer the number, then added: "Just remind the locals one more time that all we want to do is watch. We're a long way from considering Mercer a serious suspect, but at this point we can't afford not to keep an eye on him. We don't want him spooked, and we sure as hell don't need a harassment charge filed against us."

"Got it," said Russo. "We'll all just blend in and see what goes down. This guy has no idea we're on him."

"Quick question," said Nazareth. "Did Mercer have any luggage when he started out this morning?"

"Not a thing," Stormer answered. "Short-sleeve shirt, slacks, loafers, and a cup of coffee. Period."

"Okay, so he's just out for the day. But, remember, that doesn't mean a whole lot," Nazareth added, "because there's a good chance the guy we're after likes to get in and out the same day. At least that's what the FBI's profiler thinks."

"Yeah," said Russo soberly, "that and $2.75 gets you a subway ride."

29.

As I turn off the highway I notice a sleek, contemporary structure in the distance, towering over the landscape like a gigantic golden book that has been balanced on end. Since I really don't know one casino from the next — those I once visited are probably all shuttered now — I will try my luck at the Borgata. I pull up to the main entrance, and an energetic youth in hotel uniform jogs over, hands me a valet stub, and drives off. I stretch my arms after the long drive, and while doing so I notice out of the corner of my eye that the black sedan has been parked a block away next to a chain link fence that provides no cover at all.

Am I really this good, or are those two really that bad?

The casino floor is like all others I have ever seen or heard. I can't decide which is more energizing, the thousands of flashing lights or the raucous gambling machines. Hard to say, since both momentarily overwhelm my senses. It is no mistake that a casino rips you away from reality as soon as you set foot in it. Even if you just happen to stumble in, as I do today, you are immediately swept up in the illusion of ecstasy. Many of the gamblers should already be distraught, having lost sickening amounts of money that could have been spent on a mortgage, or a college education for the kids, or for a year's worth of groceries. But the carefully orchestrated spectacle somehow makes even desperate losers continue to feel like sure winners. They are hypnotized into believing that they have a right to become rich with the next hand or spin or pull. So they waste no time taking out their ATM cards and digging even deeper holes for themselves.

I experience much the same rush as everyone else, of course, but I enter this room that has been painstakingly sealed off from the outside world — try finding a window or a clock in here — knowing that I will lose no more than precisely $50. That is and always will be my limit. I consider $50 plus the price of a meal to be a reasonable investment in a day's relaxation. I didn't set out this morning looking for pleasure, except to the extent that my work results in the great joy of having rescued a suffering soul. But since this is where I am, I will stay the course. My NYPD friends can spend a few boring hours watching me feed a hungry machine whose random payoffs are scientifically designed to increase the pace of betting.

This really is a diabolical enterprise, after all. I doubt that I will mourn the passing of the last Atlantic City casino, something I expect to read about within the next five years. The entire city is on death watch.

But that is not my concern today. Or ever, for that matter. The tolling of Atlantic City's bell does not affect me, no matter what the great John Donne might have thought. At the moment I enjoy pulling a handle that no longer needs to be pulled (casino owners know that pushing a button generates more plays per hour than pulling a handle), and waiting to see whether I am richer or poorer. After several dozen tries I have neither won nor lost much, but I have carefully, surreptitiously, eyed the lovely young woman who plays the machine to my right. Unlike the cocktail waitresses who work the floor in their short black skirts and push-up tops, this woman could easily be a runway model, though better built. Neither too thin nor too plump, she wears her golden hair in a casually perfect knot at the back of her head. Moist lavender lipstick. Matching eye shadow. No other makeup to spoil her smooth, tanned face. Snug white tank top. Loose lavender skirt that barely covers firm, athletic legs as she sits. A simple seashell necklace graces the curve of her neck.

I wonder whether I can muster the courage to say something to her. But then she finishes her drink and walks into the crowd. Have I driven her off by looking too hard? If so, the greater my loss. I watch her sway deliciously as she moves off.

"She's gorgeous, isn't she?" It's the player to my left, a young man of 35 or so outfitted in a pale blue Polo shirt that clings to his large upper arms. I have no desire to make a new buddy today, so I offer only a lukewarm smile.

"Yes, quite lovely," I say curtly, then turn back to the machine.

"Also quite available," he says.

"I beg your pardon?"

"I said she's available."

"The woman who just left?" He simply nods. "I'm sorry, but what do you mean she's available?"

He looks at me as though I have just fallen off the back of that turnip truck everyone talks about.

"I mean," he says amiably, "that she's available to entertain you for a while. If you're interested, of course."

"Wait, are you a . . . ?" Before I can finish the question he says, "Marketing associate."

"You're her marketing associate? A pimp?"

"No, not a pimp at all. She's an independent entrepreneur. I just help with client acquisition," he says, sounding for just a moment like one of the stuffed sausages who serve as adjunct faculty in our business department. "There are lots of plain-clothes cops around here these days, so she employs my marketing services to help generate business."

I am an aging man, but I am not yet dead. My desires are in perfect working order, and the young woman who just disappeared into the crowd has successfully set those aflutter. I feel giddy at the prospect of actually being with her.

"How exactly does she become available?" I ask him.

"If you want to spend an hour with her, I simply call. She'll meet you in her room on the 40th floor."

"Here at the Borgata?"

"An elevator ride away," he grins.

"And what might the fee be? Is that what it's called?"

"Fee, charge, whatever you'd like," he laughs. "$500." The amount would be laughable were the woman in question not breathtakingly beautiful. Only in film have I seen a woman as remarkable as this.

"I don't carry that kind of money with me," I say.

"She's happy to take Visa, Mastercard, or American Express," he assures me. "She has a PayPal card reader on her cell phone. The charge will show as Allegro Design Consulting. The cash fee is $500, credit card $525."

"Design Consulting?"

"It's an actual company," he tells me. "She has a master's degree in interior design, but when she's not busy enough with that she comes here for a week at a time. Sometimes more, sometimes less. Makes perfect sense, doesn't it?"

"It does to me," I hear myself saying. Wait, did I say that? Does working as a hooker in Atlantic City really make sense for a beautiful young woman with a degree in interior design? How the hell would I know? In any event, I agree to the price because I believe that $525 for an hour in heaven is something I not only can afford but richly deserve. I have not had a genuine vacation for years.

30.

Russo sat ten chairs away from Mercer in a row of quarter slots. The detective alternated between slowly feeding the machine and quickly eyeballing his quarry. Mercer seemed to have settled in for the afternoon with a dish of peanuts and a tall, clear drink in front of him. Russo thought it looked like plain water with lime, but he couldn't be sure from a distance. A thin waitress with an outsized chest had brought the drink at Mercer's request and took a dollar tip in return. Complimentary water most likely. No charge for the lime or the cleavage reveal.

Detective Stormer, meanwhile, grabbed a sandwich with their new ACPD partners at a cafe just off the casino floor. So far, at least, this hadn't come even close to being a four-man operation. Before attacking the second half of his immense corned beef on rye, Stormer called Russo's cell phone to say that he'd relieve his partner in ten minutes. Russo caught the phone on the first ring, but the reception on the casino floor was quirky. Must be interference from all these fancy gambling machines, he thought. When he turned to get better reception, he accidentally elbowed his glass of Coke and doused himself as well as the guy next to him. Suddenly Russo was apologizing and wiping soda from his slacks. For about fifty seconds he was focused on his pants rather than Mercer. By the time the detective stood up and got his head back in the game, Mercer had vanished.

"Aw, damn, damn, damn," Russo swore into a dead line. He had disconnected from Stormer while trying to get the Coke off his slacks. He redialed as he took off toward where Mercer had been sitting, but at that same moment Stormer dialed him. They both got busy signals. When Russo turned the corner at the end of the slots aisle, he looked left and then right. Left was about fifty feet to the casino exit; right was at least double that distance toward the blackjack tables. No Mercer in either direction.

Russo's phone rang, and this time he connected with Stormer.

"The guy is missing, Storm. I turned my back for a second," he wailed, "and the guy is gone."

"Ah, no, man. No way."

"Aw, damn. Look, I'm heading toward the blackjack tables. You head to the lobby and see if he's there. Have the two AC guys watch for Mercer's car. He's not leaving without the car, right?"

"I hope to hell not, man. I'm moving."

The four detectives spent the next forty-five minutes criss-crossing all 161,000 square feet of the casino floor. The Borgato casino floor occupied 3.69 acres jammed with nearly 3,500 slot machines and roughly 250 gaming tables. And people. Lots and lots of people. If Mercer was among them, they couldn't find him. They hit the tables, the bathrooms, and the restaurants.

The guy had ditched them.

Stormer made the call to Nazareth and Gimble, because Russo couldn't find the courage to pick up the phone. All he could think of at the moment was a fifteen-year career swirling into the toilet because he had spilled a glass of soda. He was correct in assuming that he would not be getting a written commendation for this one. In fact, he told himself, if this guy Mercer turns out to be the killer, I'll be lucky to pound a beat in Bed-Stuy.

31.

I feel suddenly blessed not to have been drinking alcohol down at the casino, because I would not want to be anything but monastically sober as Melissa Smythe looks into my face with gleaming blue eyes and slowly removes her clothes, patiently revealing the body of a living goddess. Her name, I assume, is fake. But clearly nothing else is. Standing before me, now wearing nothing but a seashell necklace, is a woman whose beauty is genuinely, achingly perfect. I avoid cliches whenever possible. But I do feel weak. If I were not sitting on the edge of the bed, I might faint.

"We can go slow," she whispers as she leans over me and begins unbuttoning my shirt. "Or we can go even slower. One hour or two? You decide."

Her lips caress my face, and I am scarcely able to mumble, "Two."

32

Russo stood alone in the hotel lobby, looking vacantly into space. The four detectives had split up and continued to look for Mercer, who had disappeared just over an hour ago. Not a trace. But that hardly surprised anyone. Mercer was a plain-vanilla guy in a gigantic hotel filled with plain-vanilla people. It wouldn't take much for him to disappear in here.

Russo thought that things couldn't get worse until his phone rang and he saw that it was Nazareth. "I just got off with the ACPD chief," Nazareth snapped. "They've got a dead body in a home three blocks from you. Take down this address, and get over there. Call me when you know what the hell's going on."

It took Russo, Stormer, and the two ACPD guys longer to get their cars than to drive to the crime scene. As Gimble had said, the place was practically around the corner. They pulled in front of a ramshackle home on a beaten-down street and found two local cops holding back a group of twenty-five or thirty curious neighbors, a number of whom carried open cans of Colt 45. No need to flash badges. The two AC cops escorting Russo and Stormer just mumbled to their colleagues as they walked by.

They entered a murky living room whose most prominent features were tattered wallpaper from a previous century, a crumbling plaster ceiling, and several large holes that had been punched in the walls by apparently huge fists. The room looked as though it had just hosted World War

III. When Russo and Stormer crowded into the kitchen, they found much the same decor: a laminate countertop with chunks of the surface torn off, a prehistoric refrigerator that was either gray or green depending upon your viewing angle, and a vinyl floor straight from an illegal slaughterhouse in Queens.

Slumped on the floor near an open back door was a woman who appeared to be somewhere near sixty. The swollen face and blood-red eyes made it impossible to say for sure. Her neck was distorted, apparently the work of two powerful hands that had been wrapped around it until the woman died. The beating obviously had taken longer than the strangulation. Once the killer had put his hands to her neck, she was less than two minutes from death.

"This just happened, guys," said a shaken Officer Kelly Simmons, who had been first on the scene and stood alongside the body taking pictures with her cell phone. "When I got here the blood was still running from her nose. Witness thinks he saw the perp walking away."

"Where's the witness?" said Russo.

"Out back with Officer Jenkins, giving a statement."

Stormer stayed behind to get a closer look at the victim while Russo went out into the patch of tall weeds and rotted lumber that was the back yard. The witness was 72-year-old Charles Wayans, an emaciated drunk who lived next door. He had been sitting in his living room, sucking down a beer, when he noticed a white guy walking past the front of his house.

Russo identified himself, then listened in as Officer Jenkins continued questioning Wayans, who followed each answer with a nervous gulp from a large can of Bud.

"What made you notice the guy?" asked Jenkins.

"White guy?" he shrugged. "Seriously? Plus it looked like he came from the side of Martha's house."

"Martha, the woman who was attacked?"

"Yessir, Martha Tyus. Widow. Living here thirty years, maybe more. Not as long as me, though."

"What else did this guy look like?"

"My height, maybe. 5'9" or so. Kinda chunky. Not fat. Dressed okay, not some bum."

"Beard, mustache, hair?"

"No beard or mustache, I don't think. Didn't notice his hair. He had hair, pretty sure," Wayans said.

"Which way was he headed?"

Wayans casually raised his chin toward the Borgata.

"To the casino. He wasn't running, but he wasn't strolling either. Guy was bookin', you know?"

"How long did you watch him?"

"Soon as he was up the street I went next door to Martha's."

"What made you go over?"

"White guy bookin' up my street, maybe had been next door? We look out for each other here," he said, looking at Jenkins directly for the first time, "because ain't nobody else doin' it."

Stormer went into the back yard and huddled with Russo.

"Can't say for sure what this was," Stormer began. "Maybe a robbery that went bad. But it could also have been our guy. Came to AC to put down some old woman, but she didn't follow the plan. What's up out here?"

"The description fits, if you can trust it," Russo said as he shook his head in something approaching despair. "The witness was boozing in his living room and saw some white guy walking fast toward the Borgata. He went next door to check on the vic, couldn't get in the front, went around back. Walked in, she's dead on the floor."

"Any way the old guy is good for this?" said Stormer.

"In my dreams," said Russo. "He's lucky if he can pop the next Bud. No way he does what happened to her."

"Okay, bro, let me call this into Nazareth."

Russo stared down at his shoes but saw nothing. Bust your ass your whole career, he thought, and in less than a minute everything changes. How in God's name can that happen?

After finishing their call with Stormer, Nazareth and Gimble couldn't tell what they felt more — anger or frustration. They couldn't lay this all on Russo. Excellent cop with a terrific record, got distracted for one goddamn minute. It could have happened to anyone. They knew that. But they also knew that in a case like this you might only get one serious bit of luck. And if the guy who had just murdered someone in Atlantic City was Mercer, they had forfeited one of the biggest strokes of good luck in the history of police work. Out of the millions of widows this guy could have gone after, he went after the one who was just around the corner from four detectives who were supposed to be on his ass.

"I didn't make him out to be this sloppy," Nazareth said to Gimble, "but it's a high-risk business. Anything can happen."

"It's not his M.O.," Gimble answered, "but we can't rule him out."

"Okay. No choice. You and I go to Atlantic City," Nazareth said as he hit the flashers. "Tell Russo and Stormer to find Mercer. Get whatever help they need from ACPD, but find him. We'll get there as soon as we can."

"Done."

33.

I have always considered time a constant. Seconds, minutes, hours . . . all of them morphing relentlessly into eons. I now stand corrected. In Melissa's presence, time marches backward. Hours become minutes, minutes mere seconds. Our glorious time together brings immeasurable pleasure as well as memories that will no doubt live as long as I do. But the moment finally ends.

I am hardly naive. Our time together seemed much like love but was merely a business transaction, an exchange of negotiable currency for services. And I fully realize that, appearances to the contrary, no one who looks like Melissa has ever been aroused by someone who looks like me. The young man in the casino — her marketing associate, he calls himself — I presume that he is the sort she favors when not catering to the needs of a randy old man like me. Unlike me, he is probably insatiable. Perhaps he'll be up here as soon as I leave. I wonder.

Idle speculation benefits no one. I take my shower, and as I leave her room, Melissa presents me with a business card for Allegro Design Consulting. On the back she has written her private phone number.

"If you know anyone who needs interior design work," she smiles, "please pass my name along. And, of course, if you come back to Atlantic City, I hope you'll call."

"I will certainly do both, Melissa," I say. "This was wonderful."

As I walk toward the elevator I know that I will never find any design clients for her, just as I will never meet her again in a lovely hotel room looking out to the Atlantic. I am a careful planner by nature, and this is not the sort of day a careful person could ever plan. Still, it actually happened. It was not my overactive imagination. And I am extremely happy.

Are the detectives still in the casino wondering where I went? This is not my problem. I'll play the slots a bit longer, have a bite to eat, then drive home.

Much serious work lies ahead.

34

Russo and Stormer guided a six-person plainclothes team onto the casino floor while eight uniformed officers patrolled the hotel grounds and parking lots.

"The four of us will each take a corner, and you two," Russo said as he pointed to the others, "one on each side at the middle of the room. Get in position, and exactly three minutes from now we all begin walking slowly toward the center. Cover your sector both left and right. If we don't find him on the first pass, we regroup and try again."

Russo and Stormer knew exactly who they were after, therefore stood the best chance of finding Mercer if he had returned to the casino. The four ACPD detectives worked from a thorough description that Stormer had provided. Since Mercer had brought no luggage with him, he would still be wearing the clothes he had on when he left Manhattan. With luck, his clothes would provide bloody evidence of his visit to Martha Tyus's kitchen.

Mercer walked off the elevator less than a minute after the six officers began their search of the casino. In this crowd their first pass would take ten minutes or more. Mercer sat at a slot machine in the first row he reached and began to play. He planned to play for one hour or until his original $50 was gone, whichever came first. Fifteen minutes later all six officers met in the middle of the casino with nothing to show for their efforts.

"Okay, we go back the other way," Russo told them. "If we don't find him on this pass, we start hitting the restaurants, then the pool area, then the stairways. After that, if necessary, we join the guys outside. Okay? Let's go."

Five minutes into the second search of the casino floor Russo spotted Mercer pulling a handle halfway across the room. He maneuvered through a group of stoned college kids who crowded the aisle, apologized for almost knocking down a grandmother holding a bucket of silver dollars, and began to close on Mercer when his phone rang. Stormer.

"I'm about to take the bastard down, Storm. I've got him!"

"Shit, no. Stop!" Stormer yelled into the phone. "One of the ACPD guys just got the word. They found the perp in a ditch about five blocks from the murder scene. It wasn't Mercer."

A stunned Russo said, "Are you sure? I mean absolutely sure?"

"Blood on his shirt and his pants, knuckles swollen from beating on the old lady. They're bringing the neighbor over to ID the guy before they move him."

"Where are they taking him?

"Morgue, I guess. He OD'd on something. Wait," he said. "Okay, just got a photo from the lead guy on the scene. White male, fifty plus, scruffy as hell."

"I thought the witness said the guy didn't look like a bum."

"Yeah, but the witness also said he was drinking his first beer of the day when he looked out the window. And we both know that's bullshit. He was flat-ass drunk."

"I'm ten steps away from Mercer," Russo said, practically pleading.

"Don't go near him, man. DO NOT GO NEAR HIM. Trust me."

Russo punched off his cell and began rounding up the troops. Two years ago he had stopped drinking for good. But on the way home tonight he planned to buy a bottle of Johnnie Walker Black.

35.

Nazareth and Gimble were screaming toward Atlantic City when Deputy Chief Crawford called on Gimble's phone. She hit the speaker.

"Gimble here."

"Yeah, it's Crawford. Nazareth with you?"

"Yep, I'm here Chief."

"Where are you two?"

"Heading to Atlantic City as fast as we can get there."

"Nope, get to Manhattan," he barked. "East 80th. We've got a dead rich lady with a rosebud in her hands."

Nazareth and Gimble looked at each other in something close to shock.

"It looks like our guy?" Nazareth asked.

"That's what I'm told, but you two will know best. The place will be locked down until you get there. The press hounds are already on scene, so walk fast when you go in."

"All right, we're on it," said Nazareth.

He took the next turnoff hard, pointed the cruiser toward Manhattan, and stomped on the gas.

"Better call Russo and Stormer," Nazareth said. "Let them know what we've got."

Before Gimble could speed-dial Russo's number, her cell rang. It was a disgusted Russo.

"I was just going to call you," she said.

"Yeah, well, wherever you are, you can turn around," he told her. "They already have their guy down here — strung-out junkie looking for cash, killed the old lady, then OD'd in a ditch a couple blocks away. End of story. Mercer is back in the casino at the slots. No idea where he was, but he didn't kill her."

"But in the meantime," she told him, "someone killed an old woman on the Upper East Side and left a rosebud on her body."

"You can't be serious!"

"Unless Crawford was telling the first joke of his life, we've got a very dead widow in Manhattan."

"Another old woman with a rosebud?" She could hear the frustration in Russo's voice. "And meanwhile we're down here chasing junkies in Shitville."

Nazareth jumped into the conversation.

"Listen, I really need you and Stormer to stick with the plan. Hang back but keep Mercer in sight. It looks as though the guy is perfectly clean, but I'm not ready to stop watching him."

"Even though you just picked another rosebud killing in Manhattan?"

"Yeah, even though. We've gone this far with Mercer, so just hang in for the rest of the day. We can talk about him again after Gimble and I sort through the one that just went down in Manhattan."

"Understood. You know, I'll be happy to get back to Manhattan where it's safe," Russo whined. "One of the local uniforms told me that murder is the only business that's booming down here.

"I can believe it. And it's a damn shame, too. It was a great place when I was a kid."

By the time Nazareth and Gimble rolled onto East 80th the sidewalk had been strung with yellow crime-scene tape, and three TV news vans sporting satellite dishes were in place. Nazareth pulled in next to a hydrant and set the police placard on the dash. He and Gimble got out and worked their way along the street toward a well-behaved crowd that stood expectantly outside the $18-million townhouse.

"Another rich uptown lady," Nazareth said. He seemed lost in thought, as though he was working some complex calculus problem in his head. "This doesn't feel right."

"In what way?" Gimble asked.

"This guy has been super cautious, spreading things out so that we can't get a fix on him. And then suddenly he decides to hit another Manhattan widow? Midtown, Uptown, doesn't really matter. He's overworking the territory, and that doesn't feel like our guy."

"Well," said Gimble, "let's see what we've got inside."

The smell was the worst of it.

"Hey, Pete. Glad you guys could join us," said Detective Ron Pederson, who had swiped some Vicks under his nose so that he could stay in the same room as the victim. "Looks as though your boy likes fancy homes."

They walked down the hallway past a large sitting room and stood at the entrance of a lavishly decorated library whose four panelled walls housed thousands of books, mostly old, mostly rare first editions. The cheap ones probably cost $10,000 each, Nazareth thought. Two leather wing chairs, each cradling a $5,000 Persian embroidery pillow, stood at opposite ends of a large Persian rug that had most likely set the collector back $200,000. Next to each chair stood an antique Tiffany lamp worth $50,000. At the room's far end was an ornate Louis XIII sofa worth another six figures. On the sofa rested the body of Vivian Latourette, whose husband left her with something just north of $1 billion when he died five months earlier.

"This room alone is worth millions," said Nazareth, who looked like a man viewing the Sistine Chapel for the first time. "Pick the right book, and it's probably worth more than your entire pension account."

"Want a souvenir?" Gimble smiled.

"Hell," he joked, "I couldn't afford the safe deposit box."

Detective Pederson offered them some Vicks, and they both decided that was a good idea. The home was excessively warm, and that had accelerated the body's decomposition. Nazareth noticed a high-tech control module for central air, but obviously the air was turned off.

"No signs of forced entry. And according to D'Angelo," Pederson nodded toward the crime-scene specialist, "she's been dead two, maybe two-and-a-half days."

Gimble shot Nazareth a quick look. He nodded.

"Meaning Mercer was in town at the time of the murder," he said.

The body on the couch looked much like those at the other Rosebud Killer crime scenes, but Nazareth immediately noticed small differences.

"Her hands are crossed over her chest," he said as he studied the body. "With all the others the hands were crossed over the lap. But the rosebud looks about the same as usual." He bent over and looked more closely at the old woman's face and shook his head slightly.

"This is off," he said after a few moments. "Very pale around the nostrils, red blotches on the cheeks, and what looks like a small amount of dried blood at the corner of her mouth. She may have been smothered. A pillow, maybe."

"Then you and D'Angelo agree," said Pederson, clearly impressed. "I take it you've seen this before?"

"Seen it too many times," Nazareth said soberly, "but not with the Rosebud cases. Has someone checked the pillows on those two chairs?"

"Looked but not touched. You're expecting blood?"

"Hers, yeah, definitely. Mouth, maybe tongue. Smothering isn't a great way to go. If we're lucky," he added, "maybe the guy left hair or clothing fibers during the struggle. If we're extra lucky, maybe the vic scratched him. In that case we could get his blood on the pillow and tissue under her nails."

"What do you make of this?" said Gimble, pointing to a blue Tiffany gift bag that rested waist-high on the bookcase near the room's entrance. She peered into the bag and saw that it held a small blue box tied with a satin ribbon. The box was about the right size for a ring. "It's the only thing that looks out of place in this room."

"Have you checked this, Tony?" Nazareth asked.

Tony D'Angelo came over and nodded.

"I've taken pictures, that's it."

Nazareth bent over and turned his head sideways.

"The way the sunlight is hitting this shelf," he said, "you can see that the bag was pushed along after it was set down. There's a faint trail in the dust."

"I definitely didn't touch it," Tony said.

"Understood," Nazareth replied. "I'm guessing it was done at the same time the bag was put there. Instead of just setting the bag down, someone put it down while moving — forward, in that direction." He pointed toward the couch.

"Can you take the box out and give it a shake?" Nazareth asked.

"Yeah, as long as you don't think it's a bomb," D'Angelo joked.

"If someone fit a bomb into that box," Nazareth grinned, "I'll sing at your funeral."

"Oh, in that case, I can die happy."

Still wearing latex gloves, D'Angelo used the thumb and forefinger of each hand to grasp the corners at the top of the box. He gently shook the box from side to side, then up and down.

"No rattling sound. And it's really light," he said.

"Empty is my guess," said Nazareth. He walked down the hallway to the front door, then turned around and glanced back at the couch. He slowly moved back toward the library, stopping briefly to push the sitting room doors fully open and poke his face in. Finally, he stepped back into the library where the others stood and looked across the room to the couch where Vivian Latourette had been posed after her murder.

"No forced entry," Nazareth began. "So unless someone else had a key, always a possibility, she opened the door for this guy. And a rich old widow on the Upper East Side doesn't do that for just anyone who shows up."

"But," Gimble finished the thought, "she might do that for someone delivering a blue Tiffany gift bag."

"Precisely. If the guy looked respectable, she might have done that. If it had been a legit delivery, she would have taken the bag at the front door and carried it to the sitting room, where she's got a big desk, cozy chairs, and a telephone. That's where she would have opened the box and then called someone to say thank you."

"But instead," Gimble followed the thought, "the bag ended up on a library shelf, and it was put there by someone who was most likely in a hurry."

Nazareth gave her a thumbs-up.

"Right. She let the guy in, he did something that spooked her — shut the door behind him maybe — and she took off toward the library. But why the library and not the sitting room? The sitting room is closest, and she could have slammed the doors, maybe bought enough time to call 911."

"Maybe she had a gun in the library," Pederson offered.

But Nazareth was already walking the length of the library, obviously hearing nothing but his own thoughts. When he reached the library's far end nearest to the couch, he briefly examined an adjoining hallway that led toward a rear sunroom with a large skylight. He shook his head and walked back to the other end of the library. This time he paused to study the library's doorway, then turned to the nearest bookcase and looked up and down the shelves. The others could practically hear the tumblers in Nazareth's brain clicking into place.

"What are you getting?" Gimble asked.

"Composite pocket doors," he said, showing them the sliding door that was virtually hidden inside one of the door frames. "Manufactured to look like wood, but actually made of ballistic composite. Light, very strong, easy to glide open and shut. One door on each side of the doorway," he pointed, "and so inconspicuous that most people walk by without noticing."

"As we all did," said Gimble.

Nazareth nodded, then knocked on the walls that sandwiched the bullet-proof pocket doors. Instead of the characteristic hollow sound one gets from wallboard, he got a dull thud indicative of serious heft.

"Concrete on both sides, I'm guessing. Now check the bookcase." Inside a shadowy corner near the doorway, chest high, partially hidden by a signed first edition of James Joyce's *Ulysses,* was a small black control pad whose entire surface functioned as a panic button.

"This whole library is a safe room," he said. "All she needed to do was get in here and hit that pad. The doors on both ends of the room would have slammed shut. Hitting the pad probably would have also alerted an armed-response security company."

"But she didn't make it here," said Pederson.

"Tough to do when someone's already with you in the hallway. She certainly wasn't going to outrun him," Nazareth said, "and she probably didn't think to do anything else."

"What else could she have done?" asked Gimble.

"Anyone's guess," he answered. "Kicked him in the groin. Poked him in the eye. Whatever might have bought her fifteen seconds, and that's all she probably needed. But he scared her in some way, and she bolted. He was right on her as she got to the library door, shoved her as soon as she reached for the panic button, and threw the Tiffany bag on that shelf."

"I can buy the whole scenario," Gimble told him, "but it's a real departure from how the other murders went down."

"Yeah, that's what I'm not liking. All the other victims were tasered, then put down very gently — diazepam shot followed by fatal injection. This one was all strong-armed stuff," he said. "Something causes her to bolt, he catches up to her, puts her on the floor or the couch, and smothers her with a pillow. Instead of reaching for a pillow, why not the taser?"

"But if this isn't your Rosebud Killer," Pederson asked, "how did the guy know to pose the body like that?"

"See, that's the thing. He really didn't. Even if you say that for some reason our guy decided to smother her, I'd still expect him to pose her the same way as the others. But that's off, too."

"Okay, but who else would know how to get the pose even close to right?" asked Pederson.

"Even though there haven't been any public photos," Gimble explained, "I think the news accounts alone would get someone in the ballpark. How many ways are there to lay an old woman out on a couch with a silk rosebud in her hands? And that much was in the Pennsylvania newspapers from day one."

"So you're thinking a copycat?" Pederson asked.

Gimble just shrugged and deferred to her partner.

"Maybe, but it's definitely too soon to judge," said Nazareth. "Who called this in anyway?"

"Housekeeper who comes in five days a week," Pederson told him. "She has no key. She calls when she's a block away, and when she gets to the door, usually right at 9:00 a.m., Mrs. Latourette lets her in."

"I'd like to talk with her before running with the copycat idea. And let's make sure we agree that this wasn't just a slick robbery," Nazareth added, waving his hand around the room. "The place looks pretty much untouched, but anything you put your hand on in this room is worth thousands, or hundreds of thousands, or even more. We don't know that someone didn't walk out with a book worth a million."

"How do you want to follow up on that?" Gimble asked him.

"While I have a long talk with the housekeeper, why don't you track down the security company that covers this place. If it's a competent outfit, they most likely have a video inventory of every room in the house. In that case we can match the videos to the crime scene photos. The problem," he looked around the library, "is that we're talking about maybe thousands of objects in this room alone. So if someone took, let's say, five books worth a total of $1 million and replaced them with dummies, we could be at this forever."

"In that case," Gimble grimaced, "I'd better get started."

"Roger that."

36.

Darkness has fallen as I pass the toll booths at the northern end of the NJ Turnpike and swing toward the GWB after my Atlantic City adventure. The day's final die-hard commuters stream out of Manhattan like lemmings. In another hour, assuming no major traffic delays, they will reach carefully tended suburban homes where the children slaughter zombies on their video games and the wives sip Pinot Grigio while reading Nora Roberts. After hurried dinners and three Heinekens, these guy will tuck themselves in for a fitful night's sleep and the chance to do it all over again the next day.

I, on the other hand, cheerily hum along to Vivaldi after a dazzling though brief vacation by the sea. Yes, the day was unplanned, as wonderful moments often are. Yes, I spent more on my own pleasure than most reasonable people would think prudent. On the other hand, how much have I saved on future medical care by rejuvenating mind, body, and spirit in this way? I am, after all, a worthwhile investment.

A very long time ago I vowed never to be a soldier in the army of nine-to-five drones whose cars now head out of Manhattan. As far back as I can remember, I noticed nothing but hopelessness in the eyes of those who toiled at the same mindless work day after joyless day. I wondered then, as I do still, how any sane individual can interpret the incessant pursuit of food, clothing, and shelter as actual life. Although I understand the need for food, clothing, and shelter, I wonder how anyone with a mind more active than that of a sea sponge can fail to recognize that merely covering the basics is hardly living.

Are my detective escorts truly alive? How can they be? If today is a fair proxy, they spend their lives watching others live. On this particular day they have watched me drive for nearly four hours. They have watched me entertain myself at slot machines and, for the first time, win $18.75 rather than lose my $50 stake. They have watched me dine on excellent braised black cod at Izakaya. And for all I know they have even watched me tangle like a rabid hyena with my lady fair. Either way, my new NYPD friends are alive in name only as far as I can tell.

I live. They watch.

Yet the ending of this day is bittersweet. The memory of its pleasures will linger, but tomorrow I must seriously consider what having detectives in tow could mean to my holy pursuits. I already know that I will not let man interfere with God's work. Precisely how I will navigate the churning waters ahead remains a puzzle.

37

Nazareth had a patrol car bring Elva Stokes from her apartment in the Bronx to One Police Plaza in lower Manhattan. He had no particular reason to believe the 58-year-old housekeeper was involved in the murder, but he also had no particular reason to believe she wasn't. Even if she hadn't killed Mrs. Latourette, she could have set the whole thing up. Three years earlier Nazareth had worked the case of a 93-year-old great grandmother who could barely walk yet had stabbed her daughter-in-law in the heart with a steak knife, then staged the scene as a robbery gone bad. That's when he learned that you lean on every witness every time.

He showed Mrs. Stokes to a seat in the conference room and offered her coffee or water. She declined both. Nerves? Maybe. She looked considerably older than her 58 years — noticeably bent, thinner than she probably should be, gray hair, no more than 5'5" tall. A hard life in this hard city will break a body down, Nazareth thought. Would he look like this if he made it to 58?

"I appreciate your coming in, Mrs. Stokes."

"I want to help," she said timidly, "but I don't know what else I can tell anybody. I just keep saying the same things over and over."

"I understand, but the more we review the details, the better chance we have of turning up just one or two extra things that were missed. You may know something that you don't think is really important," he explained gently, "but it could turn out to be a very important piece of evidence."

"Mrs. Latourette was such a nice lady," she offered, "and did so much good for people. I know she helped lots of charities. Rich people like her sometimes just keep all their money and don't help anyone."

"Did she ever talk about those charities with you?"

"The only one I really knew about was some big hospital here in Manhattan. Five or six years ago one of my grandkids was really sick with cancer," she told him, "and when Mrs. Latourette found out she picked up the phone, just like that, and the next day my grandson was seeing the best doctor in America. I mean the best one in the whole United States of America. Can you imagine that?"

"And how's your grandson now?"

"Healthy as could be," she beamed. "Just perfect. They told me later that he would have died except for that doctor. And that doctor saw him the next day because Mrs. Latourette made one phone call." At this point the floodgates opened, and Nazareth brought Mrs. Stokes a bottle of water while she sobbed into a tissue that she took from her small purse. He took a short walk and grabbed himself a coffee. When he returned a few minutes later, he found an apologetic Mrs. Stokes waiting for him.

"I'm sorry, Detective. It just hit me hard all of a sudden. Mrs. Latourette saved my grandson's life, and then someone went and killed that fine woman." She shook her head in dismay.

"Actually I want to talk about how the guy got into her house. There were no signs that someone broke in," he said, "so that means the guy had a key or she opened the door for him."

"She wouldn't let anybody have a key, that's for sure. All the years I worked for her, she never gave me a key. If she wasn't going to be home," she explained, "I didn't have to come. But she paid me anyway. You believe that? She said it was a full-time job, so I got paid for days I didn't even work. I also got paid for two weeks of vacation every year."

"Wouldn't she have given a key to relatives?"

She shook her head vigorously.

"No way. All she has is cousins, and all they ever wanted was her money. She said that plenty of times. She said it to me, and I heard her say it on the telephone. Those cousins are plain trash, and she gave them nothing."

"Do you know if she kept a key anywhere near the front door? Maybe someone was able to reach in and grab it?"

"She kept the key in her own pocket, is where. I never saw a key except in her hand or going into her pocket. That's just how she was, especially after her husband died."

"How about letting someone in? What did she do if someone rang the doorbell?"

"Look through the peephole and walk away, mostly. You ask me, the police should do something about the people who come down a street like that knocking on doors and ringing bells. Just looking for trouble, most of them," she nodded.

"Does that happen often?"

"Every couple days, I guess. People selling something or collecting for something — themselves, probably — or just looking to see what they can get themselves into."

"And she wouldn't open the door to speak with these people?"

"Nossir, never. If she saw it was the mailman or the FedEx guy or someone like that, she'd open the door. Otherwise, no way."

"Did you ever see her open the door for a FedEx delivery?"

141

"Oh, yes. She didn't get many packages, but she always opened the door for the FedEx guy."

"Would she let him in the house?"

"Not usually. No need to, because he was just dropping off. But a couple of times in bad weather — snow or heavy rain, you know — she'd ask the guy to come in if she had to sign. And once I saw the guy come in around Christmas, because she wanted to give him a card. She was always good like that. She gave Christmas cards to a lot of people."

Nazareth seemed satisfied with the answers so far, so he turned his attention to the air conditioning that hadn't been turned on. As hot as the weather had been lately, he couldn't understand why Mrs. Latourette hadn't been using the a/c.

"Oh, Lord!" she laughed. "Now Mrs. Latourette, she was always a little funny about that air conditioning, let me tell you. For as long as I knew her, Mrs. Latourette said that air conditioning is very bad for the health. She didn't say why exactly, but that's what she thought. So she wouldn't turn the air conditioning on unless the house was already hot. Yessir, I had some warm days in that house, but it never hurt me."

"What about in the kind of heat we've had recently?"

"Well, she would never go to bed with the air conditioner on. She just opened her windows and let the fresh air in. Next day she'd close her bedroom windows and then put the air conditioner on if the house got too hot. But I don't know that it ever got too hot for her. She usually put the air conditioning on just for me."

"So you think she turned it off when you left?"

"Oh, yes. I worked pretty much from 9:00 until 5:00, and she was usually shutting the air conditioner off about the same time I was leaving. If it was 100 degrees outside, maybe she'd leave it on for a while. But usually she turned it off when I was leaving for the day."

"Okay, that's helpful. One last thing. I would like to have a detective go through Mrs. Latourette's house with you. I need you to tell us if anything important is missing, or if maybe something important looks out of place to you."

"You think somebody was robbing her, and that's why he killed her?"

"We don't know for sure, but that's certainly possible. She had a lot of very expensive things in the house."

"Well, I sure never knew what was expensive and what wasn't. I know she was rich, but most of the stuff in that house is so old it looks like it came from some charity. It sure is good at collecting dust, though."

"I'm going to ask Detective Gimble to meet you at the house later this week."

"That's fine. I hope you catch this Rosebud Killer, Detective."

"So do I, Mrs. Stokes." He looked directly into her tired brown eyes. "So do I."

38.

I am utterly fascinated by the *Times'* account of Vivian Latourette's passing. A "prominent Manhattan socialite" and a "billionaire widow" was she. Try as it might — and it seems not to try very hard — the *New York Times* cannot disguise its smugness. This begs the question of which came first, the smugness of New Yorkers or the smugness of the *Times*. Or did the two spring simultaneously into existence, a sort of Big Bang of class consciousness? Show me someone who reveres the *Times,* and I'll show you someone who's not from Iowa, Missouri, or North Dakota. In real America, as opposed to the faux America that one finds in New York City, people read *USA Today*, whose color photos and streamlined stories provide all the necessary facts without the *Times'* pretension and editorializing.

So Mrs. Latourette was a "Manhattan socialite," was she? Well, la-di-da and my oh my. In this city those words mean nearly as much as "Nobel Prize" and "Presidential Medal of Freedom." How many addled Uptown dowagers would be willing to die today, this very minute in fact, if they could be assured of earning a *Times* front-page story containing the words "Manhattan socialite"? All of them? Most of them? Impossible to know but stimulating to contemplate.

What offends me most about the reporting is the preoccupation with *what* to the almost complete exclusion of *why*. This is unmistakably clear evidence of shallow thinking, which is to say contemporary thinking.

Wondering *why* things happen has become, it appears, a rather quaint, out-dated nineteenth-century affectation. All anyone seems to care about today is the outcome, as though there's no value in considering what led from A to B, from cause to effect. All *what*, no *why*. Did television cause this deficiency of mind? Or was it the World Wide Web and its glorification of trivia? I don't know. But I loathe it.

Mrs. Latourette died for a reason. Is that reason meaningless? Should we care only about the time of death, the discovery and the condition of the body? After all these weeks shouldn't someone have at least a glimmer of an idea why widows are being shepherded into the next life? Good God, how many logical explanations can there be? Yet the entire question of why is absent from the news, and I find this extremely disappointing.

Do I know why Mrs. Latourette died? Yes, of course I do.

39.

Gimble phoned Nazareth from the Latourette residence, where she and two other detectives were attempting to determine whether anything obvious had been stolen by the murderer. They had covered half the rooms in the 4,000-square-foot brownstone, and they were slowly building up enough courage to tackle the library. The crammed bookshelves would make their work almost, but not quite, impossible.

"Well," she said, "you were right about Mrs. Latourette's security company having video footage of every room in the house. They printed out hard copies for us, and we're matching everything as well as we can. It's really slow going, and we haven't gone near the library yet."

"Yeah, the library's going to be a bitch," Nazareth agreed. "Why don't you just take photos of each shelf, then bring everything back here. I can have a couple of rookies sit down with magnifying glasses for a few days."

"That sounds really good to me. I'd like not to spend the rest of my life here. Well, not unless I can actually live here."

"You can afford $90,000 a year in property taxes?"

"Are you serious?"

"Oh, yeah. Next year it'll probably cost a hundred grand."

"In that case I'll just keep on renting."

"Sounds like a plan."

The next morning Nazareth and Gimble sat in the conference room with coffee, buttered rolls, and two thick stacks of 8x10 color photos. Before bringing in extra eyes for the project, Nazareth wanted to gauge how long the analysis might take. It took only a few minutes to get the answer. Too long.

"We've got, say, twenty-five books on each shelf, times eight shelves in each bookcase, times maybe thirty bookcases. Roughly six thousand books?" He shook his head in disbelief. "Can you imagine how much these things must have cost?"

"Forget the cost," she answered. "Just imagine how long it takes to find six thousand books worth buying. I don't think I've read six hundred books in my whole life, much less six thousand. "

"The rich really are different, aren't they?" Nazareth said as he quickly flipped through the photos.

"Tell me about it. Someone has millions of dollars worth of valuables in the house, but she opens the door because someone rings the bell. Can you explain that to me?"

"Could be anything," he replied. "It could've been someone she knew, or someone she thought she knew. Or maybe the door wasn't locked in the first place. Or maybe she was suffering from dementia, in which case all bets are off."

"Well, whatever the case," she said, "if something was stolen, do you really think it will help us find this guy?"

Nazareth gave the question some thought as he looked back and forth between two photos of the same bookshelf, one taken by the security company and one taken by an NYPD photographer.

"In most robberies I'd say definitely not. Whatever gets stolen is usually worth a couple of thousand max," he reasoned, "and it just vanishes in the huge sewer of stolen goods that runs from one end of this city to the other. But anything that gets stolen in this particular house could easily be worth six or seven figures, assuming the thief knows what he's looking for. In that case there's a very limited marketplace. If we can somehow find the buyer, we can find the seller."

"I'm having trouble believing robbery was the motive."

Nazareth shrugged. "And I'm having a hard time thinking it wasn't. Robbery may not have been the primary motive, but I believe it was one of them.

"You don't think this was another Rosebud killing?"

He shook his head more emphatically than usual.

"Not at all. Doesn't feel right. Significant details are way off. And the housekeeper has me thinking about something else that could be going on."

"And that is?"

"She remembered that Mrs. Latourette had blown off some cousins who were badgering her for money. I'm thinking that a billionaire widow who doesn't toss the poor relatives a few crumbs could generate a lot of hostility, you know?"

"Not really," she grinned. "In my family all anybody has is crumbs, so we're always happy to share."

"Yeah, I definitely know about that. But in this case a crumb could be $500K. Think about it. If Mrs. Latourette was worth $1 billion, a half million is just 0.0005% of the total. That would be like saying I have $1 million but won't toss you $500 when you really need it. Would that piss you off?"

"Well, it's your money, not mine," she smiled. "But, yeah, I can see how that could piss someone off big time. But a revenge killing?"

"Hey, in this city people get killed for pocket change."

By the next morning Nazareth had ferreted out some information that he believed could open a whole new avenue of inquiry. He came to the conference room with a single sheet of typing paper on which he had sketched what looked like an organization chart.

"Is that the official game plan?" Gimble joked.

"Close, actually. It's a tiny section of the Latourette family tree that I was able to piece together from public records on the Internet. And I think you'll find this interesting."

The family tree that Nazareth laid out for Gimble began with Ruppert and Dorothy Schuyler, both born and raised in New York City. This respectable middle-class couple had two children: a son, Emmons, and a daughter, Barbara. Son Emmons married Daphne Simmons, and their daughter, Vivian, married the heir to one of the great American family fortunes, Damien Latourette. Throughout their untroubled married life Damien and Vivian supported countless non-profit organizations, especially those headquartered in New York City, and had publicly declared their intention to leave all of their earthly possessions to four or five favorite charities when they died.

"Okay," Gimble said. "So everything on this side of the family tree is golden."

"Solid gold, yep," he nodded.

"So I'm guessing that means the other side of the family didn't turn out the same way."

"Major understatement," he told her. "Vivian Latourette's father, Emmons Schuyler, was a straight-up guy who made a lot of money on Wall Street. But his sister, Barbara Schuyler, was a booze hound who ended up marrying a West Virginia scam artist by the name of Gentry Tompkins. They had a daughter — this would be Vivian Latourette's first cousin — by the name of Beth. And Beth took after the mother, except that she favored drugs over booze."

"How the hell does the same family fly off in two completely different directions?" she asked.

"No clue. Anyway, Beth got pregnant and married a complete mutt by the name of Jesse Rivers, who spent half his life out of jail, half of it in. Felonies, misdemeanors, you name it. Nothing close to murder, though. Drugs, robberies, that sort of thing."

"A regular choir boy."

"Relative to their son, yeah," he nodded. "The son, Jesse Rivers, Jr., who by the way is now 54 years old, was put away for murder when he was 15. Took a little neighbor boy into the woods, filled his shirt and pants with rocks, and pushed the kid off a wooden bridge into a pond. Watched him drown just for laughs."

"And this record wasn't sealed?" said Gimble.

"Well," he answered, "there's sealed and then there's sort of sealed. I arranged for this one to be sort of sealed."

"Understood."

"Naturally, this homicidal piece of garbage was put back on the streets at 18, then proceeded to polish his resume: assault with a deadly weapon, menacing, stalking, possession with intent, and just about anything else you can think of."

"Except for murder."

"No other murders that we know of. But is he someone who might think that Mrs. Latourette should have shared some of her fabulous wealth with him? Yeah, for sure. His mommy is, or was — I don't know whether she's still alive — Mrs. Latourette's first cousin," he explained, "even though they probably never had anything to do with each other."

"I can't picture the Latourettes driving to West Virginia for a family reunion, can you?"

"We know that never happened. But that doesn't mean the Rivers clan didn't think about the Latourettes a whole lot. Jealous as hell. Maybe even blamed the Latourettes for their shitty lives. *If you had just given us a hand,* and so forth. Jealousy turned to hate."

"And then hate turned to murder."

"Yeah, maybe," he said. "But if that's the case, I can't picture this guy just walking away empty-handed after killing her."

"Copycat murder to cover the robbery?"

"That would certainly keep us looking in the wrong direction, wouldn't it? He'd be long gone with whatever he stole," Nazareth reasoned, "while we're back here looking for someone else. That's why I'd like to nail down whether this was a robbery before we look seriously at the cousin."

"Okay, so it's back to comparing photos of the house."

"Right, but I also want to have the housekeeper walk through the home with you. She spent fifteen years taking care of the place, so something could jump out at her."

"She and I will be all over that place tomorrow," said Gimble. "But something's still bothering you, if I'm not mistaken."

"Absolutely," he nodded. "I've pushed myself pretty hard on the copycat theory, and I know that's a mistake. My first partner, Will Haggerty, was a first-rate detective, and he had a great line that I can practically hear him whispering in my ear: 'Fall in love with your theory *after* you solve the crime.' And maybe I've fallen in love too soon. I really want to believe that the guy who murdered Mrs. Latourette isn't the Rosebud Killer, so I keep looking for signs that he's not. Which means I may have us going after two guys when we should be putting all of our energy into just one."

"The only way to find out whether we've got one killer or two," Gimble said encouragingly, "is to nail someone. If the killings stop, we had one. If we get more dead widows, we have two."

"Good thinking," he smiled.

"Let's go nail someone."

40.

Gimble said good morning to the two patrolmen who watched over Mrs. Latourette's brownstone from their parked vehicle, then accompanied housekeeper Elva Stokes up the front stairs. When they entered the home they noticed the lingering smell of death. A police crew had eliminated the worst of it, but only time and maybe a few coats of paint would get rid of the rest.

"I just don't know how much I can help you, Detective," said Mrs. Stokes. "I don't know whether Mrs. Latourette had any hidden money or anything like that."

"There's no pressure on you, Mrs. Stokes," Gimble replied. "All I want you to do is walk slowly through every room, just as though you were dusting or polishing things as usual. If something is missing or out of place, you're going to notice it. You know these rooms better than anyone, probably including Mrs. Latourette."

"Well, I'll do my best."

"You'll do fine. Now, you came here Monday through Friday, right?"

"Yes, ma'am."

"Did you work in all the rooms every day, or did you just do a few rooms each day?"

"I worked on part of this main level every day," she said. "I cleaned the hallway, Mrs. Latourette's sitting room, and the library every day I was here, just in case she had company. Except for that I had a schedule for every room in the house — I did certain rooms on each day of the week."

"Great. Let's start on this main level, then work our way upstairs one room at a time."

After two hours of carefully studying every square foot of each room they had visited, the women came to a long, imposing space on the top floor overlooking East 80th Street. At the room's far end, facing a large picture window, were an elegant mahogany executive desk and matching swivel chair. In the center of the room, back to back and facing the longest walls, were two antique upholstered museum benches. Unobtrusive track lighting revealed that the entire room was adorned by paintings hung in ornate antique frames. The room was both office and art gallery as only the ultra-rich could imagine the space. Gimble didn't know a great deal about fine art, but she knew that she was looking at it.

"This was Mr. Latourette's private office," said Mrs. Stokes almost reverently. "He worked in here every day, writing mostly. Until he got too sick, he came up here right after breakfast, wearing a suit and tie, and worked all day except for lunchtime."

"And you cleaned in here?"

"Oh, yes. This was one of my Monday rooms. And the only time I could clean it was if Mr. Latourette was in here. If he was traveling some-place," she added, "I couldn't come in here."

"Did he ever say why?"

"No, he just loved those paintings, I suppose, and he wanted to make sure I didn't do anything but dust the frames with a special little brush he gave me. A sable brush, he called it, and I kept that in its own little box when I wasn't using it."

"So you never actually touched the paintings themselves."

"Oh, sweet Lord, no!" she laughed. "Once a year he had someone from a big museum come in and do that. Otherwise, no one else ever touched those paintings of his."

Gimble studied Mrs. Stokes as the older woman walked slowly around the large desk and then moved to the nearest painting. First she stood close enough to examine the frame carefully, then stepped back to assess the painting's place on the wall. It was easy to see why she had been a trusted employee for so many years. She had a gentle and quiet way about her, and you could read the fierce pride on her face as she went about her business. Working here had never been just a job, Gimble thought. This home represented her rightful place in the world. This is where she was someone special. Not just a housekeeper. A curator, a caretaker. Never just a housekeeper.

"Frame needs dusting. If these frames don't get dusted once a week," she said, "I can tell right away. Mr. Latourette wouldn't be happy."

Mrs. Stokes moved deliberately from one painting to the next, each time checking the frame and the painting's position relative to its neighbors. As they worked their way down the first long wall side by side, Gimble glanced at the brass nameplates under the paintings: Turner, Caravaggio, Wyeth, Kandinsky. She recognized the names and knew that some of these pieces were undoubtedly priceless. Just how priceless she couldn't say. An NYPD detective will never own art like this.

About halfway down the room, just opposite the twin museum benches, Mrs. Stokes brought her face especially close to the frame she was examining. She looked up and down one vertical edge, then the other, then back. After studying the top and bottom edges, she stepped back and checked the painting's position. She tilted her head to one side and just kept looking.

"This one isn't right," she said.

"What's wrong with it?" Gimble asked.

"First off, someone rubbed away some of the dust on both sides of the frame. All the other paintings haven't been touched. This one has. And if you step back you can just make out that the top of the frame isn't level like it should be. Look at this one, and then at the ones on each side."

Gimble did so, and she saw that the top edge was just a hair away from being perfectly horizontal. It's not something she would have noticed without Mrs. Stokes' guidance, but now that she had seen it she was mesmerized.

"And you don't think it was like this?"

"No way. Mr. Latourette had some museum expert hang every one of these paintings, and they don't move, believe me. There's some kind of little sticky pad on the back to hold the painting in place."

Gimble studied the moody lavender and gray painting of what she took to be a castle of some sort. When she looked back and forth from this piece to its neighbors, she noticed that the surface seemed newer and cleaner than the others. It also appeared that the painting wasn't stretched as tightly as it should be. In fact, she noticed a very slight bulge in the canvas at the lower right corner.

She stepped back and read the brass nameplate: *The Houses of Parliament, Sunset, Claude Monet.* Gimble didn't know the painting, but Monet's name was enough to get her attention. She immediately called Nazareth.

"We need to get an art expert up here," she said with more authority than usual. "I'm pretty sure I know what's missing."

Dr. Emerson Symington, curator of European paintings at the Metropolitan Museum of Art, entered Mr. Latourette's office in the company of the two detectives. Symington had visited this room twice before during his seven years as one of the Met's top experts, and he was plainly thrilled to return.

"Very few people have ever seen this gallery," Symington observed, "yet it houses one of the world's truly great private collections."

"No argument from me," Nazareth replied. "I did some reading on a few of the artists in this room, and it's a pretty amazing lineup."

Symington simply nodded his agreement as he stood in awe before a small oil of Mont Sainte-Victoire by Paul Cezanne. For a moment he seemed to exit the real world.

"You know, detectives, Cezanne continually painted this same scene. He was thoroughly taken by it. But of all those efforts over all those years," he said, "I believe this to be the finest. This is the one that finally captured what he had to say."

"How much is something like this worth?" asked Gimble.

"Almost impossible to know, really," he shrugged, "because this painting will never be sold. I happen to know that all of the paintings in this collection will be coming to the Met, and we'll certainly never part with it."

"But if you had to take a guess at its value?" said Nazareth.

Symington thought for a moment, chin resting on his left hand.

"Fifty million? Probably more. But putting a price on it is meaningless," he continued, "because it will never come to auction. It's pieces like this that give meaning to the word *priceless*. It is truly a price-less painting. Magnificent and irreplaceable."

Gimble guided the curator to the Monet painting whose appearance had troubled Mrs. Stokes the day before.

"What do you think of this one?" she said.

"Good God in Heaven!" he cried like a man who had just met Death face to face. "This is a cartoon, not a painting."

He snatched the painting from the wall before Nazareth could stop him. Symington turned the frame over to reveal the crude work of whoever had replaced the original with a $49.95 print on cheap canvas. The painting had been carelessly stapled to the wooden stretcher like a dining room chair that had been reupholstered by a housewife in a hurry. The curator was pale and breathing hard.

"My God!" is all he kept saying.

Symington tore away at the canvas print. Underneath it were the remnants of the Monet oil that had been cut from the stretcher with a razor blade. He was numb.

"Can you give us a value?" asked Nazareth.

"I wish I could say priceless," answered Symington. "But this painting is now going to be sold to someone who doesn't care about provenance. In that underground marketplace if it finds the right middleman and the right buyer, it could sell for $70 million or more. We'll never see it again."

Less than two hours later Nazareth and Gimble sat at One Police Plaza with Detective Rob Tyler from the Major Case Squad. Tyler was NYPD's most experienced and most successful art-theft expert, and his assessment of the Monet robbery was highly encouraging.

"I'd bet my pension that this isn't the work of a serious art pro," he began, "and I'll give you three reasons. One, the absolute last thing you want to do is put a spotlight on your activity. And killing someone is guaranteed to shine a very bright light. Two, you don't go after a small collection, because the theft is tougher to hide. Three, you don't substitute a $50 print for a $70-million Monet and hope that no one will notice. What you leave behind is an expensive, top-shelf forgery that only a real expert can detect."

"In other words, the pro does everything possible to keep the theft hidden," said Nazareth.

"Exactly. It's all about buying time. One case I worked on," he said, "the painting was worth $30 million . . . and the theft wasn't even noticed until three years after it had gone out the door. Three years! The only reason they finally figured it out was that the painting was on the schedule to be cleaned. Whoever stole that painting left behind a forgery that even some experts would have said was the real thing. Scary good."

"Okay," said Gimble, "if this guy's an amateur, what do you think his next move is?"

"The pro usually has a buyer before he steals the painting. Let's say I have a dirtbag collector in Italy who wants a particular Monet from an American gallery or museum. We agree on a price," he explained, "and I try to get the painting. If I succeed, I bring it to Italy as a luggage liner. Only two people involved. I get the money, and my client in Italy gets to look at his secret Monet for the rest of his life."

"And our guy?" Gimble asked.

"Your guy obviously knew which painting he was after. Probably just read about it if he was keeping tabs on Mr. and Mrs. Latourette. Lots of rich people can't keep their mouths shut about what they own. But," he said, "this guy has no chance in hell of getting big money for the painting, because he has no buyer lined up. If he's really lucky, he finds a fence here in the City who's willing to give him fifty grand for the painting. And if you're really lucky," he smiled, "I have friends who'll know which fence we're talking about before the painting ever changes hands."

"You make it sound easy," said Nazareth.

"Let me tell you something. Your guy would have been a whole lot smarter to make off with a bunch of items worth ten grand each. That kind of merchandise he could sell. But a $70-million Monet?" he laughed. "That's hysterical. It's like trying to unload the Statue of Liberty."

A week later Tyler had gotten no tips at all on the missing Monet. His mood was markedly downbeat when he met with Nazareth and Gimble in the conference room at One Police Plaza.

"Nothing at all?" said Gimble.

Tyler shook his head gravely and studied his coffee cup longer than necessary.

"The only person who's out there talking about the painting is me," he said. "I've spoken with all the right guys, believe me, and the painting isn't for sale anywhere near Manhattan. If it was in the market, I'd know."

"And you still don't think the guy had a buyer lined up already?" asked Gimble.

"No way," he said emphatically. "This guy is strictly amateur hour. Yeah, he got the painting, and that counts for something, right? But my guess is he's staring at the thing wondering what the hell he's supposed to do next."

"So he just sits tight until he figures out how to unload the thing?" said Nazareth.

"Yeah, that's my guess. Wherever he calls home, that's probably where he is right now. The painting is stuffed in a box in the crawl space, or maybe it's under a carpet in his bedroom. Who the hell knows? He's counting his $70 million but doesn't know how to get seventy cents for it."

"Okay, then," said Nazareth, turning to Gimble. "So Cousin Jesse lives in Elkins, West Virginia?"

"Seven-hour drive each way," she nodded.

"So be it. Let's arrange for Elkins PD to take us out to the guy's house. Right now Cousin Jesse is our best shot."

"Okay, I'll make the call," she said. "In the meantime, what do you want to do about Mercer's tail? We still have guys watching him, but all he does is teach, buy groceries, and hang out in his apartment."

"Let's bag that for a while," he said. "Maybe I jumped the gun on him anyway. When we get back from West Virginia, we'll pay him a visit and see whether we think he's a real suspect."

"Okay, I'll get the word out."

Nazareth and Gimble followed Chief Terry Harrelson of the Elkins Police Department to a narrow, dead-end street at the edge of the Monongahela National Forest. Harrelson was cordial when Gimble called him two days earlier, and he had no objection to the visit as long as he was able to accompany the two detectives. Like most other long-time resident of Elkins, he knew that Jesse Rivers, Jr. had a bad history — well, the entire clan did, for that matter — so he wasn't terribly surprised that the guy was a suspect in something big.

Rivers occupied a small, run-down cabin set well back off the roadway. Running from the road up to the cabin was a long dirt driveway with a battered green pickup parked at the far end. At the back of the home stood more than 900,000 acres of picturesque mountains and valleys populated by black bear, flying squirrels, white-tailed deer, and untold other creatures.

"If you really want to get away from Manhattan," Gimble said, "I suppose this is where you do it."

"And if you really need money," Nazareth replied, "you live in a shack like this. Do I actually want to go in there? Looks as though the roof might come down any minute."

"Well, we've come all this way," she smiled.

"Yeah, for nearly eight hours of driving — one way, of course — I guess we should get our money's worth."

"Like a $70-million Monet?"

"Exactly like that."

Chief Harrelson climbed out of his cruiser and met the detectives by Rivers' front door. There was no bell, so he just pounded with the side of his fist. No answer. After a decent wait he pounded again, and this time was rewarded with a loud, "Hold the fuck on!"

"Someone's happy to have company," Gimble said.

"Probably the butler," Nazareth replied.

"Or maybe just the guy with the shotgun," Harrelson joked, then thought better of it. "Maybe we should, uh, all just move away from the door. You never know."

The door opened hesitantly, and the three officers looked into the dusky room at the outline of a man in a wheelchair trying to maneuver around the half-opened front door.

"Who the hell is it?" the man said.

"Mr. Rivers?" said Harrelson

"I know who I am," said Rivers caustically. "What I don't know is who the fuck you are."

"Uh, well, I'm Chief Harrelson, Elkins Police Department, and these are two detectives from New York City. We'd like to have a word with you."

"I'm listening."

"Would it be okay if we came in?"

"You have a search warrant?"

"Mr. Rivers, we don't want to search your home," said Harrelson. "We just want to talk with you for a bit."

"About what?"

"About Vivian Latourette," said Nazareth.

"That useless old bitch," Rivers said. "Please say you came here to tell me she's dead."

"In fact, that's exactly why we're here," Nazareth replied.

"Hot fuckin' damn," Rivers howled. "Praise God! C'mon in and tell me all about it."

They trailed Rivers as he wheeled himself across a small living room whose floor was littered with empty beer cans, old pizza boxes, and several dozen magazines, most of them porn.

"Actually, Mr. Rivers," Nazareth continued, "we were hoping that *you* could tell *us* something about Mrs. Latourette."

Rivers reached an old recliner whose damp stuffing poked out of the torn fabric. As he turned the wheelchair and began hoisting himself onto the chair, the others saw that he was missing the lower part of his right leg.

"And why the hell do you think I have anything to tell you about my dear cousin?"

"Well, uh . . . ." Words suddenly failed Nazareth.

"Oh, wait," said Rivers brightly, "you came here thinking I snuffed that worthless old piece of shit? Oh, I'm lovin' it! Yeah, you got me, Detective. I hopped out of here on my one good leg, dragged myself into the ol' pickup, drove my ass to New York City and skinned Cousin Vivian alive. Took my time about it, too. I used a dull knife. Then I hacked off her head and put it in her freezer. Did you find that, I hope?"

"I take it you didn't love her," said Gimble.

"You got that shit right, missy. I hope that nasty bitch went real slow, just like her po' cousins here in West Virginny."

"I'm not following you," said Gimble.

"Well follow this," he snarled. "Look around at this shit hole. I was born and raised here. When I was a kid I thought a hot meal was a can of beans that you left out in the sun. We had nothing but bad luck and cancer. And when Mom asked Cousin Vivian for some help, that old dried up turd told her own flesh and blood to fuck right off."

"When did your mother ask for help?" said Nazareth.

"Well let's see. First time was when I was about thirteen and starving. I don't mean I was hungry, folks. I mean I was starving. I'm here today because a couple of churches finally brought us some damned food. Second time was right after Pop got stomach cancer. Couldn't afford a hospital, so he blew his brains out right over there on that couch. Third time, let's see . . . oh, yeah. Third time was when Mom couldn't pay for drug rehab. Cousin Viv-i-an," he drew the syllables out, "said to fuck off. A week later Mom OD'd. End of family story."

"What happened to your leg, Mr. Rivers?" Harrelson asked.

"Aunt Vivian happened to my leg," he said bitterly. "I couldn't afford to see doctors. So three weeks ago they took my leg from the knee down because of diabetes. When the rot began to stink up the emergency room at the hospital, they decided they'd cut it off for free. Nice work, huh? Now all I'm good for is watching TV and drinking jug wine."

"I'm sure the county can help you out," said Harrelson.

"And I'm sure you're more full of shit than my outhouse. So tell me detectives, did Cousin Vivian have a slow, horrible death? Please say yes."

"Someone smothered her with a pillow," said Nazareth.

"Shit. That's way too fast and way too good. I was kinda hoping maybe some maniac had spent a week or so slicing off parts of her body and feeding them to wild pigs. I'll tell you what, though," he added. "You bring what's left of her to me, and I'll feed her to the wildlife this winter. Critters gotta eat, you know."

After wrapping up the interview with Rivers, Nazareth and Gimble had sandwiches with Chief Harrelson at his favorite diner and then settled into their car for the long drive back to Manhattan. If they made better time than they had yesterday when coming to Elkins, they would be back in their apartments by 10:00 p.m.

"I want to burn these clothes and take a really hot shower," said Gimble. "I don't know what made me feel dirtier, that cabin or Rivers himself."

"One of the great questions of our time," Nazareth smiled. "I'd say it's a toss-up. Equally disgusting."

"Well, at least we know we were on the right sort of track," she said. "This guy would gladly have killed Mrs. Latourette if he'd been able, so we had the profile right."

"And so did someone else."

"What do you mean?"

"The guy who killed her did the same research we did. He knew that we'd end up looking at the cousin. He played us."

"Does that really seem likely?"

"Oh, yeah. This guy found the same information I did about Mrs. Latourette's cousin," said Nazareth, "and he knew we'd head off in that direction. So we wasted time in West Virginia while he's back home disposing of a $70-million painting."

"Well hell. I'm definitely starting to hate this guy."

41.

It's a bit overcast, but the rain is supposed to hold off until late tomorrow. My trip to Ellenville, NY, should take no more than six hours round-trip, including the time I spend driving past Ellen Karcher's home. Although I'm hoping not to have an NYPD escort today, I have made careful plans in advance just in case. I certainly don't want to improvise the way I did with my Atlantic City trip, because it's always possible to make foolish mistakes when you're planning on the fly.

I will take the GWB as before, but this time, even if I'm followed, I'll turn onto the Palisades Parkway heading north. If it's obvious that I have a police tail, I will drive fifty miles or so to West Point and spend some time touring the U.S. Military Academy. Nothing at all suspicious about that. Let the detectives have fun following me through the West Point Museum for an hour or so.

If, on the other hand, I do not detect a car following me, I will take a simple precaution. About a half mile before exit 11, New Square, I will turn on my emergency flasher and carefully drive onto the shoulder. My reason for doing so, should anyone have reason to inquire, will be to reach into the back seat for my briefcase and the over-the-counter asthma inhaler in it.

After three minutes I will drive on. If my NYPD friends have been following me, I will notice them on the road ahead — most likely parked on the shoulder waiting me to drive past. If there are no detectives, I will finish my trip to Ellenville as planned.

I have always enjoyed time spent driving on the Palisades Parkway. The southernmost stretch offers superb views of New York City across the Hudson, while the northern section winds its way through hilly, heavily forested terrain that makes you almost forget that Manhattan is just a short drive away. But since I have not embarked on a pleasure trip today, I keep my eye on the rear-view mirror. No obvious police presence. So I follow my plan and stop just before exit 11. When I begin driving again after a few minutes, I am pleased to see no dark sedan either waiting for me on the shoulder or speeding onto the highway at exit 12 as I drive by. So today, in fact, I will finally complete my planning trip to Ellenville.

I am sorry for the way Mrs. Latourette had to die. My goal is to end the fear and suffering of the women I serve, not cause it. And clearly my customary process is the best possible. A few seconds of a stun gun followed immediately by a diazepam injection, and the woman is past all care. The final injection of sodium pentobarbital completes the effort efficiently and quite humanely.

But in order to assure the continuance of my important work, I needed to shift NYPD's focus somehow — had to get the detectives snapping at their own tails, as it were. So with Mrs. Latourette I altered the process in order to create the illusion of a copycat Rosebud Killer. I orchestrated what I believe was a reasonable balance between looking too much like and too much unlike my customary visit. I now trust that I created doubt in the minds of those who studied the results.

The life-ending option that I came up with for Mrs. Latourette was smothering her with a pillow. My admittedly limited research indicates that suffocation is not a terribly painful process, but naturally the fear associated with having a pillow held forcefully over one's face is extreme. I am certain that I will long remember Mrs. Latourette's eyes — wide and terrified, yet at

the same time softly pleading, like those of a doe about to be savaged by a
.240 Weatherby round traveling at more than 3,000 feet per second. I hope
never to witness this sort of thing again.

But it does appear that my ploy succeeded. The detectives, or so says
the venerable *Times*, are looking for a copycat killer along with a priceless
Monet. The longer they travel that road to nowhere, the less I need to worry
about my own heavenly path.

As I drive into Ellenville I immediately wonder whether the residents
have been evacuated by the National Guard or abducted by aliens. But, no,
I now see a few people standing outside assorted storefronts along what I
suppose is the small town's main business district. Over there two large men
with monumental bellies hanging over their belts stand under a green-and-
yellow awning, each holding a can of soda. And here by the old brick building are a graying husband and wife waiting for the traffic to subside before
daring to cross the road.

I am the traffic.

This is a sleepy hamlet marked by a church steeple, a few businesses
that survive only because the nearest shopping mall is twenty miles away, and
a whisper of human life, apparently all of it old. As I had hoped, Ellenville
is a leafy, pleasant village where Ichabod Crane would not look out of place.
I make several random turns at small intersections, just to see whether the
impression changes from one block to another. It does not. Fortunately, a
plain vehicle with New York plates attracts no attention whatsoever, so I
drive along slowly — anything over twenty-seven would most certainly
attract attention — as I get my bearings.

After a few minutes the charming female GPS voice guides me to
a neighborhood of shabby hundred-year-old dwellings on the outskirts
of town. Ellen Karcher's simple home stands on a street that runs roughly

parallel to Sandburg Creek, whose clear water flows vigorously at the end of her back yard behind a tangle of wild shrubs. I notice that the Widow Karcher is one of the few residents on this street whose property does not have a *FOR SALE* sign out front. I can think of countless reasons why owners might be abandoning this area, including old age, excessive flooding, and the downward spiral of the community's economy. But the reason is irrelevant. Whatever hardships have befallen Mrs. Karcher and her neighbors, she will not worry about them for much longer.

Her faded blue one-story home sits some thirty feet behind an over-grown hedge that stretches across the front of the property and then down the full length of the left side, separating her property from the foreclosure next door. Excellent. The fewer eyes here the better. To the right of Mrs. Karcher's home, perhaps twenty feet away, is a two-story structure whose cedar-shake siding has turned nearly black over the decades. Another home for sale. Judging from the run-down appearance, I assume that this place could be on the market for quite some time.

As I coast past Mrs. Karcher's home, the front screen door opens and out steps a gaunt, unsteady woman in a thin house dress and old-fashioned rubber galoshes that reach just above her ankles. She carries a pair of scissors and a small, clear vase. Heading out to cut some flowers, I assume. But I really can't tell because the wild waist-high hedge blocks my view. Mrs. Karcher doesn't look up as I drive by. She just grabs hold of the wooden railing and begins lowering herself painfully down the two wooden steps.

I make a right at the end of the block, then drive back toward the town center. I pull into a small parking lot behind a bakery, turn the car around, and head back to Mrs. Karcher's street. This time as I pass along the street I see no one. No one at all. It's a short block, but I am nevertheless surprised by the absence of life. Except for my brief sighting of Mrs. Karcher, the block is deserted. Well, a dog barks in the distance, but a dog will never identify my face or license plate.

I feel comfortable cruising the side streets of Ellenville. This is small-town America, where people are content to sit in their own homes and mind their own business. Life here must have been more stimulating fifty years ago, but time has a way of obliterating places like this. From coast to coast, American towns go one of two ways: they grow large enough to be called cities, or they vanish. I know which way this place is headed.

Next week, if the weather is accommodating, I shall return. In the meantime, I pull onto 209 South toward NY 17, then take the NY Thruway back toward Manhattan. But first, one last bit of business before I travel too far. I do not want to come all the way back to Ellenville only to find that Mrs. Karcher is away. This is a step I had neglected to take in my earlier work, and I continue to learn. About fifteen miles from Ellenville I pull into a gas station, and while the attendant fills my tank I use the pay phone at the far end of the building. I dial Mrs. Karcher's number, and she answers on the third ring.

"Hello," she says timidly.

"Good afternoon," I answer politely. "Is this Mrs. Karcher?"

"Yes, who's this?"

"Mrs. Karcher, this is Bob Riggins with the New York State Department of Environmental Conservation. I'm calling about some work we'll be doing next week along Sandburg Creek. Do you have a minute?"

"Surely. What kind of work are you doing?"

"Well, at this point all we're doing is mapping the area. But sometime within the next year we plan to do some additional flood-protection work along the creek."

"Well, that would be wonderful," she says enthusiastically. "We still get way too much water here after the big storms."

"Yes, ma'am, we understand. Anyway, sometime next week we're going to be photographing the area behind your home. The crew will be across the creek from you, but I wanted you to know in advance just in case you'll be home and might see them."

"Oh, thank you so much. I'm going to be here all next week, so I'll certainly see them. Will they be coming into my yard?"

"That shouldn't be necessary, Mrs. Karcher. They'll be on the other side of the creek for an hour or so. You'll see the truck parked over there. It's a white truck with a large New York State Department of Environmental Conservation logo on the door."

"Well, I'm awfully glad you're going to do some more work here. It's very nice of you to call me."

"My pleasure, Mrs. Karcher. You have a nice day."

I, for one, have had a lovely day. And I feel blessed to know that Mrs. Karcher's future is about to turn very bright indeed.

42.

Nazareth and Gimble didn't go so far as to say their long trip to West Virginia was a complete waste of time even though it felt that way. At least they had successfully ruled out one potential suspect, and that was worth something. Jesse Rivers had committed his share of crimes, but murdering Vivian Latourette obviously wasn't one of them. In his present condition he was plainly incapable of traveling to New York and smothering someone, no matter how feeble.

And in their absence two detectives from Staten Island had successfully ruled out a second possible suspect, Raphael Black, the sculptor who had attended Eleanor Martinson's funeral in Pennsylvania. Black had been traveling for two weeks recently and therefore hadn't been interviewed and ruled out as a person of interest. But that happened quickly after he returned home following a Caribbean cruise with his wife. Black had suffered a stroke five months before Mrs. Martinson's murder, and the left side of his body remained partially paralyzed. The prognosis was good: his doctors believed he would regain almost all use of his limbs. But for now he dragged more than lifted his left leg, and he was incapable of picking up a shoe, let alone a stun gun, with his left hand. This was not a man who could have wrestled a victim to the couch and injected her twice.

"So where do you want to go on this?" Gimble asked as she spread butter on a corn muffin in the conference room at One Police Plaza.

"We keep going back to the first murder," he said, "which is when this guy probably made a mistake that we still haven't caught. We continue to look at everyone who attended the funeral in Pennsylvania, with special emphasis on Mercer. I haven't seen anything to implicate him, but I also haven't seen anything to rule him out."

"Time to pay him a visit?"

"I think so, yeah. He's on the Lower West Side?"

"Right. We can drive there in ten or less."

The two detectives reached Mercer's apartment building on Cornelia Street at 10:18 a.m. and snagged a parking space across the street. They entered the lobby, walked past the unmanned receptionist desk, and took the stairs to the third floor. They rang Mercer's bell, and he opened the door almost immediately.

"Professor Mercer?" said Nazareth.

"Yes," he said mildly.

"Good morning. I'm Detective Pete Nazareth, NYPD, and this is my partner, Detective Tara Gimble." They held out their credentials for Mercer's inspection, but he didn't pay much attention to the gold shields or ID cards. "We'd like to speak with you about Eleanor Martinson."

"Ah, Lord, Eleanor!" he replied. "Yes, please come in. Chelsea said you would want to talk to me at some point. That's my sister, Eleanor's daughter-in-law."

Mercer led the detectives to a small leather couch in the combination living/dining area, and he sat opposite them on a straight-backed wooden chair that he pulled over from the dining table. The apartment was neat, lined with bookshelves, and tiny even by Manhattan standards. A bachelor professor's digs.

"Is this a good time, Professor?" Gimble asked.

"Well," he looked at his watch, "I teach a class at eleven this morning, so I need to leave in a few minutes. The academic building is just a short walk from here through the park. But if you want more time we can certainly meet later today, either here or in my office on campus. I want to help however I can."

Nazareth checked his watch.

"You know, it's a gorgeous day," he said. "Would it be okay if we walked over with you? We can talk on the way, and that might actually be enough time."

"That would be fine," said a charming Mercer. "It's the safest I'll ever be while walking through Washington Square Park."

"Oh, it's a pretty safe place anyway, Professor," Nazareth smiled.

"Safer is always better than safe, Detective. In any event, I'll be glad for the company. Let me just get my briefcase and sunglasses."

While Mercer gathered his things in the bedroom, Nazareth noticed the writing desk at the far corner of the living area. Neat, same as the rest of the apartment, except for a large, somewhat crumpled cardboard box that had been stuffed behind the swivel chair under the desk. From a distance it appeared to be about twelve inches high and twenty-four inches long. One well-worn flap was open. To Nazareth the box seemed a glaring blemish in an otherwise tidy space. He began to walk toward the desk just as Mercer came out of the bedroom, briefcase in hand and a smile on his face.

"All right, then," he said. "I'm ready for my police escort to work. Wonderful day for it, detectives."

A few minutes later the three of them had quickly covered the length of Cornelia Street and crossed 6th Avenue toward the park.

"I don't actually have to walk through the park," said Mercer as they stepped onto West 4th Street, which ran adjacent to the park, "but I find the place refreshing. It's a welcome bit of nature in the midst of much concrete, steel, and glass. But that's not why you came to see me."

"No, sir," said Nazareth, "but I certainly understand the sentiment. It's nice to be outdoors."

"Indeed it is, Detective."

"What can you tell us about Eleanor Martinson?" Gimble asked. "How well did you know her, aside from the fact that she was your sister's mother-in-law?"

"Aside from that, almost nothing, really. I'm sorry to say that the funeral in Pennsylvania was perhaps only the fourth or fifth time I was ever with her. I met her for the first time at Chelsea's wedding, and then maybe twice — yes, I think twice — at family barbecues, and then once again at Chelsea's for Christmas a couple of years ago."

"When was the last time you saw her prior to the funeral?"

"Chelsea has a better memory for these kinds of things than I do," he chuckled, "but I'm pretty sure it was last summer. I confess that I remember the steaks on the grill more than I do who was there or when it was, unfortunately. I enjoy good food, so I often associate pleasant occasions with the meals that accompanied them."

"Do you remember her as as being troubled or nervous in any way?" Nazareth asked. "Like someone who might need to look over her shoulder?"

"Absolutely not. The few times I saw her she was lively, talkative, and quite charming."

"And this was before her husband died?"

"Oh, yes. I never saw her after her husband died . . . until the funeral, that is. But I do know from speaking with Chelsea that Eleanor was not the same person after Jake's death. You would have to ask my sister for the details, though."

They reached the academic building where Mercer worked, and he invited them up. They took the elevator to the fourth floor and walked its length until they reached Mercer's office. The room was roughly the size of his modest apartment, but a large window looking onto Washington Square Park made the space look larger. Clean, beige walls. Round wooden conference table with four upholstered chairs. Fabric couch quite a bit larger than the leather couch in his apartment. Above the couch was a large framed painting whose scheme of rich golds and pale blues brightened the entire room.

"Very nice office," said Gimble. "And I especially like the painting."

"Yes, it's a favorite of mine. It's entitled *Rain, Steam, and Speed — the Great Western Railway,* by J.M.W. Turner. The design was considerably ahead of its time. Unfortunately," he laughed, "it's not the original. That's hanging in the National Gallery in London."

"It's lovely nevertheless," she said.

"Well, thank you. My senior honors class gave it to me two years ago as an end-of-semester gift. We had talked about Turner quite a lot in relation to 19th-century British literature, so the gift had special meaning for all of us."

Nazareth glanced at his watch. "I know you need to get to class, Professor, so let me ask you one last question for now."

"Ask anything you want, Detective. I want to help you find whoever did this."

"Thank you. Do you remember where you were on the day Mrs. Martinson was murdered?"

"No beating around the bush, eh, Detective?" Mercer laughed.

"In this type of investigation, Professor, I can't not ask."

"I'm teasing, Detective. I understand perfectly, and I'm glad to answer. I remember exactly, in fact. I was right down the hall, behind closed doors as a member of an oral-defense committee."

"What exactly is that?" said Gimble.

"Five senior members of the faculty grilling a Ph.D. candidate on his doctoral thesis. And the defense went badly, I'm afraid. All five of us had spent days reading the thesis and preparing our questions, and it turned out that the candidate was horribly ill-prepared. He wasted many hours of every-one's time."

"Were you here in Manhattan in the days leading up to that meeting?" Nazareth asked.

"Oh, absolutely. You don't sit on that sort of committee without being well prepared, Detective. That would be unconscionable. The committee essentially has the power of life and death over a young scholar's career, so you prepare thoroughly. I can't say what I did every minute of every day of that week, but I do know that apart from teaching, most of my time was spent getting ready for that oral defense."

"Got it," Nazareth nodded. "Last thing: could we have your teaching schedule in case we need to touch base with you again? I doubt we will, but it's always possible."

"Certainly," he said, "not a problem." Mercer jotted down the days and times. "I have a very light teaching load in the summer, and I have no vaca-tion plans other than a day trip now and then as inspiration guides me."

The detectives thanked Mercer for his time, left the academic building, and began walking back to their car outside Mercer's apartment.

"So what did you think?" Gimble asked.

"I was about to ask you the same thing," he said.

"Okay. Very calm and cool. Didn't appear to be at all nervous, either in his apartment or in his office. Answered every question satisfactorily. Nothing implausible about anything he said. But," she continued, "he's still the only guy who's even close to fitting the FBI profile."

"Well, that profile doesn't mean much to me at this point. We keep going farther down the road, and I don't see much confirmation that the profile is on point. But," he added, "we don't have anyone else worth watching at the moment."

Nazareth seemed a bit distant as he answered, and Gimble studied his face.

"Something else on your mind?"

"Small things. But sometimes small things turn out to be big."

"Which things in particular?"

"First of all, I'd love to see what was in the box under his desk."

"I saw it, but I didn't really think much about it."

"The whole apartment was neat as could be," he said. "Nothing looked the least bit out of place . . . except for that old box. I'd just like to poke my face inside it."

"And maybe find a dozen silk rosebuds?" she asked.

"Yeah, that's exactly what I'm thinking. But there's also that painting in his office."

"What about it?"

"Whoever stole the Monet from Mrs. Latourette's house replaced it with a cheap knockoff," he explained, "the same sort of thing on Mercer's wall. He said his students gave it to him, but he could have bought it himself."

Gimble was skeptical. "The painting doesn't bother me at all," she said. "How many millions of Americans must own cheap reproductions like that?"

"Granted. But it's still something to keep in mind. Anyway, I'm a lot more interested in that box under his desk. It just doesn't fit."

They slid into their unmarked cruiser in front of Mercer's apartment building. Nazareth held the key but didn't put it in the ignition.

"If we found silk rosebuds in that box," he said, more to himself than to Gimble, "we could close this in a hurry."

"Sure, but we'll never get a search warrant on the basis of a cardboard box under some guy's desk."

"Agreed. But sometimes the search needs to happen without the warrant."

"Pete, I'm really not interested in losing my shield over that cardboard box."

"Neither am I." He thought for a moment. "How long is the class that Mercer's teaching right now?"

Gimble looked at the note that Mercer had given them.

"Two hours."

"Okay. Let me make a quick call."

Nazareth reached whoever it was he was calling, explained what he needed, and clicked off. He looked over at Gimble, whose mouth hung wide open.

"Seriously?" she said.

"Seriously. Very discreet, highly skilled, and just happens to live in the neighborhood," he said. "We've worked together before on some difficult cases. Never had a problem."

"And if there are rosebuds in the box," she said, "we've still got no evidence. An illegal search gets us nowhere except maybe off the force."

"We won't be off the force, Tara. Trust me. And if we find what we're looking for, then we'll get other evidence on him. I take full responsibility."

"Well, gee, now I feel better."

"I'm glad," he smiled.

Fifteen minutes later a smartly dressed 30-something woman walked up Cornelia Street toward where Nazareth and Gimble sat in the unmarked cruiser. Elegantly proportioned and about 5'6", she had well-coiffed blonde hair down to her shoulders, a long-sleeved white silk blouse, a slim indigo skirt with expensive gold embroidery, and handsome black flats. A medium-sized Yves Saint Laurent purse hung from her shoulder by a thin strap. She walked into Mercer's apartment building looking every bit the well-heeled resident.

By the time she reached Mercer's apartment door she had slipped the HPC ElectroPick from her purse. The slender tool was nothing more than a converted Black & Decker screwdriver outfitted with a flexible lock-picking device, the whole thing powered by four AA batteries. She needed less than fifteen seconds to unlock the door and close it behind her. In another forty-five seconds she had snapped several photos, left everything as she had found it, and locked the door on her way out. She exited the building sooner than Nazareth had expected.

"That must be a world record," he said.

"What are we talking about?" Gimble replied.

"My friend just left the building."

"Miss Moneybags?"

"Right."

"She's your B&E expert?"

"She calls it intelligence gathering, not breaking and entering."

"She just went in there a minute ago."

"A little bit more than that."

"Fine, maybe two minutes," she said. "No way she was in and out of his apartment. Fifty to one says she bumped into one of Mercer's neighbors and abandoned ship."

"Large mushroom pizza from Garlic," he grinned.

"Garlic pizza?"

"No. Garlic is the name of the pizza place. And I want mushroom. That's the bet. You said fifty to one, but I'll settle for a free pizza."

"Done," she said. "Since you're buying, I'd like sausage instead of mushroom."

Nazareth gave her a smile and a thumbs-up as they watched the trim blonde walk around the corner. Twenty seconds later Nazareth's phone buzzed, and he opened the text message. The photo clearly showed that the inside of Mercer's mysterious cardboard box contained an obsolete Canon printer and a dozen or more used ink cartridges, both color and black and white. An obviously disappointed Nazareth just shook his head.

"No silk rosebuds," he said.

"Nope. The neat professor just has an untidy little secret under his desk."

"Do you think maybe he put the box there just to jerk us around?"

"Please, dial it down, Pete. This guy has given us nothing to go on. Really. You're obsessing. It's time to look elsewhere."

"Maybe so. But I'm not happy about that. On the other hand," he brightened, "I just won a mushroom pizza."

"You actually want a free pizza?"

"Damn right. It's time for lunch, I'm hungry, and I won it fair and square. I'll order it right now, and they'll have it at my place about the time we get there."

Twenty minutes later they arrived at Nazareth's apartment on East 24th Street. The two-bedroom space was considerably larger than Gimble had expected. The guy was, after all, on the NYPD payroll. The maple hardwood floors gleamed from the entry all the way to the far end of the living room, where a 70" flat-screen TV graced the wall. The galley kitchen featured stainless-steel appliances and eye-popping marble countertops with silver and gray veins swirling through a black background. The bedroom nearest to the kitchen had been converted to a high-end home gym fit for a former Marine. In the corner, standing on an expanse of thick mats, was a 6'6" kicking dummy molded to look like the bare upper body of an axe murderer on steroids. But the gym's centerpiece was a $5,000 commercial-grade BodyCraft weight machine with enough steel plates to tame the New York Giants. More than anything, Gimble noticed that Nazareth's corner of the 12th floor had an angled but unobstructed view of the East River, a feature that undoubtedly bumped up the cost.

"Wait," she said, a bit stunned by the surroundings, "you're a detective, not the police commissioner, right?"

"Yes, ma'am. I work for a living."

"But you live here?"

"I definitely do," he nodded. "I didn't just pick the lock, did I?"

She shook her head in mild disbelief as she looked around the place.

"The only thing missing, as far as I can tell, is a place to sleep," she said, "since you turned the bedroom into your own private Gold's Gym. Or do you sleep on the martial-arts mats?"

"Actually, this is the fitness bedroom. I sleep in the bedroom bedroom."

"Bedroom bedroom. As in a second bedroom?"

"True."

"Okay, my whole apartment would fit in your fitness bedroom. Are you running private security for some drug lord in the Bronx?"

"Nope," he laughed. "First of all, I'm a very good saver. Always have been. Second, after my parents died, I used what they left me to buy a house, which I later sold to get this place. And third, I get free food."

"Free food?"

The doorbell rang, and Nazareth nodded.

"Ah, yes," she said. "Free food as in Gimble buys the pizza."

"There you go."

She started toward the door, but Nazareth put his hand to her shoulder.

"No, you're my guest," he smiled, "so this time you get a pass."

"Hey, I'm not going to argue with Detective Rockefeller."

"Good. Never argue before eating a pizza from Garlic."

After polishing off a large pizza washed down by four bottles of iced tea, they headed back to One Police Plaza and began sorting through their notes on the people who had attended Eleanor Martinson's funeral in Pennsylvania. They began with forty-six names listed under the heading *Improbable*. After that, they would move on to a list marked *Impossible*.

This wasn't good. But it was the best they could do unless the Rosebud Killer got sloppy.

43

Detective Gimble is likable but, I suspect, ill equipped for the rigors of her current job. This is not to say she is stupid. I don't believe that at all. But I do believe that her grasp of the issues is paper thin. She seems to understand what's happening on the surface of this investigation, but I don't see her as one who can delve into the hidden layers, where the real story lies.

Nazareth, on the other hand, gives me pause. He thinks more than he speaks, a sign of intellect. And when he does speak, he has a habit of asking the right questions. As a taxpayer, I am glad to know that there are NYPD cops of his caliber. As the person he is hunting, however, I realize that I need to be especially wary of the man. Wariness is not nearly the same as fear, of course. There is nothing to fear in the man, since he is plainly grasping at straws. I have given him no clues worth pursuing, and I have no doubt whatsoever that his IQ is forty or fifty points shy of mine. Nevertheless, when I plan my actions, I will take Nazareth's above-average abilities into account.

I find it mildly amusing that they raised the issue of the Turner print that hangs in my office. Did they expect to trip me up with something so obvious as that? I actually hope they pursue this nonsensical "clue," since the painting is precisely what I said it is: a gift from my students. How would the NYPD go about proving that? Someone would need to speak with the registrar, find out who had enrolled in that class, and interview several former students to see if they remembered having given me the print. Yes, all of that. Probably more. And at the end of the tale they would be left sorely disappointed. They would find that I hadn't lied. Indeed, I have no reason to lie except about having visited Eleanor Martinson prior to her death. On that point they have no possibility of finding me out.

I must admit that I am surprised they didn't broach the subject of Mrs. Latourette's recent passing. This is probably a good sign, evidence that they have not linked her to the other deaths. All modesty aside, I did a highly commendable job of creating the apparition of a copycat on the loose.

Or — I must consider this possibility — were they simply waiting for me to raise the subject? And if I had done so, would they have taken that as a sign I knew more than I was letting on? No, I don't believe that.

So I am quite content. Detective Gimble is merely taking up space on this investigation. Nazareth, meanwhile, is a handsome, rather capable young man, but I calculate that his thinking is not sufficiently dimensional to match my pace. He's obviously skilled at thinking his way from Point A to Point B in two-dimensional, linear fashion. But to reach the proper conclusions in this situation he needs to work in three dimensions, factoring in themes, motives, and contexts that swirl around, and not just between, Points A and B. I am reminded of Einstein's perception of space and time. His contemporaries conceived of the universe as a Point A to Point B construct. Einstein, on the other hand, knew that the universe was actually a four-dimensional space-time continuum of startling complexity.

Detective Nazareth is not up to the challenge of understanding the multiple dimensions of this case.

Alas, the young man is no Einstein.

44.

Two days after Nazareth and Gimble visited Mercer, the Pennsylvania State Police dropped a bombshell. Their ongoing investigation into Eleanor Martinson's murder had turned up a possible suspect named Tyler Young. Nazareth took the early morning call and was suddenly more upbeat than he had been in weeks.

"PSP just caught a big break," he told Gimble when they met in the conference room. The two of them had spent more than eighteen frustrating hours studying their notes on people who had attended Eleanor Martinson's funeral. "Someone told them to take a hard look at Tyler Young."

Gimble looked quickly to her far right, grabbed some of her notes, and thumbed through them until she found Young's interview sheet.

"He's in our *Improbable* stack," she said. "Forty-eight years old, married, two kids, employed, lives in Rutherford, NJ. His wife is a long-time friend of the Martinson family, and she attended the funeral with her husband."

"What we weren't told," he said, "and what we probably wouldn't have learned without the tip, is that the guy is divorced. No big news there. But, get this, five years ago he got a twelve-month suspended sentence and three years probation for beating his first wife unconscious."

"And let me guess," she said. "The first wife called PSP when she heard about the murder."

"That would be my guess. Whatever, without the call we would never have seen the man behind the mask. But it gets a lot better."

"I'm listening."

"One," index finger high, "he's a regional sales manager who covers Pennsylvania, New York, New Jersey, Delaware, and Maryland."

"A man with easy access to all of the murders."

"Oh, yeah. But two," he gestured, "the company he works for is LifeBest Pharmaceuticals, and one of the generics they manufacture is injectable diazepam."

"No way!"

"Yes, ma'am. A very presentable salesman who can probably talk his way into anyone's home, has a reason to be all over the map, and has easy access to drugs."

"And," Gimble added, "apparently doesn't mind a little violence in his life."

"There you go," he nodded.

"Okay, let me find out where he is."

"That may not be hard," Nazareth smiled. "LifeBest is headquartered in Queens, as in our jurisdiction."

"It just keeps getting better," she said. "Lovely day for a drive to Queens."

An hour later Nazareth and Gimble sat with Jeremy Irons, Personnel Director for LifeBest Pharmaceuticals in Queens. The detectives downplayed the urgency of their visit, since they had no hard evidence linking Tyler Young to the Pennsylvania murder. They couldn't risk jeopardizing the job of a man who might prove to be innocent. This seemed all the more important because the personnel guy struck both detectives as a nasty twerp who had probably enjoyed torturing small animals as a kid. Irons had Tyler Young convicted and jailed before Gimble had finished four sentences.

Nazareth interrupted Irons' rant about books that can't be judged by their covers.

"Excuse me, Mr. Irons," he said, "but you're not understanding Detective Gimble. We're not looking to speak with Mr. Young because he's a murderer. We're interviewing everyone — repeat, everyone — who attended a particular funeral in Pennsylvania. Mr. Young is on the list, so we want to check off that box. Understood?" The personnel guy seemed chastened . . . but also unhappy that he couldn't get someone fired today.

"Yes, Detective, I understand," he whined. "Let me see if Tyler Young is here today or on the road. He's usually in the field, but I'll find out."

Irons used the computer at his desk to pull up the travel schedules for every member of the sales team, then printed out one that showed where Young would be for the next two weeks. He also printed a 5x7 color photo of Young taken from the employee database. He walked over to Nazareth and handed him both sheets.

"You're in luck, Detective," he said. "Mr. Young will be on the road for almost all of the next two weeks beginning tomorrow. But today he has a lunch meeting in Manhattan with one of our clients. In case you've never met him, here's a recent photo."

Nazareth quickly scanned the pages. "Excellent. So lunch at noon today at the Grand Hyatt. Then two weeks spent traveling around the territory — down to Maryland, then back up through Delaware and New Jersey."

"That's pretty normal for our regional sales managers, Detective. If they're not on the road, they're probably not hitting their sales numbers."

"One other thing. Could you print out his schedule for this past May?

"Uh, sure. I should have that." He tinkered at the keyboard for a moment, then printed what Nazareth wanted.

"Much appreciated. Do you happen to have his work cell phone number?"

"Yes, of course." Irons once again went back to the computer and read the number off to Nazareth.

"Got it. Well, thank you for your time, Mr. Irons. And please remember," Nazareth said, "that this is a routine, informal inquiry. Mr. Young is simply one of dozens of people we're speaking with in order to get some leads."

"Yes, I understand," he nodded. "I appreciate your reminding me." The look on his face didn't show much appreciation but the detectives let it go.

As soon as they left the building, Gimble turned to Nazareth and said, "What a complete asshole."

Nazareth laughed. "You've got that right. On the other hand, don't you wish we could get a few judges like that?"

"The guilty-until-proven-innocent type?"

"Yeah," he smiled.

"God help us all."

When Nazareth and Gimble arrived at the Grand Hyatt's main restaurant they had no trouble spotting Tyler Young. The guy was extremely fit, neatly dressed in a tan suit, and looked more like 38 than 48. This was not someone who would automatically be taken for a wife-beater, but the detectives knew for a fact that looks are often deceiving.

Young and his client were sitting closer to each other than necessary at a quiet table in the corner of the restaurant. Young held a glass of white wine, and his guest held a champagne flute alive with tiny bubbles. The client was an extremely attractive blonde woman of 30, or perhaps slightly less. She wore a tight, sleeveless blue dress that showed off a sparkling necklace that drew attention to her beautifully tanned chest. The two made a lovely couple as they traded glowing smiles and gentle laughter. Anyone with eyes could see that the two of them had something other than pharmaceuticals on their minds.

"Since they're talking business," Nazareth joked, "why don't we just hang outside until they're finished? No sense ruining his sales pitch."

"I sure hope he hits his sales numbers this month," she mocked. "After all, he has a wife and two kids to feed."

Nazareth just grinned. "I think he definitely hit the jackpot today."

When Young and his lunch mate finished eating, they strolled shoulder to shoulder through the hotel lobby and moved toward the elevator bank. Nazareth and Gimble held back, waiting to see whether the couple parted company. When it became clear that the lunch meeting was going to continue upstairs in a pricey room, the detectives discreetly introduced themselves to Young and his wide-eyed blonde friend.

"We'd like to have a word with you about Eleanor Martinson," said Nazareth, "if you can spare just a few minutes."

Young looked stricken, while the young woman looked utterly confused.

"Uh, Miss Reinert," he said to her, "why don't I just say goodbye here?"

"Of course," she said gently as she boarded the elevator. "Thanks very much for lunch."

Young accompanied the two detectives to a corner of the lobby, where they sat around a coffee table on overstuffed chairs.

"How did you even know to find me here?" Young asked.

"We didn't mean to interrupt your business meeting, Mr. Young," said Gimble, not answering the question. "But we believe you might be able to help us with our investigation into Eleanor Martinson's murder."

"Sure, I'm happy to help," he said, clearly flustered, "but I have no information that would be helpful."

"What kind of information *do* you have?" she asked soberly.

"I mean, I don't have any information at all."

"Sometimes the people we interview know more than they think," she said.

"Okay, fine. Let me know what I can tell you."

Nazareth liked the fact that Young was nervous, but he couldn't judge whether the nervousness came from having murdered Eleanor Martinson or having been caught wining and dining the young babe on the company's dime. So he decided that the first-strike method was most appropriate.

"Well, specifically, Mr. Young," Nazareth intoned, "I would like to know where you were on the day Mrs. Martinson was murdered."

The question slammed into Young like a hard punch to the midsection. He looked like a man about to lose the fine lunch he had just eaten.

"Oh, Jesus," he said, "you think I had something to do with her murder?"

"Did you?"

"No! Hell no! Why would anyone think that?"

"I'm not sure we do yet," said Nazareth, "so just tell us where you were on the day she was murdered."

"I don't even know when that was."

"That would have been April 21st or 22nd," Gimble offered. "We're pretty sure it was the 22nd, but it's possible she was murdered the day before."

"I don't know," he stammered. "Traveling probably. I spend most of my life traveling."

"Don't you keep a record of your travel on your cell phone calendar?" she asked.

"No, I keep everything on my laptop."

"Okay, then look at your laptop."

"It's, uh. I don't have it with me," he said.

Nazareth jumped back in. "You're at lunch in Manhattan with a client, and you don't have your laptop? That seems odd."

"I must have left it . . . ."

"In your car?" Gimble asked quickly. "We'll walk you over to get it."

"No, uh, look detectives. I think the laptop is up in the room."

"Your room?" she said.

"No, my client's room. That's where the meeting started."

"So you left your laptop in the hotel room when you went for lunch?"

"Yeah, I didn't want it at the table."

"So you planned to go back to the room to get it after lunch?"

"I guess, yeah. I mean, yes, that's what I was going to do."

Gimble laid a cold stare on him. The guy was a complete mess.

"Well, let me help you out, Mr. Young," Nazareth offered. "I have a printout of your April travel dates."

"How can you have that?"

"We're detectives, remember?"

"Yeah, but . . . ."

"According to this schedule you were in Delaware on both April 21st and April 22nd. So that means if we call the people you met with on those days, they'll be able to tell us that you were there. Is that correct?"

"I'd have to think about who I met with."

"Is that information on your laptop upstairs?" said Gimble. "If so, let's go up and get it."

"No, I mean, we don't need to go get the laptop. Just let me think about who I met with on those days."

"That's fine," said Nazareth. "Just give us the names and phone numbers, and we'll call from here in the lobby."

Young had been backed into a corner, and he knew it. His face grew red, and his eyes actually seemed just a bit moist.

"I wasn't in Delaware those days," he said softly.

"See how easy it is to remember things?" said Nazareth. "Now remember where you were if you weren't where you told the company you were."

"I was in Florida for most of that week."

"Are you responsible for Florida sales too?"

"No," he said, "I was with someone."

"Not on company business?"

"No," he shook his head disconsolately.

"So personal business?"

"Yes, it was personal."

"Where in Florida?"

"Miami."

"Hotel?"

Young paused. "The Setai."

"Okay, give us the person's name, and we'll verify that you were in Florida when Mrs. Martinson was murdered."

Young thought for a moment, considered adding another layer of nonsense to his predicament, then thought better of it.

"Her name is Laura," he said, "and you don't have to call her."

"And that's because?" said Gimble.

"Because she's up in her room."

"The woman you just had lunch with?"

"Yes. Look detectives, I'm happily married and . . . ."

"And you have a traveling companion that your wife and your employer don't know about?" she fired back.

Young stared off into space. He didn't really see anything. He simply sensed the good life collapsing all around him. In the space of a few heartbeats he saw an ugly divorce, an unhappy blonde girlfriend, and an employer that would sue him for bilking the firm on a regular basis.

"No one knows about her but you," he said.

"Well, since we all know each other," Nazareth said, "let's go up and talk about your trip to Florida."

"Do we really have to get her involved?"

"You strike me as a smart man, Mr. Young," Nazareth said as he drilled the guy with his eyes, "but you and I both know that wasn't a very smart question."

Young nodded. They walked toward the elevator bank.

"She's married," he said. "Her husband will go crazy if he finds out."

"Your problem," Gimble smiled, "not ours."

Young shook his head, then began to punch in a number on his cell phone. "Stop, please," said Nazareth. "Who are you calling?"

"I'm calling Laura to let her know we're coming up."

"Oh, I don't think so. Detective Gimble and I are going to speak with her before you do. If there's evidence in the room, we don't want her tampering with it."

"But . . . ."

"There's no *but* Mr. Young. Either we go up and speak with her unannounced, or she'll come speak with us Downtown while you're in a holding cell. Those are your options."

Young was in no position to call Nazareth's bluff, so he grudgingly entered the elevator with a detective on either side of him.

Laura Reinert came to the door of the $1,000-a-night suite only half wearing a plush Grand Hyatt bathrobe. She yanked the front tightly around herself when she saw that Young had brought company.

"Tyler, Jesus!" she yelped.

"I'm sorry, they wouldn't let me call first," Young apologized. Laura was already stomping off to the bedroom when he added, "The detectives need to speak with you."

While they waited for Reinert to find her clothes, Nazareth and Gimble studied Midtown from the hotel's twenty-fifth floor.

"Manhattan looks positively livable from up here, doesn't it, Mr. Young?" Gimble asked. "How much does a room like this go for?"

"A little over a thousand a night," he said glumly.

"Must be spectacular at night, eh?"

"Yeah," he whined, "it's just great."

When Reinert rejoined the others she wore an expensive outfit different from the one she had worn at lunch. Gimble wondered how many days Young and Reinert had been here . . . and whether the mini-vacation had been irreparably spoiled.

Nazareth let Gimble handle the questioning, since it was obvious that she was itching for a chance to rake the blonde over some hot coals. And for the next twenty-five minutes that's exactly what she did. She began by implying, very gently, that the young blonde might actually be a suspect along with Young. That put the woman in a highly talkative mood. Soon thereafter a teary Laura Reinert had admitted to partying in Florida with Tyler Young during the week that Mrs. Martinson was murdered. That was the easy part. From that point she found it much more difficult to explain why someone on the staff of the Setai Hotel would be able to remember that Reinert and Young had been there.

"So you think the concierge will remember that you two were there?" said Gimble.

"Yes," said Reinert. She looked nervous, and Young look puzzled.

"Why do you think the concierge will remember that you two were there, Miss Reinert?" Gimble asked. "I'm sure a concierge works with thousands of guests in the course of one year."

"Probably because of the room we stayed in," she said.

"What about the room?"

"It was one of their ocean-front suites, and they tend to remember who stays in those."

"Why is that?"

"Because they're expensive, I guess."

"You guess they're expensive?"

"No, I mean, I know they're expensive. That's why they remember the guests who stay in them."

"How expensive is expensive?"

Young tried to warn her off with a stern look, but she didn't notice.

"About $3,500 a night."

"Ah," said Gimble, "I guess they might remember that."

From here the going got quite a bit tougher for both Young and Reinert. When Gimble announced that she was about to phone the concierge — Aldo Montilla was his name — to ask him a few questions, Reinert broke down.

"Oh, God," she sobbed. "He's not the one."

Gimble was puzzled. "He's not the concierge?"

"Yes, he's the concierge."

"Okay, I'm not following."

"He's not the one who can tell you I was there."

Interesting, thought Gimble. Suddenly it's *I* and not *we*.

"Miss Reinert," Gimble said a bit more forcefully than before, "I want you to stop playing games and give me the facts. If you can't do that, we'll end up holding you and Mr. Young on suspicion of murder."

"Oh, God. Tyler, I'm sorry." She looked at Young, who was as baffled as Nazareth. Gimble, it seemed, was the only one who knew where this was headed.

"Miss Reinert?" said Gimble.

"I was at the hotel a couple of days before Tyler . . . and a couple of days after."

Young still seemed utterly lost. But it could simply have been an unwillingness to add two plus two.

"I was staying with someone else, another guy."

"Laura!" Young jumped up and moved toward Reinert, but Nazareth stiff-armed him back into his seat.

"You were with someone else before and after your stay with Mr. Young?" Gimble asked.

"Yes."

"But you weren't with him when Mr. Young was in town?"

"Most of the time, no."

"But you were with him some of the time? Meaning, when Mr. Young wasn't around?"

Reinert nodded but said nothing.

"And when I speak with this man, he'll be able to provide me with an airtight alibi for you?"

Another nod.

"Okay, let's make the call."

After Reinert's other Florida lover had provided an alibi that satisfied Nazareth's curiosity, he closed his notebook and prepared to leave the hotel room with Gimble.

"We appreciate your cooperation, Miss Reinert. If you think of anything else that might help us with the investigation, please call either of us." He and Gimble handed her their business cards. Young sat seething on the couch, obviously eager for the detectives to leave.

"I think you should go with them, Tyler," Reinert said firmly.

"What?" he said. "What the hell are you talking about?"

"You're angry, and I don't want to deal with that right now. So you should leave."

"I'm the one who's paying for this fucking room." Gimble assumed that the double entendre was purely accidental.

"Fine, I'll pay for the room. Just please go. We can talk later."

"No, we'll talk right now."

She turned to Gimble. "I'd like him to leave with you."

"Understood," said Gimble. "Mr. Young, she has agreed to pay for the room, and she wants you to come with us. So please get your things."

Young stormed off to the bedroom and returned with his laptop as well as a pair of slacks and a short-sleeved shirt on a hanger.

"Call me later," Reinert said to him.

"The only thing I'll do for you is wring your fucking neck!"

Nazareth cut the argument short. "I'll add that threat to my notes, Mr. Young. If anything should happen to Miss Reinert, you'll be the first person we look for."

"I didn't mean I would actually wring her neck, Detective," he said sarcastically.

"You said what you said, Mr. Young, and I make a hell of an impressive witness."

Young pushed past the detectives and angrily left for the elevator. Gimble turned to Reinert.

"You play a dangerous game," Gimble said.

"Not dangerous," she grinned. "Just interesting."

Gimble wanted to pound her fist into the elevator door but thought better of it. She was angry, frustrated, and feeling like someone who had earned a break.

"Two for two now: right guy, wrong crime," she said.

"Yep, two complete dirtbags," Nazareth answered. "One in West Virginia and one in Manhattan. But this is what we do, Tara. We follow leads, most of which take us nowhere. If we stick to business and catch a break, the right lead comes along and we see it for what it is. We'll nail this guy. He's probably made a big mistake already, and we'll eventually find it."

"Hope you're right."

"I know I'm right. We keep going back to the beginning," he said, "until somewhere in all those notes and photos we find the clue that's really worth something. In the meantime, I'm hungry."

"We missed lunch, didn't we?"

"Nope. Just postponed it. How about some Chinese?"

"Chinatown. I know an excellent dumpling house on Lafayette," she said. "Then I'm going back to all those notes and photos."

"Sounds like a plan."

45.

eriods of heavy rain in tomorrow's forecast, so I won't be going to Ellenville. But the next day looks positively wonderful. Sunny, clear, 82. Probably a touch cooler in the Catskills. I love the Catskills, though I don't often get there. When people throughout the country hear the words *New York,* most of them think immediately of noisy avenues, homicidal cab drivers, and street-corner drug dealers. But that's New York City, a world apart from the small-town America one finds in the Catskills.

I remember traveling through the Catskills by bus when I was in college — narrow two-lane roads winding their way up steep hills, dense forests, and even a vigorous waterfall now and then. Most of all: empty space — what America looked like before places like Manhattan and Chicago and, God forbid, Los Angeles began reaching to the sky. Here's a fact: the population density of many Catskill towns is less than 200 per square mile. Manhattan, meanwhile, is 72,000 per square mile . . . and counting. 72,000 humans per square mile! Is it any wonder that bad things happen in Manhattan? If you stuff too many sardines in the can, some are bound to get mangled.

My plan for the visit to Ellen Karcher's home in Ellenville is as uncomplicated as I can make it. Simpler is better. I will leave Manhattan in early evening, drive to a quiet spot in a park less than ten miles from my destination, and there replace the New York plates on my vehicle with the stolen Maryland plates that I have kept for just such a purpose. Darkness will have fallen by the time I arrive at the old woman's front door, and she will be pleased to let me in when I show her my Department of Environmental Conservation ID.

Less than thirty minutes later I will be back in the park changing the license plates once again, then heading to Manhattan. I plan to eat a late dinner at a simple roadside restaurant that I noted during my earlier trip. The place gets fine reviews on Trip Advisor, and the prices are reasonable.

By anticipating complications, I will avoid them. My chief concern is the potential for another police tail. But since I'll still have ample daylight for the early part of my journey, I can change direction if I detect an NYPD presence. My plan in that event will be to divert to the Palisades Center Mall, near the Tappan Zee Bridge, have dinner at the Cheesecake Factory, and shop for some fall clothing. So either way, this won't be a wasted trip. But I have a strong preference for the successful completion of another mission of mercy.

46.

The detectives returned to One Police Plaza after grazing on dim sum for a half hour or so, then settled back into the unglamorous but necessary task of sifting through the notes that they had sorted into uneven piles from one end of the long conference table to the other. Gimble meticulously reread every word that they had written during their interviews with people who had attended Eleanor Martinson's funeral in Pennsylvania. She was now primarily focused on individuals who lived in or near Hallstead, PA, since she and Nazareth had already struck out with a few of the more distant suspects.

Maybe, she told herself, this whole thing was simpler than it seemed. What if the murderer had begun with a grudge killing in his own back yard, decided he liked the thrill, and then expanded his territory? Had the investigation been led astray by the FBI profile that suggested the killer was from New York City? And why exactly did the FBI profiler think that the killer was based in the City anyway? The original profile was based on minimal evidence, after all, so it could have been way off the mark. It was just as likely, Gimble told herself, that the murderer lived in Hallstead and happened to feel comfortable in Manhattan.

While Gimble read, Nazareth examined photos taken at all of the crime scenes. He looked for similarities, differences, and anything that seemed remotely out of place. Again and again over the next three and a half hours he moved 8x10 photos from one pile to another, then back. Along the way he used a large magnifying glass to get a closer look at details that hadn't caught the crime-scene photographer's attention. He was about to call it quits when he remembered the photo that his break-in expert had taken in Mercer's apartment. The cardboard box under Mercer's desk had been a tantalizing but worthless clue. Still, he thought, I've gone this far, so I might as well look at that picture again too.

He was surprised to find more than one photo. On the day of the illegal search of Mercer's apartment he had only opened the first of what had actually been several images. He now emailed himself the full set and opened them on his desktop computer. The final photo of the group made his head spin. He cropped the photo to show only what was of interest to him, and he turned to Gimble.

"God bless Miranda," he smiled.

"As in Miranda warning?"

"No, Miranda as in the young woman who checked out Mercer's apartment for us."

"Ah, the burglar blonde."

"Intelligence consultant, remember?"

"Yes, I remember you said that."

"Well," he continued, "you're about to see that she's more than just a B&E guy. When I looked at her photo of the cardboard box under Mercer's desk, I was disappointed and figured we had just reached another dead end. So I didn't even notice that she had sent me a few other photos."

"Photos of the box?"

"To my great surprise, no. She clicked off a few extras for us while she was near the desk. Check this one out."

First he showed her an image of Mercer's entire desktop as it would look to someone sitting down to work.

"Okay," she said. "Desk lamp, coffee mug, pen holder, pile of papers, a small sheet from a sticky note." She looked more closely. "Is that writing on the sticky note?"

"You bet. I cropped out everything but that, and here's what I got."

The enlarged image was a bit fuzzy, but the writing was still clear enough to read. Written in blue ink on the white note paper were three cryptic lines:

ellen

1:57

sandburg

"Ellen Sandburg?" Gimble said.

"Maybe, maybe not. If so, why did he separate the two words like that?"

"Okay, so we're not sure about the two names. But we've got one minute and fifty-seven seconds. Less than two minutes. What do you do in less than two minutes?"

"Beats the hell out of me," he said as he sent the enlargement to his printer. "The whole thing could mean absolutely nothing, or it could mean a lot."

"It's not much to go on, Pete."

"Something's better than nothing, right? And I've been saying that maybe we failed to notice a clue that was right there in front of us the whole time. Well, here's something that I should have caught earlier but didn't."

"Yeah, I get that. But this note could take us in a million different directions, and it may just be something he scribbled about one of his classes. He's meeting with a student named Ellen at 1:57 to discuss her paper on Carl Sandburg." She was obviously not sold on the merits of the new clue.

"In all likelihood that's what it is, or something close to it and completely unrelated to the murders. But look again at the entire desktop. See this over here?"

He pointed to a stack of graded student papers and enlarged an essay belonging to a student named James Nevers, who had gotten a C+.

"Let's assume he's sitting at the desk grading papers," he began. "The one on top belongs to James Nevers and is probably the last paper he's graded, right? If he's planning to meet with a student named Ellen, why isn't her paper on top? Or why didn't he attach the sticky note to her paper and move it to the side as a reminder?"

Gimble shrugged. "Yeah, okay, but I think you're reading an awful lot into a three-inch-square sticky note."

"No question about it. But," he added, "something that doesn't make sense on this note is the word *sandburg*."

"And that's because?"

"Mercer teaches English lit, and Sandburg's American."

"Interesting. But why would he leave a note like that on his desk if it's related to a murder? Whoever killed these women has been super careful so far."

"Well, the note could be nothing," he nodded. "We agree on that. But suppose he's our guy. First, he wasn't expecting us, so he had no particular reason to take the note off his desk. Second, the note doesn't actually tell us anything. If we had seen it and asked him about it, he could have made something up, just the way you did when you first looked at it. Correct?"

She nodded. "But why have a note like that in the first place?" she asked. "You think he was sitting there planning a murder and wrote a note to himself about it?"

"Not exactly. Think about it. As you just said, the killer has been extremely careful. That being the case, would he really plan murders on his own computer? No, not at all. He'd be afraid someone might search it."

"He would use a different computer," she said, beginning to see why the note could matter to their investigation.

"Exactly. Like one in an Internet cafe, or in the academic building, or in the campus library. And there's no way we would ever find the right machine. But," he continued, "if he does his research away from home, he needs to take some notes. Just the essentials. Maybe just a few words that would mean nothing to anyone else but are enough to remind him of key details about his plan."

Gimble remained skeptical. "I give you an A+ for ingenuity, Pete, but I don't know if you can stretch the facts that far."

"Possibly not." He thought a bit. "Okay, probably not."

"But we're going to try anyway, right?"

"Hey, I'm still too full for dinner anyway."

"Fine by me. But I would like to go home and sleep sometime tonight, okay?"

"Possibly," he grinned.

For the next forty minutes they brainstormed, each feeding the other any idea that might have some connection to either *ellen, sandburg,* or *1:57.* When that took them nowhere, they tortured Google for information on "Ellen Sandburg" and spent another half hour looking at some of the 250,000 search results that popped up. Then they aimed for anyone named Ellen at Sandburg College. And finally they listed anyone named Ellen who was involved in research on Carl Sanburg's poetry. Nothing they found made any sense, especially when linked to the cryptic *1:57* shown on Mercer's note.

"I can almost — emphasize ALMOST — get my head around a few of these Ellens, but I keep bumping into one minute and fifty-seven seconds. Or 1:57 p.m. Or 1:57 a.m. The numbers in that note could mean anything, Pete."

His eyes widened as he pointed at her. "You just hit it," he said.

"I said the numbers could mean anything."

"Right, and you listed some of the things they could mean. But," he smiled, "you didn't say one hour and fifty-seven minutes. Change 1:57 to hours instead of minutes, and we might get somewhere."

"Damn, I've been thinking minutes ever since I saw the note."

"And I didn't argue the point, because I used to be a middle-distance runner. To me 1:57 was a really good half-mile split time when running a mile. So we both saw the same thing when we looked at the note."

"But if we're talking hours instead of minutes . . . ."

"Then maybe — since we're basically grasping at straws anyway — maybe we have a time associated with one of his murders."

"It took an hour and fifty-seven minutes to get to Midtown and back, for instance?"

"Exactly. Except there have been no Ellens or Sandburgs involved in the murders we're working."

"But there could be in the next murder."

"Bingo." Nazareth sat quietly for a bit, and Gimble decided not to interrupt his thought process. She knew that when he fell silent like this, his brain was usually on afterburner.

"The 1:57 in the note could still mean anything, but I'm willing to bet it's a drive time. Think about it. If someone asks you how long it takes to drive to the Hamptons, for example, you'd say?"

"About two hours without traffic."

"Precisely. You wouldn't normally say an hour and fifty-seven minutes. The only time you would get that specific is when you're calculating a drive time on your GPS."

"Or something like Mapquest."

"There you go. If you're thinking about killing someone, your research would certainly include the drive time. That would be extremely important, especially to someone who wanted to get in and out the same day. And if our killer is based in Manhattan, every one of the murders so far could easily have been an out-and-back trip. No hotel records or credit cards. No overnight bag or change of clothes. No one at your garage asking how your trip was."

"I'm still not liking Mercer," she said, "but I agree we need to follow up on the note. Can we dig in tomorrow?"

Nazareth glanced at his watch. "Yeah, that probably makes sense. We're going to need hours for what I have in mind."

"Which is?"

"Tomorrow we'll need the biggest map I can find."

When Gimble arrived at the conference room at 7:03 the next morning, two coffees and two bagels in hand, she found Nazareth in the final stages of a high-tech installation of some sort. He was tinkering with an enormous computer screen that was mounted to a wheeled stand.

"Today's your lucky day, Pete," she said as she set his coffee and bagel on the table. "Breakfast on me. What's with the big screen?"

"Ah, thanks for the food. I haven't eaten anything yet," he said. "I've been at this for a while. Anyway, this is a ridiculously expensive 80" high-def computer monitor that I borrowed this morning from the Major Case folks. Very portable, as you can see, and also perfect for what we'll be doing. Assuming, of course, the screen actually talks to my laptop."

"Wireless?"

"So they say. We're about to find out."

He turned the screen on, tapped a few keys on the laptop, and suddenly they were looking at the largest Google page they had ever seen.

"Whoa! Now that's what I call a big screen, Pete."

"Yeah," he nodded, "this is definitely going to make our lives easier today."

He went into Mapquest and called up a map of Cornelia Street in Manhattan. "What I propose is this: we begin with Mercer's note about 1:57. Let's assume it's one hour and fifty-seven minutes, then round up to two hours even."

"Okay."

"Then you and I sit here until we find something that a) is within a two-hour drive of Mercer's home and b) somehow connects with either Ellen or Sandburg.

He called up a map of the tri-state area and looked for a town that he thought might be about a two-hour drive from Manhattan. He chose New Paltz, NY. On his laptop he then pulled up Mapquest driving directions and found that a one-way trip from Manhattan to New Paltz took about an hour and a half.

"Okay, just a bit short. Let's go farther north to, say, Kingston." He typed in the new destination. "Roughly two hours. Good. North takes us to Kingston. I'd estimate, let's see, that west for two hours would get us a little past Allentown, PA. And south would take us to just past Philly to maybe Chester, PA, or maybe a place like Mystic Island, New Jersey."

"Also along that two-hour line," said Gimble, "it looks as though we'd have Hartford to the northeast and maybe Scranton to the northwest."

"Yep, we might just be able to touch the edge of Delaware and Maryland. But those look to be something more than two hours. Worth considering, though, especially since we've already had one murder down there."

"So now we hunt?"

"Right. What we need to do is overlay the map with our imaginary two-hour driving radius," he said. "Then we enlarge the map, sector by sector, and look for absolutely anything that echoes either Ellen or Sandburg."

"Or Rosebud."

"Yeah, sure, why not? I don't think he'd be that obvious," he smiled, "but I'll gratefully accept all the obvious leads he'd like to give us."

"Assuming he's our guy, of course."

"Assuming that, of course."

"But if he's not. . . ."

"Then you and I become experts on whatever is a two-hour drive from Manhattan. Plus. . . ."

"Plus we've got nothing else to go on," she grinned.

"You've heard that line before."

"I have."

The project that Nazareth and Gimble embarked on was one they quickly realized could take days to complete, and they understood all too painfully that the odds were stacked against them. First they would need to identify every city or town that fell on or near the two-hour radius line. Then for each of those places they would need to conduct an exhaustive online search for references to either *Ellen* or *Sandburg*. They would be wading through torrents of information, all in the hope that Mercer was actually involved in the murders. If he wasn't, then they had just embarked upon a monumentally time-wasting journey.

They decided somewhat arbitrarily to begin searching at the northeast end of the two-hour radius, near New London, CT, then drop down to the southeast segment, around Atlantic City, and then continue alternating north and south until they finished somewhere around Scranton, PA. As they proceeded in this fashion they gathered mountains of interesting but absolutely useless information. They learned, for instance, that there's an Ellen Sands Lane just outside New London, CT. In Appleton, MD, Ellen Sandburg died five months ago at 101. The College Club of Hartford was the first to invite poet Carl Sandburg to Connecticut in 1922. And the Carl Sandburg Middle School of Levittown, PA, has a lovely website.

After nearly four hours of this, Gimble reached into her purse and took out a small plastic bottle of eye drops. After putting a couple of drops in each eye, she turned to Nazareth.

"I don't believe in suicide," she said, "so I'm begging you to shoot me. Please, just put the gun to my head."

"How about if I buy you a couple of hot dogs at the stand around the corner instead?"

"Okay," she said in mock resignation, "just this once I'll go for the hot dogs. But I reserve the right to be shot if we're still doing this two days from now."

"I'd like to help you out, Tara, but New York really isn't big on assisted suicide."

"Fine. Then buy me four hot dogs."

"Death by hot dog. Great title for a novel."

Sameer Khan manned his cart Monday through Friday, January through December, in rain, sleet, and snow. "Just like mailman," he liked to say. But he brought a lot more to the table than the average mailman. His hot dogs were legendary, at least among Downtown cops. Khan had somehow rigged up a griddle in his cart, so he offered hot dogs that were grilled, not soaked in greasy, week-old water. And he made all of his own sides: sauerkraut, onion relish, and even chili. "The chili, this not in my country," he confessed, "but still best in New York anywhere." If you planned to kill yourself by OD'ing on hot dogs, this was where you wanted to do it.

"You really want four?" Nazareth asked as they stepped up to the cart.

"Well," she took an exaggerated deep breath, "I think the fresh air — or the fresh exhaust — has made me a little less suicidal. So I'll go for two. One with sauerkraut, the other with chili."

"Can't make up your mind, can you?" He shook his head. "Hey, Sameer, two for the young lady — one sauerkraut, one chili — and I'll have two with chili."

"My pleasure, detectives." You knew you had arrived when you were on Sameer Khan's short list.

They ate as they walked, and Gimble stayed ahead of him by half a hot dog the whole way. "Maybe you should have gone for the four," Nazareth said, much impressed with Gimble's appetite.

"I'm not usually a four-hot-dog date," she smiled, "but these are so good I could probably do it."

"Tell you what. When we solve this case, we'll come back and celebrate with four each. My treat."

"I love your optimism. And I accept."

An hour and a half later they were staring at the huge computer monitor and analyzing the northern section of their imaginary two-hour radius. Same routine as before: pick a city, and then search online to find any *Ellen* or *Sandburg* links. The process was maddeningly slow, and by late afternoon they estimated that at this pace they'd still be working on the map three days later.

Gimble was working the left side of the screen, taking a hard look at White Lake, NY, whose chief claim to fame was being the town nearest the Woodstock Music Festival of 1969. She was unimpressed by that particular detail, since she hadn't been born yet when Jimi Hendrix, Janis Joplin, Jefferson Airplane, and all the others had rocked Max Yasgur's farm. Nazareth studied the right side of the screen and Litchfield, CT. When he searched Google for *Ellen* and *Sandburg*, he learned that Ellen Vastopopoulos was the principal owner of the largest real estate agency in town. An overdose of this sort of trivia could probably drive a man insane.

Gimble saw it first. On the huge screen, a few inches to the right and slightly north of White Lake, was Ellenville, NY.

"Oh my God," she said, grabbing Nazareth by his left arm. "I can't believe this."

"What've you got?"

"What *we've* got," she pointed to the spot, "is Ellenville, NY. That's Ellenville as in Ellen-ville!"

"Hot damn! Let's blow that map up." He zoomed to street level. Due east of the town's center they heard the other shoe drop loud and clear. "Sandburg Creek," he said, as astonished as Gimble.

"Ellen-ville and Sandburg Creek." She punched Ellenville into her laptop and checked Mapquest for the drive time from Manhattan. "According to Mapquest, in current traffic conditions it should take one hour and fifty-five minutes to get from Manhattan to Ellenville."

Nazareth just stared at the screen, stunned by the discovery.

"Ellenville," he said, "near Sandburg Creek, 1:55 from Mercer's apartment. Almost identical to his note."

"This would be one hell of a world-class coincidence, wouldn't it?" she asked.

"Nothing is this coincidental," he said, shaking his head. "But what we still don't know is whether this has anything at all to do with murder. Maybe Mercer's got a girlfriend up there."

"Yeah, that may be. But right now who the hell cares? Let's jump on this and see where it goes."

"It goes north, Tara," he grinned. "Due north."

47

On days like this — sunny, clear, a high of 81 — I am glad to be on the far side of the Hudson. I get out of the car at the Alpine overlook on the Palisades Parkway and savor the view of the Manhattan skyline from a distance. On most days I am quite pleased to be part of the energetic thrum of New York City. But the occasional respite is beneficial to one's mental health.

After today's English Lit class I deserve time away. I wonder where civilization is headed when college students can name every brand of vodka ever bottled but cannot distinguish between two lines of Shakespeare and two lines of Tennyson. More to the point, they seem to care only about vodka and not at all about literacy, their own or anyone else's. Was I asleep for twenty years under a tree when iPhones were substituted for the human brain? Did I miss the day when humans stopped speaking and began texting? While it is true that I am paid to teach these cretins, it is also true that I am not paid enough.

Yet, somewhat miraculously, after a few breaths of clean outdoor air all that is behind me. Here on the shady overlook alongside the highway I confess to feeling just a bit like Rip Van Winkle setting off for a day in the Catskills with my faithful dog Wolf. To the Catskills I do, in fact, go today. In little more than ninety minutes I will find myself in the midst of nearly 700,000 acres of protected wilderness, safe from the prying eyes of the NYPD, while I seek out Ellen Karcher — my own substitute Dame Van Winkle, in a sense — for our blessed tryst.

Five gray-and-white herring gulls soar above me as I walk slowly back to my car. For one rapturous moment they become a heavenly flock of liberated souls escaping their earthly woes.

Ellen Karcher is among them.

48

"So how do you want to play this?" Gimble said as she checked her watch. "It's a little after four right now, and I don't know whether we can get a whole lot done about Ellenville until tomorrow. If we start on it early in the morning, we can touch base with the local police and drive up if it seems worthwhile."

Nazareth studied the large computer screen, then his watch, then the screen. Lost in thought again.

"Part of me says we're going to end up spinning our wheels one more time," he said, "because we keep looking at this guy and coming away thinking he's clean."

"And the other part?"

"Right, the other part is telling me that the note from his desk is too big to ignore. Maybe he has a perfectly innocent reason for thinking about Ellenville. And, of course, it may be that we've completely misinterpreted the business about *ellen, 1:57,* and *sandburg.* Maybe we just tortured that note until it happened to fit Ellenville, in the same way we probably could have made it fit a town in Maryland or Connecticut."

"Too much of a coincidence, Pete. You know that."

He nodded. "Does Mercer teach today?"

Gimble checked the schedule that he had given them. "Already finished for the day."

"All right. What we do first," he explained, "is find out whether Mercer is home. If he's home, then I'm comfortable waiting until tomorrow to get on this. If he's not home, I want to know whether his car is at his garage. If it's not, then I think we need to call the Ellenville PD and see how they react."

"Want me to call Mercer?"

"Sure. If he's there, just let him know we'd like to meet with him again tomorrow to ask a few more questions. If he's not there, we drive over to the garage."

Gimble called Mercer's home number, then hung up when voicemail kicked in.

"Not there," she said. "Let's check out the garage."

49.

I am delighted that the NYPD has decided to leave me alone today. By way of several clever starts and stops and quick turns, I have satisfied myself that no one is following me, so I am completely free to do the Lord's work. I whisper a joyful prayer: "Thank you for the glory of this day and for the power to end someone's suffering."

A few miles short of Bear Mountain I turn off the Palisades Parkway onto US 6 West. I pass through the thick woods of Harriman State Park, where everything is hilly, green, and remarkably lovely. To my left is Stockbridge Mountain, where I took a solitary and quite challenging three-hour hike several years ago. To my right is Long Mountain, which I have not yet hiked but have been told offers breathtaking views. It has been too long since I last hiked. Especially on a day like this, I am reminded that nature's healing presence is always near. I should reach out to it more often.

50.

Nazareth pulled to the curb directly across from Summit Parking, where Mercer kept his car. As he and Gimble crossed the street, Ramon took one last hit and flicked his joint toward the gutter.

"Good morning, officers," he smiled.

"Not too hard to make us, huh?" Nazareth replied as he and Gimble reached for their wallets.

"Not unless you're blind and from, like, Kentucky."

"And I take it you're not?"

"Got that right. Born and raised right here on the streets of this fine city, officer." He eyed Nazareth's shield. "Make that detective, Detective." He gave Nazareth a thumbs up.

"Listen," Nazareth said pleasantly, "do you know a guy named Thomas Mercer?"

"Yeah, sure. The professor, right?" Nazareth nodded. "He's one of our monthlies. Real nice guy. What, he shoot somebody when I wasn't looking?"

"Nothing like that," said Gimble, taking out her notepad. "We missed a 3:00 o'clock appointment with him, and we just want to find out whether he's still in the neighborhood. If not, we'll catch up with him tomorrow."

"Hey," said Ramon as he raised both hands, "whatever you say, Detective. Man's innocent 'til proven guilty, right?"

"The professor is just someone we've been talking with." She gave him the stop-busting-my-chops stare.

"That's cool. Yeah Prof. Mercer left here about, oh, maybe two hours ago. I brought the car around for him," he said. "Dude doesn't drive much, but he hands me a five every time he comes here. Real good guy like that." He raised his chin toward two other attendants who were sharing a can wrapped in a brown paper bag. "I won't let one of these other clowns go near him, believe me."

"Did the professor say where he was going?" Nazareth asked.

"Nope, never does. I don't ask. None of my business."

"When he goes out, is it usually overnight?"

"Like he's out killing zombies or some shit?"

"You should be writing screenplays instead of parking cars," Gimble said. "As far as we know the professor isn't an axe murderer or zombie hunter. We just want an idea of whether he'll be back tonight, that's all."

"Okay. I'd say yeah, he'll be back tonight. He's usually back the same day, but it's after my shift. I check his car the next morning to see that no one has screwed with it."

"Do the people who work here usually screw with the cars?" Gimble asked.

"Depends on how messed up they are," he laughed. "Ain't easy parking cars if you're too high."

"Ah, I get you," she nodded, wearing her best Judge Judy face. "There's a difference between high and too high if you're parking cars?"

Ramon glanced at the gutter where the remains of his most recent joint floated in a murky puddle. "Uh, I really wouldn't know about that, Detective."

"What does the professor drive?" Nazareth asked.

"Beige Nissan Altima," Ramon said quickly. "Clean, low mileage, no dead bodies in the back seat." A comedian, Nazareth thought. If he only knew.

When they were back in the cruiser, Gimble began clicking away on her iPad.

"I take it we speak next with the locals up in Ellenville," she said as she waited for the Ellenville PD web page to load.

"Correct," Nazareth replied, stomping the gas to get into the traffic ahead of a fully loaded garbage truck. "Let's hope Mercer is out doing his Christmas shopping early and not on his way to the Catskills."

"Amen to that." She turned around to look through the rear window. "I take it you don't like riding behind garbage trucks?"

"Most definitely not in June, July, or August." He thought about that for a moment, then said, "I'd like to be picking up some trash today, not riding behind it."

51

A t the border of Harriman, NY, where US Route 6 and NY Route 17 join, I turn off at a sign for Maggie's Coffee Shop and drive into the small town. I get out at Maggie's and walk into a tidy place that serves several varieties of coffee along with homemade baked goods. The woman behind the counter wears her hair in what earlier in the day might have been a beehive but now looks more like a large round bale in a soggy hay field. I order a medium black coffee and a splendid cheese danish. I permit myself this modest excess since I didn't eat much for lunch. Besides, I need to keep my energy up. I'll be eating dinner later than usual tonight.

One danish and two wrong turns later, I find myself driving slowly along a heavily wooded stretch of Route 17M looking for a place to stop and switch the GPS on. Suddenly the woods on my right give way to a large parking lot. At the front edge of the lot stands a tall steel post atop which is an immense green and black Enterprise Rent-A-Car sign.

I pull into the lot and begin programming the GPS device. But something catches my attention, and I look up through the windshield just as a magnificent red-shouldered hawk, its wings outstretched and feathers fanned in the late-day sunlight, lands gently on the Enterprise sign. I can scarcely breathe. It is like the very hand of God reaching out to touch me. Have I been guided to this specific place at this specific moment for a reason?

Something I have indeed pondered during the past twenty-four hours is whether to use my own car for my trip to Ellenville. That still seems the wisest course. If I rent a car, someone could easily track me down through my credit card. Yes, I could pay cash as I did in Maryland. But that transaction raised a few eyebrows. After all, who pays cash for anything nowadays? Who wouldn't notice a person who did? So here I sit. I'm not willing to pay cash, and I'm not willing to use my credit card. I have my answer.

I force myself to look away from the hawk and drive back toward the main highway.

52

Back at One Police Plaza it took Nazareth nearly twenty minutes to get Chief Dan Montagne of the Ellenville PD on the phone. First the dispatcher said the chief was gone for the day. Then he said, no, wait, I think he's next door. Finally, after Nazareth said he'd just hang up and call the state police, the dispatcher decided that he could probably reach the chief on his cell phone no matter where he was.

The chief turned out to be an amiable sort who seemed ideally suited to the pace of life in a small Catskill village. Nazareth heard squealing kids in the background, along with the occasional deep splash of what might have been a successful cannonball off a five-foot diving board.

Nazareth quickly outlined the Rosebud Killer case — something Chief Montagne had not heard about — and, without mentioning Mercer's name, explained that something bad might be approaching Ellenville's southern horizon.

"Well, I appreciate your call, Detective," Montagne said. At this point in the conversation Nazareth thought he detected the sharp fssst of a can being popped open. "But what exactly are you hoping to get from us?"

Nazareth looked at Gimble as if he had just intercepted a call from another galaxy.

"If this suspect is actually the killer," Nazareth explained patiently, "you probably need to begin knocking on the doors of every widow in town."

"Let me tell you, Detective," Montagne chuckled, "if I could do that with my sixteen officers, only seven of which are on duty right now, I should be playing Las Vegas as a magician. There is no way, none, zero that I can have my guys visit every widow in town. Well, maybe I could get it done in a week," he allowed, "but sure as hell not in one day or one night."

"There may not be that many widows, Chief."

"I really have no idea how many widows we've got up here. But we've had lots of funerals over the past year, so I'm guessing we have lots of widows."

"But if you look for older women — maybe 65 plus — who lost their husbands in, say, just the last six months," Nazareth said gently, "you might come up with a manageable number."

"Here's the thing, Detective. First off, you said yourself that you're not even sure that this guy's a reasonable suspect yet. And that note you read me," he said pointedly, "could mean damn near anything. In my professional opinion, that note has absolutely nothing to do with Ellenville. It's sure as hell not something that's going to get me sending my entire force blazing around town tonight with lights flashing. I appreciate your concern and all, but I don't have the resources to run with something like this."

How many times, Nazareth wondered, in how many different settings had he heard the same lame excuse for doing nothing?

"All right, what about calling in the state police?" Nazareth asked.

"No, we do not," said Montagne testily, "repeat, we DO NOT call in the state police. Bringing them in is my decision. And I have no intention of making a complete jackass of myself by getting them involved because of this secret note you found. Ain't gonna happen."

"Chief Montagne, this is Detective Tara Gimble."

"Good afternoon, Detective."

"Chief, Detective Nazareth and I feel strongly enough about this that we're willing to drive up there ourselves, but only if you have no problem with that."

"Detectives, if you want to chase wild geese all the way up here to the Catskills," he replied calmly, "you're absolutely welcome in Ellenville. I'll gladly show you around town tomorrow and buy you lunch. But we're not going to be knocking on doors and getting people in this town all stirred up over some phantom killer."

"Understood, Chief," said Nazareth. "If we do get up there tonight, should we phone you?"

"No need to do that, Detective. But feel free to give me a call in the morning, and we'll set something up. You both have a safe trip and a good night."

After hanging up, Nazareth just stared at the phone. "What really hurts," he said, "is that he's probably right. We're stretching the facts to fit our story. Always a mistake."

"Always?"

"Okay, maybe not always." His fingers drummed the conference room table. "Let's get a couple of rooms in Ellenville for the night. And we should pick up sandwiches to eat on the way."

"And coffee. Lots of coffee."

53.

The drive to Ellenville seems to me a voyage into America's past. In this part of New York State the trees outnumber people a million to one, and the very names of the towns I pass strike me as relics of a bygone era — places like Kiryas Joel, Scotchtown, Pine Bush, and Otter Kill. My favorite, though, is Goshen. Ah, yes, the Land of Goshen. And Moses led the Israelites out of Egypt and slavery! Let our souls soar, dearly beloved. I momentarily fancy myself a traveling preacher healing the sick and lame under a tent at the edge of town. Maybe after I retire from teaching.

Before reaching the southern edge of Ellenville I head east toward Minnewaska State Park and its deep, dark woods, streaming waterfalls, and rocky outcroppings. I follow a narrow winding road through the forest and turn into a secluded bare-earth clearing that is virtually hidden from the road by tangled bushes and a wall of oaks, maples, and pitch pines. This is a wonderfully secluded spot that I had found during my first visit to Ellenville. In the dusk I quickly remove my New York license plates and attach the Maryland ones.

It's 8:25 p.m. and still a few minutes too early to visit Ellen Karcher, so I walk a narrow path that meanders through the woods for thirty or forty feet until it reaches a granite ledge overlooking Ellenville. From high on the mount I gaze down upon Ellenville, where the lights of civilization have begun to twinkle in the darkening valley. I can't say for sure which is Widow

Karcher's mournful home, but I imagine that at least one of the glimmering lights belongs to her. Is she in her kitchen, washing a single dish after another lonely dinner? Does the light from her window shine on the water of Sandburg Creek as it flows gently toward its union with the distant Hudson? Will the passage of her soul be like the resolute journey of a mountain stream?

I stand at the edge of the rocky outcropping and reach my hand out toward one of the distant houses. From this perspective the dwelling seems tiny enough to fit in my palm. Peace washes over me as I gently close my fingers around what could be Ellen's home.

I feel the power.

54.

At 7:40 p.m. Nazareth double-parked in front of the Stage Door Deli on Vesey Street while Gimble went in to pick up their phone order. She came out with a large brown bag containing a massive ham and provolone on rye and a formidable turkey BLT on whole wheat toast. She also carried a cardboard cup holder with four large coffees.

"A bag that big for just two sandwiches?" Nazareth asked as he sped off toward the West Side Drive.

"Well," Gimble grinned, "they're big sandwiches. Plus I got us a bag of Cape Cod potato chips. It's a long trip, right? Tomorrow after work I'll hit the gym."

"Oh, yeah, four hours in the gym should just about get the job done," he taunted.

The detectives figured they would make good time since they had already missed peak rush hour, but that plan went south in a hurry at the George Washington Bridge, where an accident was being cleared from the roadway. By the time they really got rolling they had lost a half hour, but at least they had been able to eat their sandwiches and most of the chips in relative peace."

"So," Gimble said as she set down her first empty coffee cup of the night, "when we get to Ellenville tonight, we cruise the streets and look for Mercer's car?"

"Absolutely. If he's there, he could already be minutes or hours away from his next victim — unless, of course, he's not the killer. In that case, he'll probably end up filing charges against us for harassment. Do I really think he's our guy?" He slowly shook his head. "I kind of doubt it. The only thing that makes me think there's even a chance is that note. And as Chief Montagne reminded us, the note isn't much to go on."

"It's a frustrating business, isn't it, Pete?"

"At the moment, yeah," he nodded thoughtfully. "But if we keep following whatever lead comes along, sooner or later the frustration ends."

"Hope you're right."

"I can't afford not to be, can I?"

55.

I leave my mountain hideaway, drive the darkened roads, and at 8:45 p.m. park directly in front of Ellen Karcher's house. From the front door all she'll see is the profile of my vehicle, and at night even that will be indistinct to her aged eyes. There is certainly no possibility that she will notice the white Maryland plates.

The street is absolutely still. More *For Sale* and *Foreclosure* signs in this neighborhood than people. No barking dogs. No street lamps. No evidence of life other than the dim light that emanates from several of the old homes, including Ellen's. I don't know her floor plan, but I judge that an overhead kitchen fixture is on at the back of the house facing the creek, while a small table lamp, perhaps a floor lamp, lights a front living room that is hidden behind blinds and drapes.

I lift my briefcase and carefully remove the key contents. First is a latex glove, which I stretch onto my left hand. With the gloved hand I tuck a silk rosebud into the right inside pocket of my sport coat. Next is the syringe filled with diazepam, and that goes into the right outside pocket. Then comes the syringe of sodium pentobarbital for my left outside pocket. The last item I remove is the stun gun, which I hold in my left hand and conceal under a brown file folder that contains a meaningless document.

Thus equipped I walk to Ellen Karcher's front steps and ring the bell. I wait in the dark. As she unlocks the cheap aluminum interior door I notice a light fixture above me, but she doesn't turn it on. The bulb probably burned out months ago and hasn't been replaced. This is good.

She is gray, thin, and stooped. She wears a simple flowered house dress and a stained blue apron that has done battle with many meals over the years. Balanced on the front of her nose are wire-rimmed bifocals, and she squints at me through the screen door.

"Yes, can I help you?" she says sweetly, remarkably unperturbed for a vulnerable old woman standing face to face with a stranger in the dark.

"I certainly hope so," I reply in my warmest voice as I hold up my phony ID for her perusal. "I'm Bob Riggins of the Department of Environmental Conservation. Are you Mrs. Karcher?"

"Yes." She looks puzzled but not alarmed. I go gently.

"Oh, wonderful," I smile like an old friend. "I spoke with you last week about some work our department will be doing along Sandburg Creek."

"Oh, yes, I remember. You said they would be working across the creek from my back yard."

"That's correct, Mrs. Karcher. Am I catching you at a bad time?"

"No, not at all."

"Great. Well, unfortunately, we've been unable to reach the owner of the property across the way, so I'm hoping that you will be kind enough to allow two members of my crew to walk through your yard to take some photos early tomorrow afternoon. They would be in and out within fifteen or twenty minutes at the most."

"You're not talking about big trucks or anything, are you?"

"Oh, no, ma'am. Just the two uniformed workers, and they'll walk in. They will *both*," I emphasize, "show you appropriate identification."

"Well, that seems fine."

"Wonderful, Mrs. Karcher. Thank you so much. If it's okay, I need to get a signed release form from you." I lift the file folder a couple of inches toward her, but she pays no attention to it. "It's half a page, and it simply says that you give permission for us to come onto your property in order to take photos for a New York State flood-zone project. It also says that you have no responsibility whatsoever for our crew. So if one of them falls into the creek," I laugh, "that's my problem, not yours."

"Oh, I hope that doesn't happen," she laughs with me. "Come in. Let me get a pen."

56.

Nazareth pulled into a convenience store on Route 52 and began topping off the gas tank while Gimble headed for the ladies' room. By the time she came back, he was ready to go in and use the facilities himself. On the way out he bought two bags of salted peanuts, just in case his body's protein demands hadn't been satisfied by the huge sandwich he had inhaled earlier.

When he got back behind the wheel he saw that Gimble had bought each of them a cold bottle of water.

"Hey, great minds think alike," he said as he handed her a bag of peanuts.

"I hadn't expected to gain ten pounds on this trip," she replied. "I'm not the one with a fancy health club in my apartment."

"Peanuts are good for you. Seriously. Lots of protein — 38 grams in one cup actually — monounsaturated fat and antioxidants." He glanced over at his skeptical partner. "Hey, I'm not kidding. I also read recently that peanuts actually help you *lose* weight, not gain it."

"Uh, huh. How many calories in this bag?"

"I never check calories."

"And that's because?"

"I always burn more than I eat."

"Because you have your own private health club."

"Guilty as charged."

"By the way," she said after she stopped chewing her first handful of peanuts, "did you notice the name tag on the woman behind the counter back there?"

"Let me guess. Alison Monet."

"Very observant, Detective. And what did that mean to you?"

"Same thing it meant to you, I suppose. We're still missing a priceless painting that may or may not have been stolen by our killer."

"Bingo. I haven't given that painting much thought, but it's certainly a loose end, isn't it?"

"Yep, but not my loose end. The Major Case guys can run with that for as long as they want. My guess is that it's now hanging in the private collection of some ultra-rich goofball who gets off on owning things that no one else can see."

Gimble went back to the project that had occupied much of her attention during the trip. She read every online obituary that she could find for Ellenville, NY, beginning twelve months ago. In many instances the summary didn't contain any information about surviving relatives, so she had to cross-reference those death notices with information found through separate online searches. It was a slow process that kept turning up plenty of nothing.

But her patience was finally rewarded. She reread the obituary just to make sure she hadn't imagined it, then ran another search to check the facts as best she could.

"I think this may be what we're after," she said as she jotted down the key facts in her notebook.

"What have you got?"

"Nine months ago, Harvey Karcher died at age 88. Sole survivor is his wife, Ellen Karcher."

"Ellen as in Ellenville?"

"The very same," she smiled broadly.

"Damn, Mercer's note is an even better fit now," he said, pushing the cruiser up to 85. "I'm beginning to think we're finally on the right track."

"How about if I let Chief Montagne know what we have? Maybe this will get him moving."

"Absolutely. Go for it. He can't NOT be interested."

Gimble dialed Montagne, who picked up after eight or nine rings.

"Montagne," he said.

"Chief Montagne," she said, "this is Detective Gimble, NYPD."

"So are you guys coming up here, or did you decide to pass?"

"We're very much on our way, and I think I've come across something that you'll want to hear." After laying out the results of her online search, she floated the idea of having an Ellenville officer visit Ellen Karcher's home.

"Detective," Montagne replied, "at this time of night I have just three officers watching over nearly 5,000 area residents. Two of those officers are in patrol cars, and as we speak the third one is at the hospital interviewing a robbery suspect who had part of his ear shot off by the owner of a liquor store. I mean no disrespect, but I have more to worry about than some guy you told me isn't really a suspect and a note that means nothing at all."

"Chief," Nazareth interrupted, "I now believe there's a really strong chance he's the guy we're after."

"Then please tell me again why he's coming to Ellenville to murder someone when he has his pick of millions of people in New York City."

"He's choosing random locations to keep us off his ass, Chief. But there's nothing random about the victims. They're all old widows. And I don't believe there's anything random about Ellen Karcher."

"Is she the only widow named Ellen in this town?" Montagne asked.

Nazareth looked over at Gimble, who shrugged.

"We can't say that right now," he answered.

"Then why don't we do this. You keep looking online for other widows named Ellen, and I promise you I'll have one of my guys drive by her house before midnight. How's that, Detective?"

"That's a good start, Chief," Nazareth answered, "but midnight could be too late."

"If I thought so, Detective, I'd drive over there myself right now," he said, annoyed by what he viewed as meddling. "And I have to tell you, up here the buck stops with me. I make the calls and live with the fallout. So as I said earlier, you're welcome to come into town, drive around, have lunch with me tomorrow, and do whatever else you want to do — as long as you don't knock on doors or otherwise spook the residents. I don't need that."

"Would you mind if we call Mrs. Karcher?" Gimble asked.

"I absolutely *would* mind," Montagne replied. "You call this old lady and tell her she's about to be murdered, and she'll drop dead from a heart attack. Then I'll have to explain to the mayor and the village board why I thought it was okay to have a couple of New York detectives do that. And, by the way, I'd be having that conversation just before I collected my final paycheck. And in case you don't already know it, this is the only police chief's job in town. My wife and three kids would like for me not to lose it."

"Okay, Chief," Gimble said, shaking her head. "We'll be there before long, but we won't do anything but look around."

"Now you're talking."

Nazareth had the cruiser up over 90 with the lights flashing. He glanced over at Gimble, whose hands were clenched into fists.

"I wonder," she said, "if Chief Montagne has ever seen a dead body."

57

As soon as Mrs. Karcher turns her back to me I push the front door closed with my shoulder and drop the file folder to the floor. I move quickly toward her and wrap my right arm firmly — but I hope not too firmly — around her slender neck. She inhales sharply, startled by the assault, and with my left hand I press the stun gun to her chest. Her upper body stiffens as the muscles spasm painfully, and I half push and half lift her toward the well-worn living room couch. I regret the pain she suffers from the stun gun, but in another minute she will feel pain no more.

She yelps and struggles feebly when I release the trigger, so I apply another shock, longer than the first, and she is a dead weight as she drops to the couch. I remove the diazepam syringe from my right pocket and inject the contents into the crook of her right arm. The effect at high dosage is virtually instantaneous, and I can relax. Ellen Karcher is temporarily beyond pain. The next injection will last for eternity.

I reach toward my left pocket and the sodium pentobarbital syringe when crippling pain tears at the right side of my forehead. Immediately blood pours over my right eye, and amid the numb confusion I hear someone yell, ". . . bastard!" I have no idea what else may have been said, because I feel as though I have fallen from the top of my apartment building and landed head-first on the concrete.

As I drop to my left knee I look up and see an old man preparing to deliver a second blow with a heavy wooden cane. I can actually feel the hatred in his bulging eyes and scarlet face as he brings the cane down toward me. I lurch forward onto both hands, and his blow glances off my back. He loses his balance for just a moment, and I frantically grab one of his legs and pull as hard as I can.

He is nearly six feet tall, wiry, and an obvious menace. But age is against him. He drops heavily to the wood floor and struggles to regain his feet. I grab the lower shaft of the cane that has fallen to his side. Now on both knees I take a ferocious swing with the cane, and the curved handle makes a sickening crack as it lands on the left side of his face, tearing open his mouth and shattering several teeth. He falls to his back, and I leap on him.

Holding the cane with both hands I jam it against his exposed throat and lean forward so that my entire weight presses his neck against the floor. He grabs at the cane futilely. He struggles to breathe but chokes on the blood that floods into the back of his throat. And then he lies motionless beneath me. I maintain the pressure on his throat for another minute, making sure that he can cause me no more trouble.

When I am certain he is dead, I stand and wipe blood from my forehead and face. The shock of being attacked slowly subsides, and I look toward the kitchen, which must be where the old man had come from. I walk into the kitchen, and on the table I find an open copy of *The Joy of Perennial Gardens*, two cups of coffee, and a dish that holds a half-eaten slice of apple pie.

A drop of blood falls from my forehead to the vinyl floor. I look back toward the living room, and the bottom falls out of my stomach. A trail of spattered blood marks my passage from the living room to the kitchen. I grab a damp dish towel from the counter by the sink, and as I press it to my forehead searing pain courses through my entire body like a lightning bolt. I desperately need to see how bad the cut is, but first I need to finish my work with Ellen Karcher.

She remains immobile on the couch. For all I know she is already dead, having succumbed to a combination of sustained voltage and a major dose of diazepam. Either way, I administer the sodium pentobarbital as quickly as I can, because I am now running horribly behind schedule.

I leave Ellen Karcher slumped on the couch and rush to the kitchen in search of cleaning supplies. Good God, my blood is everywhere! Under the sink I find a large plastic bottle of vinegar and decide that this will suffice. I grab a pot holder from alongside the stove, soak it with vinegar, and get down on my knees to begin cleaning up the floors. First I do the kitchen vinyl, then move onto the living room hardwood, where I clean up my own blood as well as the old man's. Here and there I pick up a bit of tooth. I use nearly half the bottle of vinegar. The mess is shocking.

Just when I believe my cleaning chore has ended I notice blood stains on the couch and on the worn rug under the coffee table. I douse all of the spots, let the vinegar soak in, and then blot them with the pot holder. I'm no expert on DNA analysis, but I hope that undiluted vinegar will mask my presence in the Karcher home. Damn! I notice drops of blood on Ellen's clothing, so I soak those as well. I check her over carefully to make sure I haven't missed anything.

I toss the pot holder and the bloody dish towel onto the dead man's chest. He is the last bit of evidence I must remove.

58.

"What have we got up here?" Nazareth said as he noticed the flashing lights a few hundred yards ahead of them. He decelerated quickly when he saw a lone state trooper facing off with five men who had climbed out of two vehicles. The men had fanned out around the trooper, but they held back when Nazareth skidded to a stop with his lights shining on them.

"Need some help here, Trooper?" Nazareth said as he and Gimble climbed out of the cruiser, their shields and IDs held out for the officer to see. "Detectives Nazareth and Gimble, NYPD."

The young trooper kept his eye on the five men, who ranged in age from nineteen to twenty-five and appeared to be stoned out of their minds.

"I'd be grateful. Routine speeding stop until the second car pulled up," he said nervously, "and things started to get ugly. Glad you came along when you did. I haven't been able to call for back-up."

"Why don't you do that while Detective Gimble and I keep an eye on things?"

"That's works for me."

Before the detectives could draw their weapons, one of the thugs charged Nazareth, who calmly delivered a ferocious side kick to the man's front knee. The guy went down as though he had been hit by a truck, his kneecap fractured and the neighboring tendons shredded.

Nazareth pulled his Glock 19 just as the largest guy in the group, a 250-pounder whose arms, neck, and forehead were covered with prison tattoos, looked as though he might want to try his luck. He stopped and glared when he saw the weapon pointed at his enormous chest.

"The exit wound," Nazareth calmly explained, "will be approximately the size of a bowling ball. I'd be happy to prove that to you and your asshole friends."

The guy slowly lowered himself to his knees and pressed his hands to the back of his neck.

"Maybe next time," Nazareth grinned.

By the time three other state police vehicles were on scene, Nazareth and Gimble had lost nearly twenty-five precious minutes. They had done what needed doing, but they worried that Ellen Karcher might be the one picking up the tab.

Nazareth crushed the accelerator and had the cruiser over 90 in less than twenty seconds.

59

I don't know how much the old man weighs, but it's considerably more than I would have guessed. Lifting him is out of the question, even though I am reasonably fit for someone my age. Dragging him by his heels across the hardwood floor will be a challenge, but getting him to the car will be much worse. I consider leaving him but immediately reject the notion. Surely my fingerprints are on him. I don't know where, but they must be there. Maybe fibers from my clothing as well, or perhaps a strand of my hair. And without question my blood has mingled with his, whether on his face or his shirt. Impossible to know. He is literally a body of evidence. Somewhere on him is proof that I was here, so I cannot leave him behind.

I go out to the car, checking to make sure no neighbors are strolling the streets of Ellenville tonight. When I am satisfied that I am alone, I open the trunk and attempt to unscrew the small bulb that might attract someone's attention. It refuses to budge, so I smash it with a small umbrella that I keep in the car.

Back in the house I firmly grab the man's ankles and begin backing toward the front door with him. He glides smoothly over the wood floor, yet my lower back complains anyway. Dragging him over the door sill is difficult, but I manage. His head makes a hollow clunk as it bounces onto each of the front steps. By the time I get him to the trunk, I am covered with sweat and severely out of breath. But I need to move quickly while I am still alone out here. I wrestle the body to a sitting position, with the old man's back leaning against the car's rear bumper. Then I wrap my arms around the torso in a makeshift lifeguard's carry. The old man and I are eerily face to face as I shift my weight forward and hoist his upper body onto the ledge of the trunk. His body balances there tentatively as I grab his thighs, then lift and shove until the entire thing thuds into the trunk like a deer carcass.

I go back into the house and quickly check for blood stains I may have missed. At the far end of the living room I pause to look into a rectangular wall mirror. On my forehead is a raw open wound at least three inches long. The tissue is torn, not sliced, and the bloody gash is frighteningly wide and deep. It is an oozing mess that requires medical attention, and most certainly stitches, but I have no time to seek medical care tonight.

I have a body to dispose of.

60.

The call came in on Gimble's cell phone: Sergeant Sherry Pearsall of the Ellenville PD. The sergeant sounded rattled as she worked hard to make herself heard over loud background voices.

"What can I do for you, Sergeant?" Gimble said, putting the phone on speaker so that Nazareth could hear the conversation.

"We're at a crime scene," she yelled into the phone. "Well, a murder scene, actually, and Chief Montagne said you would probably want to come straight here when you get to Ellenville."

Nazareth tightened his grip on the wheel and shook his head in disgust.

"What's the victim's name?" Gimble asked, already knowing the answer.

"Ellen Karcher. She's a . . . ."

"I know who she is, Sergeant. And I have her home address. Is that where the body is?"

"Yes." Pearsall repeated the address anyway.

"Do you have anyone in custody?"

"No, but we're pretty sure we know who did it?"

"Oh? And who's that?"

"An old guy who lives in her neighborhood. We know for a fact that he had gone to see Mrs. Karcher, and now he's gone."

"Missing?"

"Yes, ma'am. Looks as though he killed Mrs. Karcher and then took off."

"Sergeant, do you happen to know whether the killer left a silk rosebud on the body?" Gimble asked.

"I sure didn't see a rosebud, Detective. I was the first at the scene, and Mrs. Karcher's body was just lying on the couch."

"Okay, we'll be there in about twenty minutes," said Gimble as she eyed the GPS. "Should we ask for you when we get there?"

"Me or the chief," Pearsall replied. "The chief said to tell you he'd be here when you arrive."

"Okay, see you shortly."

After Gimble disconnected, she looked over at an obviously angry but also puzzled Pete Nazareth.

"She was killed by a neighbor?" Gimble said.

"That piece sure as hell doesn't fit," Nazareth replied as he stared down the highway. He thought hard for a moment. "I guarantee you that if Mercer is up here, he did it."

"And if he's not up here?"

"Then after eleven years on the force I start to believe in coincidences."

61.

I force myself to pull away from the Karcher home much more slowly than I would like. I want to step on the gas and get this awful day over with. But I cannot behave like a man who has a body in the trunk of his car. Remain calm, I tell myself, and don't attract attention during the ten-minute drive to the woods. I'll have plenty of time later on to think all of this through and come up with a sensible plan. For now, just drive. Breathe. Stay calm.

I put my right hand to my chest, where my heart pounds away like a pile driver. As I do so, my arm presses on the silk rosebud that I have forgotten to remove from the inside pocket of my jacket. I pray for Ellen Karcher's forgiveness. In my haste I was unable to show her the proper respect.

I vow to do better next time.

62

Nazareth and Gimble turned onto Ellen Karcher's street, where the garish lights of police cruisers produced a surreal carnival atmosphere in this lonely neighborhood at the edge of town. Uniformed officers, flashlights in hand, scrambled through the yards nearest the Karcher home, scouring the ground and bushes for evidence of the killer's escape. The detectives count six official vehicles — four from Ellenville PD, two from the state police.

"An hour ago Montagne couldn't spare one goddamn cop," Gimble snarled as she slammed the car door behind her. "And now he's got everyone but the National Guard here."

"I'm with you," said Nazareth, "but we need to stay cool. If we yank Montagne's chain too hard, we'll be invited to leave. And we definitely want to be here."

Gimble nodded as she strode purposefully toward the front door. She and Nazareth flashed their shields to a young cop and asked for Montagne. They were pointed toward a heavyset, fiftyish guy who stood solemnly alongside the couch chatting with one of the troopers. As they entered the room, both detectives noticed the sharp odor of vinegar.

"Chief Montagne?" Nazareth said as he extended his hand. "Pete Nazareth. My partner, Tara Gimble."

"Oh, right, Detective," he said, taking Nazareth's offered hand. "I'm glad you guys got my message. This here's Bud Carpenter from the state police." The officers all nodded to each other.

"Your sergeant told us you have a local suspect," Nazareth said.

"That's right, Detective. A woman from down the other end of the street, Charlene Ryan, called us when she came by here and found the body. Looks as though Charlene's husband did this." He pointed to Ellen Karcher on the couch.

"I'm not following you, Chief," said Gimble.

"Well, her husband told Charlene he was coming over here for just a few minutes to work on some sort of design for the community garden downtown. Ned Ryan and Mrs. Karcher here have been on the town's garden committee for years," he explained. "When he didn't come back home for a long while, she called and got no answer. So she walked down and found Mrs. Karcher dead on the couch, and her husband had taken off."

"The husband was driving?" Nazareth asked.

"Nope. Old guy with a cane. Walked here, did what he did, then walked off. We'll catch up with him soon enough. Couldn't have gotten very far."

"Has Ned Ryan ever been a problem for you before this?" Nazareth asked.

"He could be a real nasty pain in the ass sometimes, always calling about kids that were hanging out at the creek behind his house. And if you ask me," he offered confidentially, "I think he's been getting a little lost upstairs, if you know what I mean. He's an older guy, you know."

"Cause of death?" Gimble asked.

"Haven't touched the body. We're waiting on the county medical examiner. But her neck looks kinda red to me, so maybe she was choked."

"Is Ned Ryan strong enough to strangle someone?" Nazareth asked.

"A woman this size? Yeah, sure. He's a pretty big guy."

"What do you make of the vinegar smell?" Nazareth asked.

"Didn't really notice it, to tell you the truth," Montagne said as he sniffed the air. "Same smell at home whenever my wife cleans the floors. She used to buy all sorts of expensive cleaners, but now it's just vinegar and water."

Nazareth got down on all fours and began smelling the floor near the couch. He covered a section about four feet by four feet, leaned over to smell the rug, then went back to smelling the hardwood floor.

"Part bloodhound, eh, Detective?" Montagne chuckled as he winked at Gimble.

Ignoring Montagne, Nazareth put the side of his face to the floor and looked across toward the wall. He crawled closer to something that he had spotted, reached for the clean handkerchief in the back pocket of his slacks, and grabbed the tiny object. He stood up, studying whatever it was he had found. Gimble took a small evidence bag from her purse and held it open for her partner.

"The vinegar that we smell," Nazareth told them, "is only on a small section of the floor. So this was definitely just spot cleaning. And there's a heavy vinegar smell on the rug under the coffee table. Looks like the rug is still wet in one small section.

"And this," he motioned to the evidence bag, "appears to be a tooth fragment. Looks to me like the very tip of a canine tooth, but we can let the ME say for sure."

"A canine tooth?" said Montagne.

"Right," said Nazareth. He opened his mouth and pressed his thumb against the sharp upper tooth. "Canine tooth."

"Ah."

"It's not the sort of thing you normally find lying on a living room floor," Nazareth said. "So if, in fact, it's part of someone's canine tooth, I'm guessing it was knocked out of that person's mouth."

"A punch?" Gimble asked.

"Could be, especially if the person's teeth were clenched when the punch landed. Otherwise, it could have been a blow from a solid object — a lamp, bookend, something hard but light enough to swing."

"Maybe like Ned Ryan's cane?" Gimble said.

"Yeah, exactly like Ned Ryan's cane. Swing a cane at forty or fifty miles an hour," he said, "and you can leave bits of teeth everywhere. If major leaguers can swing bats at eighty miles an hour, I'm guessing the average person could swing a cane at forty."

"I'm not following you, Detective," said Montagne, shaking his head. "How does all of this relate to Ned Ryan killing Mrs. Karcher?"

"Ned Ryan didn't kill Mrs. Karcher, Chief. Thomas Mercer killed her," he continued, "and he also beat Ryan with his own cane, cleaned the crime scene with vinegar, and then took the old guy with him."

"As a hostage?" the chief asked.

"Doubtful. My guess is that Mr. Ryan was dead or dying when he left here. But let's hope you're right. Either way, he's with Mercer. It's possible that Mercer was trying to buy some time by making us think that Ryan was on the run. Can't say for sure," Nazareth said as he began tapping keys on his cell phone.

He held up his phone to show Montagne a road map of the Ellenville area. "Where would you go if you had an old man's body with you?" he asked.

63

I drive to the woods, park in the same secluded spot I had used earlier, and get out to pace in the dark. The place looks and sounds unimaginably different at night. In place of songbirds I now hear only the relentless buzz of insects and the intermittent rustling of dried twigs and leaves as small animals wander by. The trees, whose comforting greenness made me feel secure earlier in the day, are now ghastly black shapes that reach toward the moonlit sky. Surely this is the sort of primeval darkness that the first Anglo- Saxon writers had in mind when they described simple peasants being savaged by ravenous beasts.

God, no! Fifteen feet away from me two enormous, unblinking eyes glow in the moonlight. My brain screams for me to jump back into the car, but I am paralyzed by fear. I am easy prey for whatever beast prowls these woods tonight. As the eyes move closer, a large branch snaps under the weight of the thing that comes for me. I shriek without meaning to — a primitive wail triggered by some ancient reflex. The eyes disappear. An immense buck bolts from the undergrowth and bounds off into the forest across the road.

I lean back against the car and cry. The tears are nothing more than a simple biological reaction to the adrenaline rush that now begins to subside. Nevertheless, I cannot remember the last time I cried.

My brain suddenly floods with images of a mission of mercy that has gone horribly wrong. Ellen Karcher's crumpled body. A seething wound on my forehead. A trail of blood across the wooden floor. Bits of broken teeth. A body in the trunk. And police. Surely there will be police.

My careful plans have been brutalized by an old man who just happened to be in the wrong place at the wrong time.

I am terrified, no doubt about it.

I drop to my knees and pray.

64

Chief Montagne studied the map on Nazareth's cell phone, seeing in his mind's eye each of the roads from behind a steering wheel.

"Routes 209 and 52 are the fastest ways out of town," he told Nazareth. "If Mercer hit one of those as soon as he left here, he could be anywhere by now."

"That doesn't answer my question, though. If you had a dead body in your car, where would you go?"

"Exactly where I told you. I'd take the fastest route out of town, then get rid of the body far away from Ellenville."

"And where would that be?"

"Uh, well, I can't say for sure. I don't know the other areas as well as I know Ellenville and the hills to the east."

"That's my point, Chief. If Mercer scouted this area before killing Mrs. Karcher, he probably found a safe place, or maybe even a couple of safe places, that he could run to if it became necessary. I don't think he'd leave that to chance."

"Well, in that case," Montagne reasoned, "I'd probably head for South Gully Road and go up into the woods. From there I've got a whole spiderweb of back roads that I can follow to Poughkeepsie or Newburgh or a hundred other places without having to drive on a main highway. Once you're up in those hills," he nodded, "you can get lost for a hell of a long time."

Nazareth took his time studying the map, first enlarging it and then scrolling north, south, east, and west. When he looked up, he stared at an unseen point far from Ellen Karcher's living room.

"Are you up for a suggestion, Chief?" he asked as he pocketed the cell phone.

"Could be. What are you thinking?"

"I'd get roadblocks on 209 and 52, both north and south of town. If he's still here someplace trying to dump a body — assuming he killed Ryan, that is — then he may head back to one of the main roads once he's finished. He may not want to take his chances on the long way through the state park."

"Okay, let's say we block the two highways," said Montagne, gesturing for Sergeant Pearsall to come over. "What if he's up in the woods and decides to stay there?"

"If he doesn't come to us," Nazareth replied, "then we go to him."

Montagne thought about that for a moment, then said, "Any idea what sort of vehicle we're looking for?"

"He's driving a beige Nissan Altima unless he rented something else on the way up." Nazareth read the skepticism on Montagne's face. "Right, I can't be sure about the car. But I'm damned sure about who's driving it."

"Okay, then." Montagne turned to the sergeant. "We need roadblocks on 209 and 52, north AND south of town. Let's get that done. And ask Jeff Turner to come over and see me."

65.

I send up a brief prayer for the souls of both Ellen Karcher and the old man who gave his life trying to protect her. Then I turn back to the more mundane but essential task of saving myself from life in some repulsive prison. It would be a short life, no doubt. After being gang-raped and beaten senseless by the common trash that one finds in such places, I would find a way to kill myself. But that would leave undone all of the work that God has set before me. And by abandoning that work and committing suicide, I would be doubly damned.

I cannot — will not — allow that to happen.

I climb back into the car so that I can sit quietly and think. Although much has already gone wrong, I realize that much can still surely go right if I follow my instincts. Instincts are, after all, the original word of God. Nothing could be more fundamental than His divine will built into our very genes, empowering us to overcome whatever dreadful trials are set before us. So I clear my mind and listen.

Before long the facts fall neatly into place as surely as if a shaft of sunlight has pierced the night sky to reveal the surrounding forest. If I am to continue life as I know it, I must eliminate all traces of evidence from the corpse in my trunk. And the most expeditious method of doing that is to cremate the old man's body. I take a small LED flashlight from my glove compartment and walk across the road deeper into the forest. After three or four minutes, having hiked no more than fifty yards, I come across a large clearing, near the center of which is a narrow gully whose rocky bottom sits seven or eight feet below the surrounding forest floor. I study it from several angles. Yes, this will work. If I line the bottom of the gully first with dry leaves and twigs, then crisscross layers of increasingly larger branches, I will in short order create a highly satisfactory funeral pyre. Dragging the old man over here will be a challenge, yes, but with God's help I can do it. Once I have placed the body in its final resting place, I will set the fire and calmly drive off. I calculate that it will take at least twenty minutes before the fire is large enough to be noticed in town, and by then I should be sixteen or seventeen miles down the highway.

Ten minutes later, having filled the gully with enough fuel to burn for several hours, I return to my car and open the trunk. Pitch black. I now remember smashing the bulb back at Ellen Karcher's home. So I turn on my small flashlight, hold it in my mouth so that the light shines into the trunk, and with both hands tug at the old man's upper body until it shifts toward me. What I see causes me to release the body and stagger backwards in shock. A puddle of the old man's blood has soaked into the trunk's carpet, and I realize immediately that my car now holds as much damning evidence as the corpse. Why had I not anticipated this? Why had I not put something down before loading the man into the trunk? Why had God placed the man at Ellen Karcher's home in the first place?

No time for that! This new crisis demands my immediate attention.

Cremating the body is no longer enough. I also need to remove the carpet from the trunk and get rid of the blood somehow before making my escape. Do I dare drive back to Manhattan tonight? No, impossible. What if the detectives are waiting for me there and see the carpet? Not likely . . . but possible.

Is it even wise to pass through Ellenville now? If by some stroke of luck they have found Ellen Karcher, the police could even now be on the highway searching vehicles. The bloody carpet would be the end of me. No, I refuse to take that chance.

On my cell phone I pull up a map of Ellenville, and my spirits soar at what I see. Yes, I can follow this mountain road north through the woods for another six or seven miles until I am safely on the other side of the state park. Once there I will have my choice of roads and can easily, though cautiously, work my way toward civilization. Tomorrow, before driving back to Manhattan, I will locate a Nissan dealer and replace the trunk carpet. Once I have done that, I can return home without fear.

The sooner I destroy the evidence, the sooner I can be on my way.

66

Officer Jeff Turner, a lanky, athletic guy of 28, joined Montagne and the detectives in a relatively quiet corner of the living room.

"This here's Jeff Turner, detectives," Montagne said as the others shook hands. "When he's not on the job, there's only one place you can find him. That about right, Jeff?"

"Just about, yessir." Jeff said good-naturedly.

"Jeff here must've been a real mountain man in his former life, because he damn near lives up in those woods — camping out, hiking, rock climbing, hang gliding, kayaking, you name it. If it's up there to be done, Jeff has done it."

Nazareth laid out the situation for the young officer, then once again called up the map of Ellenville on his cell phone.

"So here's the deal," Nazareth said, handing the phone to Turner. "We have a killer who probably knows the bare minimum about this area. But he may have a body he needs to dispose of. Where would he go up in those hills?"

Turner studied the map, tilted his head a couple of times, then zoomed in on the state park.

"In this area here," he said, pointing to a section of forest due east of Ellenville, "there are at least eight or nine turnoffs where you can park while you're hiking. And almost every one of them is well hidden from the road.

You're really not supposed to park there, but I've never heard of anyone being hassled over it."

"Those turnoffs appear to be spread out over a couple of miles," Gimble said.

"Right, but that's only if you stick to the main road," Turner said as he scrolled farther east on the map. "When the main road ends, you come to a jeep trail that runs damn near forever. Depending on what you're driving, you could just keep going."

"Could a Nissan Altima handle the jeep trail?" Gimble asked.

Turner thought about that, then pretended to flip a coin. "Fifty-fifty," he said. "If you weren't concerned about a few dings to the exterior and maybe a dented muffler, you should be able to get through. But that," he stressed, "is in daylight. No way you do that at night. There are some really dangerous areas. Make one bad turn, and you're airborne for seven or eight hundred feet."

"But if you stick to the main road," Nazareth said, "that's something you could easily drive in the dark?"

"Oh, yeah," Turner answered. "It's pretty much the same kind of road you've got right outside this house. Dark, narrow . . . just a lot longer. And more animals, of course. But if this guy has a spot picked out already, he'd have no problem finding it at night."

Nazareth thought for a moment, then turned to Montagne.

"Chief, I suspect that Mr. Ryan is already dead, but we should proceed as though he's a hostage. And that," Nazareth said, "tells me we need to go up into the hills and try to find him."

"I'm with you on that," Montagne said, as he turned to the young officer. "How long would it take for us to search each of the turnoffs on the main road?"

"In the dark," he said, "probably an hour or more. They're pretty well hidden from the road, so we'd have to get out and hike around each one."

"In that case," Montagne said as he gave Turner a quick thumbs-up, "let's get going. Jeff, I'll ride with you. Detectives, why don't you follow us, and we'll hit every turnoff that Jeff can find."

67.

I scramble out of the gully after placing the old man gently onto the layered branches. Now I need fire. I have no matches, since I do not smoke, but I do have the cigarette lighter that came with the car. I objected to that when I bought the vehicle three years ago, but it now seems to me clear evidence of divine intervention. An accursed cigarette lighter will become the means of my salvation.

Hiking in this overwhelming darkness is remarkably difficult. My LED flashlight illuminates only a short, narrow tunnel in the wilderness. My footwork is unsteady — and often dangerous — because of the rocks, branches, and pine cones that litter the forest floor. The air is filled with the unsettling noise of night creatures that seem to be drawing nearer. I half expect to see another pair of eyes glowing in the blackness. I have read that there are mountain lions — fearsome night hunters — in the Catskills, and my insides are roiled by the prospect of being torn apart and eaten alive in the dark.

I reach the car and search the ground for a dry twig long enough to reach well into the car's gas tank. I find one, strip it bare, then poke it down through the filler tube. Once the twig has soaked in the gasoline, I remove it and use the cigarette lighter's glowing orange coil to ignite a highly satisfactory small torch. It won't last long, but it will last long enough.

I return to the gully and carefully touch the flame to the dried leaves amid the stacked branches. The leaves ignite immediately, and the flames begin licking up toward the larger twigs. By the time I settle behind the wheel of my car, I can see the yellow glow of fire poking through the woods across the road.

I turn out of the clearing and drive north.

This nightmare is nearly over.

68

Officer Turner killed the flashers on his police cruiser once he reached the mountain road. The four officers hoped to surprise Mercer if possible, thereby avoiding a long night of cat and mouse in the dense woods. Nazareth and Gimble followed Turner up the road and around two sharp curves when they noticed the bright, unsteady glow on the horizon no more than a quarter of a mile away. By the time they parked on the road near the scene, flames five feet high were writhing against the night sky like angry specters. The acrid, metallic smell that hung in the mountain air told Nazareth all he needed to know about the fire.

"We no longer have a hostage situation," Nazareth said to no one in particular.

"You think he set Ned Ryan on fire?" Turner asked.

"Somebody set someone on fire," Nazareth answered, walking toward the gully while doing his best to stay clear of the awful smoke. "You smell this once, you don't forget it."

"God help us," said Montagne as he slowly shook his head in dismay. "How in the hell can someone do that to another human being? Has this guy completely lost his mind?"

"On the contrary," Nazareth answered. "Ryan's body most likely contained evidence that Mercer couldn't get rid of with vinegar and a rag. So now the evidence is gone. By the time this fire gets put out, Ryan will be nothing but ash and a few pieces of bone."

"I have a fire extinguisher in the trunk, Detective," said Turner.

"Don't waste your time. This fire's burning way too hot, and whatever evidence was on Mr. Ryan is already gone."

"I'm wondering how long ago the fire was set," Gimble said as she peered into the gully from a respectable distance.

"It looks to me as though this fire is still reaching its peak," Montagne answered, "so I'd guess maybe fifteen or twenty minutes ago. What do you think, Jeff?"

The young officer nodded. "Yeah, Chief. Fifteen or twenty max. There's a lot of fuel left, so this fire is still pretty young."

"In that case," Nazareth reasoned, "Mercer is still up here. No one drove past us on our way up, so his car is either in one of the turnoffs or up ahead on the road."

"We're right across from the first turnoff," Turner said as he pointed back to where they had parked their vehicles. "And there's no car there. I checked before coming out here."

"Then he's up ahead," said Montagne hopefully.

"Unless he drove back down with his lights off while we're all out here," said Turner.

"Aw, shit, don't say that," the chief said as he looked back toward the road.

"No way," said Nazareth. "Too risky. He couldn't be sure that one of us wasn't watching the road. No, I think he's got two choices left. One, he tries driving the jeep trail. Two, he abandons the car and takes off into the woods."

"But if he dumps the car," Gimble said as she looked to Nazareth, "we've got all sorts of evidence — fingerprints, DNA, fibers — even if it's a rental. And if it's Mercer's own vehicle, he's finished."

"He definitely keeps the car," Nazareth told the others, "and he's definitely up ahead. Let's go get him."

69.

By my rough calculation the drive to the far eastern edge of the state park should take no more than eighteen minutes, assuming an average speed of only twenty miles per hour. That assumption strikes me as quite conservative since I'm currently doing thirty and could easily do forty. I deliberately keep the speed down, though, because the last thing I need to do is broadside that large buck I saw earlier.

Besides, now that I have calmed down, I no longer feel pressured by time. It strikes me as highly unlikely that anyone will discover Ellen Karcher's body before tomorrow. And the disappearance of her elderly boyfriend — I assume that's what he was — might go unnoticed for days. Eventually the local police will wring their hands and wonder who could have snatched the life of an old widow here in rustic Ellenville. But by then I will be teaching an English Lit class. As for the old man's cremated remains, perhaps they will never be discovered. The woods are indeed lovely, dark, and deep.

All things considered, a frustrating night has ended well.

I cut my speed as the road snakes through the deep woods. Some of the turns are extremely tight, even for my nimble Nissan, so I proceed cautiously. At the same time, though, I marvel at the fine condition of this road. New York City is surely the pothole capital of the universe, while up here in the boonies even the most insignificant of mountain roads is neatly paved. This is quite fascinating.

As I come out of yet another tight bend in the road, I notice a small sign ahead, prominently displayed at driver's eye level. I roll up to it and am stunned by what I see.

Jeep Trail. 4WD Only.

A jeep trail? By all that's holy, how can this be a jeep trail? The map on my cell phone said nothing about a jeep trail. I grab my phone from the passenger seat and study the map once again. There's the road, plain as can be, running smoothly from one side of the state park to the other. I enlarge the image, and still all I see is a road like any other on the map.

This cannot be a jeep trail! It's supposed to be a paved road just like the one I have been traveling on!

How much can one man do? Every careful step I have taken has turned out to be the wrong one today. Is this a trial? Is God testing me? But why would He do that? I have done everything asked of me, and I am prepared to do more. Why should I be challenged like this?

Once again I find myself obsessing over useless questions while precious time slips away. I need to muster the energy to face things as they are.

I can turn around and drive back toward Ellenville and the main highway. I'm probably being absurdly overcautious in thinking about the local police searching vehicles tonight. And it's ridiculous to think that those two NYPD detectives might want to look inside my car's trunk. They have no reason to suspect me of anything, and if they ever do I will have had the bloody carpet replaced long before then. So why should I struggle along this dirt trail at night?

Because that's the safer of the two choices, and safer is always better than safe.

My original estimate for traveling the breadth of the state park was eighteen minutes at twenty miles per hour on a paved road. If the rutted dirt road that now stretches before me allows only ten miles per hour, I will still be free of the woods long before anyone from Ellenville thinks to search up here. So I put the car in gear and drive on.

The road is impossibly bumpy and generously strewn with rocks the size of baseballs. Here and there the narrow dirt track is crowded on both sides by bare pine branches that claw the paint as my car pushes through. Each time one of the front tires drops into a deep pothole, the chassis slams into the ground like a 747 landing on its belly. I don't know how many more times this can happen before the muffler and transmission are torn from the undercarriage.

The worst, however, is the senseless twisting and turning of the road-bed. Hardly a roadbed. It's nothing more than a dirt path that was never meant to be here — an accident created haphazardly by generations of off-road vehicles that slammed through the brush and scarred the soil. I squeeze the steering wheel so tightly that my hands ache, and I am drenched with sweat. I struggle to follow the trail as it twists through a maze of large oaks when suddenly my right front tire drops off the road. I slam on the brakes just before the car and I plunge into nothingness. The trail has vanished. My headlights illuminate nothing but empty blackness.

As I sit here, frozen, the car's front end shifts further to the right, grating against bare earth and rock. The vehicle now teeters on the edge of an abyss. I am certain that my next breath will be enough to send the car toppling into the valley below. Terror overwhelms every nerve in my body, and I am scarcely aware of having lost control of my bladder.

Suddenly I am eight years old. A gray morning. I stand at the doorway of that smelly upstairs bedroom. My mother doesn't know I am here. She hovers over the bed and screams at a skeletal old woman who lies there.

"You've pissed yourself again!" my mother screams. "Goddamn you, you've pissed yourself again!"

The old woman mumbles something that I cannot hear. My mother screams again, then leans over the old woman — I now see it is Nana — and pushes on her face with a pillow. My mother keeps screaming. She keeps pushing on the pillow. Then she stands there crying. I back away from the door before my mother knows I saw.

I have never remembered this until now.

Oh, God! The car shifts again as I grab the door handle.

As gently as possible I open the door, throw all my weight to the left, and topple onto the dirt. By the time the car stops sliding, the front end has dropped another few inches. I frantically scrabble away from the car on my butt until I am stopped by a thorny bush that tears at my bare hands and exposed neck. The sharp pain pulls me back from some dark, nightmarish place that my brain has run off to, and I am able to think clearly again.

I crawl toward the vehicle as my eyes grow accustomed to the moon-lit landscape. The right side of the car hangs precariously over a dirt ledge that has been partially washed away by runoff from a summer storm. Had I traveled just another few inches, the car would have become my steel tomb in the forest below.

As dreadful as this mission has been, I yet find reason to give thanks. God has saved me for a greater purpose.

All hope of returning to New York and my simple life as a professor is now gone. If I leave the car where it is, the police will soon find it, and the evidence within — my registration, insurance papers, and the bloody carpet included — will set them on my trail. But if I try to push the car over the ledge, I run the great risk of falling with it. Worse than death would be lying there crippled for days on end, an easy meal for whatever carnivores happen to come by.

The decision is obvious. I stand, pluck thorns from my bloody palms, and begin to walk toward the far side of the state park and freedom. I have my health and, thank God, both cash and credit cards in my wallet. Whatever lies ahead will be revealed to me according to His will.

Hiking this path in the night is safer by far than driving, and I maintain a healthy pace even though I am not dressed for the outdoors. Now and then I think I see angry eyes watching me from the deep woods, but I am careful to keep my imagination in check. All I need to do is keep doing what I am doing, and before the sun rises I can be on a bus headed far away from Ellenville.

I am more sad than angry over having to leave my comfortable life behind. Starting over will not be easy at my age. Yet I have complete faith that I can depart this present life and be reborn into an even better one. And I will have money . . . more than enough to keep me going for quite some time. I can easily transfer my savings from my brokerage account to a bank somewhere in the middle of America. My cell phone can easily accommodate that sort of transaction.

Losing my sister will hurt the most, I know, and that particular pain will linger for the rest of my life. I hate that she will think of me not as the caring brother who helped raise her but rather as the man who, at least in her eyes, murdered her mother-in-law. Will I ever be able to explain to her that it was something else altogether, something quite different from murder? If I write to her, will she even open my letter?

My thoughts are interrupted by a dim light glowing in the woods. No more than two hundred yards ahead of me, virtually hidden behind the enormous trees, I am barely able to make out the moonlit silhouette of a small house. A light shines from a rear window. I follow the jeep trail until I come to a dirt turnoff that leads up to what appears to be a rustic cabin. And as I walk cautiously toward the front door, I notice an old Jeep Wrangler parked off to the right of the building. I stop for a closer look. The tires seem to be in good condition, so it's likely the vehicle is still being used. How easy it would be to drive out of here at daylight, this time negotiating the trail in a four-wheel-drive vehicle designed for this sort of terrain. I can abandon the thing just before reaching civilization in case someone there might recognize it. And I can then catch a bus to my new life.

I am surprised but grateful that whoever lives out here in the deep woods does not have a dog. Certainly a dog would have been barking long before this, so I am perfectly at ease as I creep around the side of the cabin and peer through a curtainless window. A dumpy woman with short brown hair stands at the far end of an open room, working at the kitchen counter. Her back is to me. She wears a faded blue short-sleeved shirt over her thick upper body. Loose jeans cover her heavy legs and ample rump. It's quite late, yet she's preparing dinner. Odd. But that's her business, isn't it? All that matters to me is gaining my freedom and assuring the continuance of the work that God has set before me.

I knock sharply on the screen door. Will she allow me in at this time of night, or will I have to smash a window? Either way, I will have that Jeep. I am surprised but elated when she opens the door. No more than 5'6" and perhaps 60 years old, she wears a disgustingly stained green apron with two deep pockets. She apparently feels safe behind her flimsy screen door, and I cannot imagine why.

"Who the heck is it at this time of night?" she asks with a caustic edge to her voice.

"Ma'm, I'm terribly sorry, but I've been in an accident." I gesture toward the wound on my forehead. "I just need to call the police."

"An accident where?" she says, looking past me into the dark.

"About a mile back," I answer. "My car went into a gully and I got pretty banged up."

"Why didn't you call the police from back there?"

"I tried, but my cell phone isn't getting any reception up here."

"Well, that sounds about normal," she huffs. "What kind of vehicle are you driving up here at night?"

"I'm embarrassed to say it's a Nissan sedan. I'm not from around here, and I thought the paved road ran all the way through the park."

"Well, I've lived up here for nearly eighteen years, and you're about the fifth person who's tried the same damn thing. But you're the first one who's tried it at night. You're lucky you didn't kill yourself."

"I almost did," I laugh. "For a while there I wasn't sure I would make it."

She unlocks the screen door and opens it for me.

"Let me get my cell phone," she says. "Up here you need AT&T. Nothing else works."

Before she can turn away I close my hands around her throat.

"His will be done," I whisper.

70

The pavement ended, and the four officers stood looking at the jeep trail's warning sign.

"Unless we somehow missed him as we came up," said Nazareth, eyeing the dirt road ahead, "he's out there."

"We didn't miss him, Detective," Montagne answered. "We went real slow up that road, and I guarantee you this here spotlight would have shown us something if it was there." He nodded proudly toward the six-inch halogen light that was mounted on the driver's side of the cruiser. "This baby is so bright you could probably grill a steak with it."

"All right, then we work on the assumption he kept driving. Officer Turner, you said it was 50:50 whether he could make it on this jeep trail. You still firm on that?"

"Maybe 50:50 in daylight. Right about now," Turner shook his head, "no way in hell he gets through with a damned Altima."

"How far up there can we drive?" Gimble asked.

"If by *we* you're including me," Turner said, "we don't go ten feet. There are very few things in these woods that truly scare me, Detective, and that trail is one of them. Whole sections of it can wash away after heavy rain or melting snow, and you never know when it's just going to disappear from underneath you."

"I second that," said Montagne. "If you want to drive out there when the sun comes up, we can come back with a couple of Jeeps and guys who really know how to handle them. But we're not driving out there tonight."

"Do either of you have a problem with hiking for a while?"

Montagne and Turner looked at each other. When Montagne shrugged, Turner said, "As long as we have good flashlights with us and take our time, it won't hurt to walk a mile or so."

"Oh, shit," said Montagne.

"What, Chief?" Turner asked.

"Ann McGrady is what."

"Damn, I didn't even think about her."

"Who's Ann McGrady?" Nazareth asked.

"Woman who lives in a cabin out there," said Montagne. "Her husband was a park ranger — died about eight or nine years ago. She's up here alone now."

Nazareth looked stricken.

"I didn't know there were homes in state parks," Gimble said.

"Technically she's just outside the boundary" Montagne explained, "but, believe me, she's deep in the woods."

"How far ahead is she?" Nazareth asked.

"A mile, maybe a bit more."

Nazareth said nothing. He quickly began following the beam from his flashlight down the jeep trail. The others followed.

71

Mercer was surprised by the firmness of Ann McGrady's neck as he began to squeeze the life from her. She was feistier than he had expected, and when she drove her heavy chin down onto his hands, he was barely able to hold on. Only when he shook the smaller woman furiously back and forth was he was able to tighten his grip.

With her left hand McGrady clawed wildly at Mercer's face. When her fingers found their way to the deep cut on his forehead, she plunged them into the raw wound and began to rip at his flesh. Mercer screamed as the blinding pain annihilated his senses, but with animal fury he squeezed even harder on McGrady's throat. They were locked in a vicious embrace that only one would survive.

While she tore at Mercer's face with her left hand, with her right hand McGrady groped frantically for the pocket of her apron. Time seemed to stop in a moment of intense clarity and perfect joy as her fingers wrapped around the familiar bone handle of her well-used Timberline skinning knife. With all of her remaining strength she plunged the three-inch fixed blade, cutting edge up, into Mercer's soft lower belly. When he loosened his grip, she leaned hard into him and jerked the razor-sharp blade upward through his pink flesh toward his chest.

Mercer staggered back against the wall as his intestines began to spill out of the twelve-inch gash that ran from his bladder up to his breast bone. The last thing he saw was McGrady maniacally swinging the blade toward his throat. He fell to the cabin floor, a pile of guts drenched with the blood that spurted from his carotid artery.

72

When the officers arrived, they looked through the screen door to find a bloody Ann McGrady sitting on her old wooden rocker near the kitchen. Her head was back and her eyes were closed. They thought she was dead until they noticed the cell phone in one hand, the bottle of Genesee Cream Ale in the other.

"Mrs. McGrady, it's Chief Montagne," he yelled to her. "Are you all right?"

She opened her eyes and blinked at the light.

"How in God's name did you get up here so fast?" she called back.

The officers stepped gingerly around Mercer's bloody remains as they entered the cabin.

"What do you mean *so fast*?" Montagne asked.

"Well, when I called ten minutes ago your dispatcher said it might be an hour before someone got here."

"Oh, okay," the chief replied. "Well, it turns out the four of us were already up here looking for this guy."

"Well, you found him," she said calmly as she took a long pull on her beer.

While Gimble and the two local cops interviewed McGrady, Nazareth wandered silently through the small home. In the kitchen sink he found a bloody skinning knife and the gray-brown pelt of the eastern cottontail rabbit that Ann McGrady had been prepping when Mercer showed up. Its pink carcass was still on the counter, waiting to be wrapped and placed in the refrigerator.

Nazareth looked back toward the dead meat that was Mercer.

Wrong widow, wrong night, he thought.

73

Three days later Nazareth and Gimble celebrated the closing of the Rosebud Killer case with three hotdogs each at Sameer Khan's stand around the corner from One Police Plaza. They sat on a bench in the shade, where the temperature was 92 but felt hotter because of the humidity. On his lap to collect the inevitable spills Nazareth had spread the most recent edition of the *Shawangunk Journal,* which young Officer Turner had overnighted to Gimble. The glowing page-one story told how Turner and his boss, Chief Montagne, had cracked the case of the infamous Rosebud Killer.

"How are you going to frame that news article if you get chili on it?" Gimble taunted. "I mean, it's not often you have your picture on page one."

She referred to a large color shot that featured the two Ellenville PD officers proudly leaning against their cruiser the morning after Mercer's bloody end. Readers with especially keen eyesight could make out, though just barely, a fuzzy image of Pete Nazareth, who stood in the background eating an egg sandwich from the local diner.

"Hey, you want to reimburse me for your hotdogs?" he said as a gob of chili slopped onto the newspaper. "Just keep it up."

"Aw, don't be like that. You even got your name in the paper."

"Right," he nodded. "Detective Peter Nazarene."

"Don't be sour. Nazarene is pretty close to Nazareth."

"Okay, Detective Gumbo. I'll remember that," he laughed as he turned his attention to the next hotdog, this one with sauerkraut.

When they had finished eating, Gimble asked, "What are the Major Case guys saying about the Latourette murder and the missing Monet?"

"Unless Mercer left a journal or diary somewhere," he said, "which I sincerely doubt, we'll probably go to our graves wondering whether he killed Vivian Latourette. Some pieces fit. Some pieces don't." He shook his head. "No way of knowing.

"As for the painting," he continued, "Major Case has pretty much written that off. Paintings of that calibre are rarely recovered. Some sick but very rich SOB is probably sitting in his private library having an orgasm over the latest addition to his collection."

"The rich really are different," she smiled.

"Yeah, and lots of them really are sick, just like anybody else."

"Though not as sick as Professor Thomas Mercer."

"Oh, baby, now that was one extremely sick specimen. No telling exactly what set him off," he said as he began balling up the newspaper with his napkins inside, "but Ann McGrady gave us an interesting clue."

"That business about *His will being done*?"

"Right. Maybe he thought that killing widows was helping God in some bizarre way." He shook his head, thoroughly puzzled. "But, in the end, I really don't care much about motives. All that matters to me is getting one more psycho off the streets."

"And then waiting for another one to take his place."

"Funny you should mention that," he smiled as he removed a folded sheet from his pants pocket. "Chief Crawford gave me this about an hour ago."

74

In late September Chet Bradbury and his fiancee Amanda Giddens celebrated their new apartment on Cornelia Street. For three days they had hauled and lifted and shoved all of their earthly possessions into the former home of Professor Thomas Mercer. They knew nothing about the previous occupant and didn't need to. They were ecstatic over having found a terrific apartment at a reasonable price in this neighborhood near Washington Square Park.

Amanda was in the kitchen working on their first official meal in the new home. She preheated the oven to 450 while she removed the frozen wild mushroom tartlets from the box and placed them carefully on a baking sheet. Then she did the same with a box of frozen caramelized onion and gorgonzola tartlets. She slid the tartlets into the oven, then sat down on the couch next to Chet, who popped a $200 bottle of Taittinger champagne that Amanda's parents had given them as a housewarming gift. After champagne and appetizers, Chet was going to prepare his signature spicy shrimp and vegetable stir fry.

Halfway through their first glass of bubbly they noticed the awful stench. They went to the kitchen, opened the oven door, and released a cloud of foul dark smoke. Amanda put on an oven mitt and removed the tartlets, which surprisingly were not burned.

"It's not the tarts," she said, shaking her head in disgust, "so there must be spilled junk from the previous tenant. The smell is making me sick."

"Same with me," Chet said. "Tell you what. Let's take the champagne and finish it in the park. Then we can walk to dinner someplace."

"Fabulous idea. I'll run the oven-cleaning cycle while we're gone."

When they returned four hours later, the same terrible odor filled the apartment. Amanda opened the oven door, looked in, but saw nothing unusual.

"Isn't there an oven light?" Chet asked her.

"Must be burned out."

He went to a cabinet drawer and removed a large black-handled flashlight. "Let's get serious about this," he said good-naturedly.

They spotted the item standing on its end in the oven's far right corner. It looked like a dried corn husk, only taller, and it rested in a small pile of gray ash. Amanda reached in with the oven mitt and extracted what appeared to be a roll of canvas. Both curious, they placed the object on the stovetop and gently unrolled it. Flakes of dried paint fell from the canvas as they did so.

"Well," Amanda said brightly, "I guess we now know that the previous tenant was an artist."

"Artists dry oil paintings in the oven?"

"Well," she smiled, "here's the evidence."

Chet shook his head and picked up the charred remains of the painting.

"Make you a deal," he said. "You spray the apartment with anything you can find . . . ."

"While you bag that smelly thing and put it out with the rest of the garbage!"

"Great minds think alike," he grinned.

At 7:53 the next morning a large New York City Department of Sanitation truck growled to a stop in front of the apartment building. Less than a minute later veteran sanitation worker Hector Nunez had tossed the bagged canvas onto the back of his truck along with the rest of the garbage.

After applying the hydraulic trash compactor, Nunez lit a cigarette, took one long, satisfying drag, and drove off into the splendid autumn day.